He stared dow

"She's so innocent, Lizzie, and it's a helluva lousy world out there."

Elizabeth touched his arm, taken aback by the unmistakable fierceness beneath his words. "But she's not out there. She's here with us."

Zach was silent for a moment, then asked, "What about a father for her?"

She wanted to say that he would make a perfect father, but she doubted that was what he wanted to hear. "I haven't really thought about it. I'm certainly not going to marry a man just to give her one."

He cleared his throat, reached down and smoothed his hand over the quilt, making sure it was tucked in.

"Maybe after this is all over..." He let the sentence trail off.

Dear Reader,

Once again, Silhouette Intimate Moments has prepared a stellar list of books for your reading pleasure. So go ahead, sit in the sun (or the shade, if you prefer) and treat yourself to a few hours of enjoyment.

First up, Kristin James finishes her trilogy called "The Marshalls" with *The Letter of the Law,* featuring James Marshall, the last of the brothers to have his story told. And don't forget—if you missed *A Very Special Favor,* the first of the series, you'll be able to find it in bookstores in September. Rachel Lee made her first appearance as part of the "February Frolics" new-author promotion, and you won't want to miss her second novel, *Serious Risks.* It's a wonderful blend of romance and white-knuckle suspense. I think you'll love it. Dee Holmes spins a warm tale (despite its wintry setting) in *Maybe This Time,* a story proving that love can, indeed, conquer all. Finally, one of your favorite authors, Kathleen Korbel, is back with *A Rose for Maggie.* I don't want to give anything away about this one, so I'll satisfy myself with saying that this is truly one of those books that will bring tears to your eyes as you share the very special love of this family in the making.

As usual, we're keeping an eye on the future as well as the present, and you can count on seeing more of your favorite writers in months to come. To name only a few, look for Nora Roberts (next month!), Emilie Richards and Marilyn Pappano. And also next month, look for Judith Duncan—a name that many of you may recognize—to make her first (but not her last) appearance in the line.

As always—enjoy!

Leslie Wainger
Senior Editor and Editorial Coordinator

DEE HOLMES

Maybe This Time

SILHOUETTE·INTIMATE·MOMENTS®

Published by Silhouette Books New York

America's Publisher of Contemporary Romance

SILHOUETTE BOOKS
300 East 42nd St., New York, N.Y. 10017

MAYBE THIS TIME

ISBN: 0-373-07395-X

First Silhouette Books printing August 1991

Printed in the U.S.A.

Books by Dee Holmes

Silhouette Intimate Moments

Black Horse Island #327
Maybe This Time #395

Silhouette Special Edition

The Return of Slade Garner #660

DEE HOLMES

would love to tell her readers about exciting trips to Europe or that she has mastered a dozen languages. But the truth is that traveling isn't her thing, and she flunked French twice. Perhaps because of a military background where she got uprooted so much, she married a permanent civilian.

Dee is an obsessive reader who started writing casually, only to discover that "writing is hard! Writing a publishable book is even harder." She has since become involved in her local RWA chapter, and says that she loves to write about "relationships between two people who are about to fall in love, but don't know how exciting it is going to be for them."

To Suzanne,
a more than extraordinary daughter.
To Pat Coughlin,
for all those late nights and words of wisdom.
And to Reinier,
both wise and extraordinary.

Chapter 1

Ransacked was too hollow a word, Zach Stone thought grimly as he surveyed the carnage in Elizabeth Healy's living room. Slashed upholstery. Pictures torn off the walls and flung aside. Furniture overturned. Ashes from the fireplace swept out as though someone hoped to find a hidden door in the hearth's floor.

He bent and picked up a jagged piece of sculpture that had been part of a work Elizabeth had titled *Newborn*.

On his way inside the white, blue-shuttered colonial house, he'd passed a gathering crowd of neighbors who, despite the frigid December temperatures, were both curious and naturally worried about a burglar running loose.

Zach would have liked to believe that a random thief had coincidentally chosen a house owned by a cop's widow, but he knew better. Even if Gordon Healy hadn't called him so urgently, Zach's gut instinct would have kicked in. In fourteen years of police work it had rarely failed him—except once. Not a day went by that he wasn't plagued with unanswered questions about that one time.

He drew in a long breath, and glanced up at the sound of footsteps. He brushed his fingers over the broken piece of sculpture before laying it on a nearby table.

"Hey, Zach, I thought you were on R and R after that undercover job over on the south side. No one told me you'd been assigned to this one." Buzz Potter was a lieutenant and an eighteen-year veteran of the police department of Liberty, Rhode Island. He shook Zach's hand.

"I just heard. I was about to grab about twenty hours of sleep. The old man called," Zach said in a distracted voice. His eyes swept across the mess that spilled from the living room and into the dining room.

On the rectangular mahogany dinner table lay a broken Christmas tree centerpiece. Zach stared for a moment, his thoughts cold and unfeeling. The reminder of the coming holiday brought the inevitable search through his mind for a single Christmas in his thirty-eight years that had been worth a damn. He found none. That was the primary reason why he worked during the holidays, he told himself, turning his back on the red and green and silver decoration.

Potter shook his head in amazement. "The call just came in to the station an hour ago. How did Healy hear about it way the hell up in New Hampshire?" Buzz's voice had a crocodile rasp from his two-pack-a-day cigarette habit. He had a sagging fleshy face, a thick neck and a rumpled body that gave an impression of shoddy police work, but his dedication to ridding the streets of punks who ripped off old ladies was legend in the department.

Zach shrugged. Beneath his sheepskin jacket, his shoulders ached and his neck felt as though he'd spent the past thirty hours clamped in a vise. "Cricenti called him. You know how Gordon likes to stay on top of anything concerning Elizabeth and Julianne. He was livid when he called me. Ranted on about incompetence in the department, and where in hell were the cops when some sleaze could break into a house in a nice neighborhood in broad daylight and get away with it.''

''I don't suppose the fact that the house belonged to his daughter-in-law and his only grandchild had anything to do with his reaction?'' Buzz asked, lifting both eyebrows in a so-what's-new gesture. He patted his shirt pocket and drew out a semicrushed package of cigarettes. Pulling one from the box, he stuck it into his mouth and searched another pocket for a lighter.

Normally Zach would have grinned and agreed with Buzz. Gordon Healy had no objectivity when it came to Elizabeth and Julianne, but then Gordon made no secret of his love and protectiveness toward his deceased son's family.

Jim Healy had been Zach's partner on the fifteen-month investigation of a statewide narcotics network that centered on drug dealing in Liberty. On their final assignment, Zach had worked backup, and Jim had gone in to do the drug buy. Buy and bust, the department called such operations, and both men had done them more times than they could count, but this time something had gone wrong.

Zach had described the disaster at the time in crudely explicit terms, and with a rage that was directed as much at himself as toward the bastard who had shot and killed Jim in the crack house more than a year and a half ago.

Elizabeth had been a month pregnant with Julianne when Jim died, and for a few weeks it had been touch and go as to whether she would lose the baby. She hadn't, and although Zach had little personal contact with her, Gordon had kept him informed. Her sheer will to hold on to her baby, the one final part of Jim, had forever locked her into Gordon's heart.

Liberty had been outraged by Jim's murder. Cop killing, in the public's opinion, showed the absolute arrogance of the criminal. And to the local anger was added the frustration that months of investigation had produced few clues. The killer had never been caught.

After Gordon's call, Zach had little doubt that the mere possibility of a threat to Jim's family would be reason enough for Gordon to demand they be protected.

"You'd feel the same way, Buzz, if it was your family."

Buzz narrowed his eyes and flipped the half-smoked cigarette into the fireplace. "I'll kill the SOB."

"No doubt," Zach muttered, and thought, not for the first time, how dangerous emotional involvement could be for a cop. His own rage over Jim's death had brought that truth home in all its raw reality. If he'd been in the crack house and witnessed the shooting, he knew he would have killed Jim's murderer as sure as his name was Zachariah Stone.

He dragged one hand through his thick dark hair, which he wore longer than regulation so as to be able to blend in on the street. His image was carefully maintained. Scuffed black boots and snug jeans that were worn and torn in places but often caused women to turn and look twice. Zach rarely noticed, or if he did, he ignored their reaction. He didn't mix women and work. Ever.

His sheepskin jacket hung open to partially reveal his black sweatshirt with white lettering that spelled Boston Celtics. His eyes were gray-blue, but a suntanned blond lady lawyer from Cape Cod had once described them as a deep smoky blend of smolder and secrets.

He glanced now in the direction of the stairs that led to the second floor. He was surprised Elizabeth hadn't appeared, but was somewhat glad she hadn't. He swore silently at his own mixed reaction, angry that he had any reaction beyond an objective concern.

"Where's Elizabeth?"

"She should be right back," Buzz replied, turning a couch cushion to its unslashed side and sitting down wearily. "I told her I'd wait while she went to a neighbor to get the baby. She took Julianne over there after she called us. She's pretty upset. Not hysterical but angry. She'd been Christmas shopping and when she came home she saw someone race across the backyard and disappear behind another house."

"Any description?"

"Just a dark jacket and dirty-blond hair."

Zach planted his hands low on his hips. "That should narrow it down to only about a million possibilities."

Buzz picked up a framed picture of Elizabeth's family in Virginia, which had escaped breakage, and set it upright on an end table. It was a grouping of her parents, her three brothers and their wives and kids. Elizabeth held center stage with month-old Julianne in her lap. Zach recalled looking at the picture at the time of Julianne's christening and being somewhat puzzled by the strained expression on Elizabeth's face.

Buzz said, "They lifted some prints around the back door where he came in. But they'll probably turn out to be only those that should be there. The job was pretty professional so we're not holding out much hope."

That professional look had nagged at Zach since he'd walked in and seen the mess, but he was even more disturbed by the ransacking. This wasn't a burglary where the objective might have been jewelry and cash, or electronic equipment that could be fenced. A ransacking meant that the intruder had had something specific in mind. He'd broken into Elizabeth's house and torn it apart searching for something. But what?

"If she saw him running, he must have heard her car drive in," Zach commented.

"Probably. Appears he hadn't gotten to the upstairs yet. Kinda weird, huh? Usually the bedroom is the first place they head. Anyway, the thoroughness of the search makes it look like more than a simple housebreaking with vandalism, but until she can assess what's missing, we're just dealing with theory and speculation."

"I'm gonna look around," Zach said, stepping over more broken sculpture pieces. After checking the kitchen and a small downstairs bathroom, he went into the den.

Dark-paneled with heavy furniture, the room had a cozy atmosphere that made him wonder how it would feel to stretch out there in the leather chair on a snowy day with a tumbler of Scotch in one hand while he waited for a woman.

He smiled. The thought wasn't surprising considering his mood. He'd been working too many crazy hours, eating too much lousy food and getting too little sleep. Scotch and a woman, in no particular order, but plenty of both, had been his plan for tonight, followed by about three days of sleep.

He shrugged out of his coat, tossing it on a chair he righted. So much for tonight's plans as well as any he had for the next few days, he decided with grim resignation. Gordon Healy had seen to that.

A pair of poinsettia plants had been dumped from their stands on either side of a console television. The red flowers were broken, the dirt already trampled into the carpet. The bookshelves that covered one wall had been emptied, a lone volume that remained on the third shelf looking naked and abandoned.

The desk top was piled with the contents of the drawers. Lying on its side on the floor was a sign with a picture of the barrel of a gun aimed straight on that said: *Don't you dare put another thing on this desk.* While Jim had been precise in doing detailed reports and had kept extensive notes on any investigation, he was known in the department for having a desk whose surface challenged the cleaning staff, and

Zach had brought the sign for his partner from a street vendor.

Now Zach placed it back on the pile, and wondered if the ransacker had gotten some weird pleasure out of deliberately trashing the desk. Or had he just been frustrated?

Why? he asked himself. Why now? Had the intruder waited and watched until Elizabeth went shopping? And since he'd only been through the downstairs, would he be back? And what was he looking for? The questions came; the answers didn't. Zach closed his eyes for a moment, considering the possibility that the break-in was connected to Jim's death. But how?

"Buzz said you were here."

Zach turned around to face Elizabeth Healy. She came slowly into the room as though she were a stranger who'd come upon something she didn't want to understand. Her eyes never wavered, and in them he saw tiredness and sadness and questions.

Her white wool coat was unbuttoned, revealing a nubby gold sweater and a darker gold turtleneck topping tailored black jeans encased in leather boots. She wasn't tall. Five-five to his six-one. The top of her head just cleared his chin. He knew that because the day he'd come to tell her Jim was dead he'd held her for a brief moment while she struggled not to scream.

"Scream, Lizzie. Scream," he'd whispered, wanting to hear her vent her rage as furiously as he felt his own. But she'd only sobbed, which had been heartbreakingly worse. Zach had never forgotten it.

Shoulder-length auburn hair swirled around a face that defined beauty with more depth than model-perfect features. Milk and whiskey, he decided, and felt baffled that he should have seen so quickly that she was a combination of nurture and intoxication.

He hadn't seen her in four months, hadn't spoken more than a few dozen words to her in the past year, and yet some thin permanent thread sprang taut and definite between them. No word seemed to fit what they were to each other— not strangers or acquaintances or friends. Whatever this wired reaction that tightened silently between them was, it had no name.

Zach rubbed his hand across the dark stubble on his cheeks. He probably looked more like the intruder than a cop. "Gordon called me. Is the baby okay?"

Elizabeth nodded, the ghost of a smile appearing and then sliding away. "Yes. I just put her in her crib. With the po- lice in and out, the house was cold and I didn't think she needed all the confusion, so I took her over to Betsy Mc- Gann's."

She shivered. Her cold-reddened cheeks had faded, leav- ing a pale wanness. "I'm just glad I didn't leave her home with a baby-sitter," she said, a tremble in her voice as she raised her hands and covered her eyes.

He saw her shoulders slump, but he didn't move, and he wasn't sure why not. Certainly not because he wasn't sym- pathetic. If she were another cop's widow he would have quickly crossed the room and drawn her into his arms to comfort her; to let her cry or get angry or at the very least draw support from him.

Watching her, he damned his reticence and shoved his suddenly chilled hands into his back pockets.

Official and rational was better, he reminded himself. He was supposed to stay objective, not give sympathy. But he knew it wasn't that. If a few moments of solace were all that were involved, if this were simply a few moments of talking to her, offering some encouragement, perhaps even taking the step of holding her . . . then he could probably handle it.

He dragged one hand across his eyes, pausing to rub his thumb and forefinger against the bridge of his nose. Doing as Gordon had requested wasn't a major deal. It was simple and direct. Hell, of course he could handle it.

But still he didn't move. With Elizabeth Healy, he had a sense that objectivity would be a struggle he could easily lose. Keeping an emotional distance meant keeping a physical distance.

Zach listened to the sounds she made. She didn't cry as much as she sobbed. It made her seem more vulnerable, more invaded, but at the same time strong. Buzz said she hadn't been hysterical, only angry. Zach thought she had the right to be both.

He made his way to the liquor cabinet. Some of the bottles lay on the floor and most of the glasses had been broken. He found an unopened bottle of brandy and a champagne flute. He broke the seal and poured the dark liquid into the glass.

Crossing back to Elizabeth, he pushed aside a torn drapery panel that had been tossed across a chair and urged her to sit down.

"Here, drink this."

She sniffled, dug into her coat pocket for a tissue and swiped at her eyes. Not a dabber, he noted and he liked that. No hysterics, as Buzz had said, but definitely anger.

After another sniffle, she pushed her hair back, and looked at the glass and then at him. Light brown eyes with a touch of gold that made them more expressive than beautiful, he decided thoughtfully. Yes, she was a woman with strong emotions who was not afraid to show them.

She asked him, "Why would someone do this?"

He handed her the glass. "Could be a lot of reasons. Drink."

She frowned. "Brandy in a champagne flute?" At his nod she shook her head at the incongruous match and sipped, then sipped again. "What reasons?"

"Money. Stuff he could fence for drug money. Vandalism because the guy gets off trashing other people's property."

"But why me?"

"Perhaps simply because you weren't home. Thieves risk
a lot in a break-in. They're not going to do it unless they can
be sure they'll get something worthwhile. This is a mid-
priced house in a manicured middle-class neighborhood.
The contents and the interior aren't cheap or secondhand
like he'd find if he went into some dump on the south side."

She nodded, sipped a third time, and Zach felt his own
inner tension loosen. She was satisfied for now.

Buzz tapped on the open door. "Sorry to interrupt. I'm
gonna split. Don't forget, we need a list of missing items,
Elizabeth."

"I don't think anything is missing, Buzz. Mostly just
broken."

Zach met Buzz's eyes, a silent concern passing between
them. "Thanks for sticking around. I'll give you a call
later," Zach said.

"Sure." Buzz turned away and a few seconds later the
front door opened and closed.

Elizabeth looked up, curious. "I didn't expect you to be
here."

He moved to the wide window that looked across the
backyard. A low hedge and some winter-protected rose-
bushes separated Elizabeth's property from the McGanns'.
Backyards should be inviolate, he thought, allowing himself a deep anger at the intruder. Yards were family places—
places where gardens were planted in the spring, where
summer laughter meant children and plastic swimming
pools and barbecues, where autumn leaves fell from the
giant trees.

The maple tree in her yard rose stark and proud despite its
December-naked branches. He watched it shudder from the

wind. Perhaps it was the shape or the size or the fat level branch about fifteen feet up, but he was reminded of a tree that had stood in the yard of the last foster home he had been sent to, and the tree house they wouldn't let him build.

Must be twenty years since he thought about that tree.... Zach halted his thoughts abruptly. God, what was he doing?

He shoved the memory back into the darkness, and deliberately glanced up at the thick sky. "Too bad the predicted snow hadn't come a day early. A few footprints would have helped," he muttered before turning to look at her. "I heard about it and I wanted to make sure you were all right. You and Julianne."

"No one reported that we were hurt, did they?"

"No."

"Then why did you come?"

"Why do you ask so many questions?"

She raised very eloquent eyes. "Because the premier undercover cop in Rhode Island doesn't just appear on an ordinary police matter." Whether it was the brandy or her energy returning, Zach wasn't sure, but he couldn't help his inward pleasure at her flippancy.

"Is that what I am? The premier undercover cop?" Zach had heard himself called a lot of names but this was a new one. "Too bad I don't get a premier paycheck to go with it."

"You're going to evade my question, aren't you?"

Better to just get this over with, he decided, walking back to the bar. He searched around for some Scotch. Finding none, he opened a bottle of bourbon. Since she had the only glass, he lifted the bottle and took a short swig. He hadn't eaten except for a bowl of chili and two cups of heavily creamed coffee about four hours ago. And he would need his focus sharp for the next few hours. When he glanced up, she was staring at him.

He brought the bottle away from his mouth, gripping its neck so he didn't drop it. He stared back, and immediately knew he'd made a mistake. Unbidden, unwanted and impossible images wove into his thoughts and lay hot and raw as if reflected across a thousand mirrors.

He gripped the neck of the bottle tighter, his mind quick to search for an escape. It had to be the thirty days of abstinence, he decided, not sure if he was embarrassed or shocked, but the fantasy still broke over him like spilled handfuls of liquid silk. . . .

Sex and magic. Lace riding high on her thighs. Her mouth under his, lush and wild like lightning. Drowsy desire coming in whispered whimpers.

Had her cheeks gotten redder? His felt fiery. No way. Hell, there wasn't a chance she could know his out-of-nowhere thoughts. Images he didn't want. Possibilities he wouldn't consider.

She took a sip of brandy, her lashes fluttering down. Zach didn't move, he didn't raise the bottle, he didn't blink, but he methodically shattered each image and each possibility with two realities. Who she was and why he was here.

When she finally spoke, he felt as though a century had passed. "Gordon's the reason you're here, isn't he, Zach?"

He found his usual ability to remain emotionless was eluding him. Taking another swig of bourbon, he nodded.

She came to her feet. "I should have known. I should have known the moment Buzz said you were here."

"I don't want any arguments from you, Lizzie."

He watched her pace and sensed her determination to take care of herself build.

She swung around, her coat spreading open and then settling back around her. "Don't you think the two of you are overreacting?"

"Of course." He braced the bottle against his thigh. "When you care about someone the way Gordon cares about you and his granddaughter, overreaction is normal. Would you rather he just shrugged this off as no big deal?"

"I would like to know what's going on. Gordon tends to steamroll through things without getting anyone's opinion as to whether they want his—" She stopped, her voice breaking a little as she regathered her composure. "I know he means well, Zach. I know he loves us and worries about us."

"He'd like you to move up to New Hampshire so you'd be closer to him and Naomi. He's told me that more times than I can count."

"And my parents would like me to move back to Virginia." She sighed, leaving unsaid the question Zach wondered about. Who had asked Lizzie what she wanted? "Thank God, Naomi understands," she continued. "If it weren't for her, I think Gordon would have sold the home they'd bought and retired right here in Liberty."

"Naomi is a wise lady. She probably knew that when Gordon wasn't parked on your doorstep, he'd be down at the station giving unasked-for advice, opinions and criticism to the new police chief."

"I don't understand why Naomi didn't stop Gordon from calling you."

"She's worried, too. And in this situation, you're lucky he isn't down here personally."

She sagged back down in the chair and retrieved the flute of brandy from where she had set it on a side table. Frowning slightly, she held it balanced on the arm of the chair. "I know he means well," she said in a resigned voice. "But my art store is here. My friends are here. And I have to live my own life. I don't want Julianne to ever forget who her father was, Zach, but if I moved up there I'm afraid they'd smother me. Maybe not Naomi, but I know she'd like to see more of Julianne than she does. I love them and I would never do anything to hurt them, but . . ." She paused, took another sip, then stared into the almost empty glass.

Zach capped the bourbon bottle and waited. The "buts" were always the core point of any argument. He could guess this one: But I won't move to New Hampshire.

Slowly she lifted her eyes. "I've been doing some dating." She regarded him closely as though she were ready to defend herself if he offered one critical word.

Zach watched her swallow and stopped himself from asking who. Not that who she dated mattered to him one way or the other. She deserved a new beginning. God knew, she'd been through hell and had been courageous and strong and . . .

Who was he kidding? For no reason that made a dime's worth of sense, he didn't like the idea of Elizabeth dating. He thought of Gordon's comments over the past few months about the probability that someday Elizabeth would marry again. Those comments had been accompanied by pointed hints that neither he nor Naomi would be displeased at having Zach as a son-in-law.

At first Zach had been stunned by the idea, but he had been quick in his dismissal of it, also. No situation he could think of was more binding than marriage, and he avoided any situation he couldn't easily get out of.

Since he had no intention of giving a thought to any involvement with her, he should have been pleased she was dating. But he wasn't. With a dark scowl, he tried to dismiss his scrambled reactions. None of your business, Stone. This is a job you're doing for Gordon and nothing more. No one cares whether your opinion is positive or negative.

He shifted the bottle to his other thigh. "Seriously?"

"Just dinner a couple times," she said softly, as though she hadn't considered "seriously" a possibility. "I met him at the McGanns' at Thanksgiving." She paused, then added almost as an afterthought, "He sells insurance."

Zach felt a wave of relief. It wasn't serious. Lizzie and some insurance salesman simply didn't fit. How he knew that was something he didn't want to examine. "You're kidding."

She blinked, her confusion evident. "That's a strange reaction."

"Forget it. It's none of my business."

"You don't approve, do you?" She got to her feet again, a little unsteady because of the brandy, but clearly annoyed. "If you don't, then Gordon won't and probably Naomi, too, and... Dammit, I shouldn't care...but I do...." She took a steadying breath as though not sure she could explain how she felt.

"You care because you care about them," he offered, feeling as if he were spouting words from some sentimental greeting card.

Elizabeth glanced up at him, her eyes wide. "You understand, then?" Was that relief he heard in her voice?

He wasn't sure if she meant her dating or her caring about the Healys, or both.

She continued before he had a chance to answer. "I loved Jim. I wish with all my heart he was here with me to watch his daughter grow up. But he's not. He never will be again."

It was the brandy, or perhaps the ransacked house. Or even perhaps that his being here with her reminded her too realistically of Jim.

She sighed.

So did Zach.

The wind stroked a tree branch against a window of a nearby room, the scratchy sound eerie and lonely.

Finally he put the bottle down, moved across the room and took her arm. She shook his hand away, and he saw a sudden defensiveness in her eyes. He kept his voice low and steady. "Lizzie, I know it's been tough."

"I'm sorry. I probably sound a little off the wall."

"No apology needed. The ransacking and Gordon worrying about you probably brings back all the sadness."

"I have a lot to be grateful for. I have a beautiful baby, a business that is doing better every month, good friends, my own family in Virginia. Gordon and Naomi, but..." Her eyes misted and Zach didn't even want to try a guess on this "but."

"Look, coming home to this kind of mess can be pretty upsetting," he said, annoyed that all he seemed able to say made the obvious sound trite.

She gave him a long look, and then whatever had caused the outburst was gone. "You're right. Either that or brandy at three in the afternoon." Then she began to pace again, finally stopping at the window and gazing out.

"I'll call Gordon and tell him we're all right. Betsy McGann wants us to go over there and spend the night. I think I'll do that. I don't think I could sleep here with all this mess." Pausing, she glanced back at him. "I appreciate your concern in stopping by to make sure we're okay, but you don't have to hang around. I'm fine."

He didn't move.

"I said I'm fine." She tipped her head to the side, but the back light of the window made it impossible to read her expression.

For one instant he wished for the days before women's rights, when he could have gotten away with simply sweeping up her and Julianne, tossing them in his car and driving them to New Hampshire.

Gordon's words echoed in his mind with the precise crispness that had left little doubt about what he wanted. "I want them safe, Zachariah, not down there where I don't know what in hell is going on. And since you're the one person I can trust to do this and do it right, I want you to handle it. And for God's sake, use the four-wheel drive vehicle, not that damn sports car. I'll expect a call from you later to let me know you're on your way."

Zach glanced at his watch. Three hours. Get her and Julianne packed, stop at his apartment to get some clothes, let his assignment chief know he'd be gone a couple of days, get gas for the four-wheel drive...

When she rested her hand on his arm, he jerked in surprise. He blinked and realized he'd been so caught up in what Gordon wanted and what he had to do in the next few hours that he'd forgotten she didn't know what was going to happen.

"Please don't worry about us," she said, obviously taking his silence to mean just that.

"I don't intend to."

"Good. Now, I want to go upstairs to check on Julianne." She moved past him and toward the door.

She was almost out of the den. "Lizzie?"

She turned slowly, her head tipped to the side in a puzzled manner. "You keep calling me that. No one ever has."

That wired threat he'd felt earlier tightened measurably. Why did he call her Lizzie? he wondered. The reasons seemed simple enough on the surface. Lizzie fit her. And he'd never heard Jim or Gordon or Naomi or anyone call her anything but Elizabeth. Subconsciously, he knew he'd chosen Lizzie because it had no attachments, no baggage, no significance.

She licked her lips, her voice an unsure murmur. "I don't know if I like it. When you say it, it sounds as if we're, uh..." She hesitated, biting lightly on her bottom lip. Zach found his mind rushing unrestrained through the possible choices she pondered over. Lovers. Intimate. Involved.

"Close friends."

He let out the breath he hadn't realized he was holding and ignored the leap of anticipation he felt.

Never had he been close friends with a woman. He hadn't the slightest idea how or what he was supposed to do. But she'd said "as if." Since lovers was out of the question and close friends hadn't happened yet, then what were they?

This was the second time since she'd walked into the den that he'd tried to define what they meant to each other and failed. He shoved the mystery aside.

At least why he was here was no mystery.

Keeping his voice crisp and detached, he said, "Pack warm clothes for yourself and Julianne. At least a week's worth. Snow is on the way and I'd like to beat the storm."

Chapter 2

Elizabeth stared at him in disbelief.

A thousand memories of ... Do this, Elizabeth.... Be careful, Elizabeth.... We love you, Elizabeth, that's why.... rushed through her mind as though once again she were a child back in Virginia. Once again she was the recipient of too much concern. Once again she was made to feel that danger lurked beyond the confines of the Clayton family nest.

Because she did love her family, her pursuit of independence had been a slow evolution rather than stubborn rebellion. Oh, she'd tried the rebellion, she'd tried begging, she'd tried tears. Nothing had worked. Finally she had simply nodded and smiled and then tenaciously gone her own way.

Now, with one stroke of a verbal pen and one tense, momentary recollection of being smothered, childlike, in a cocoon, she felt her defenses come rushing forward. She was a responsible adult, and she didn't think it too much to expect to be treated like one.

A single glance at Zach, however, was enough to convey the message that he was rarely questioned. She had little doubt that he considered his blithely given orders to be a fait accompli.

"Pack for what?" she asked warily, but she was already bracing herself for the answer she feared.

He had picked up the telephone, balanced it on the same thigh where the bottle of bourbon had rested, tucked the receiver between his ear and his shoulder and punched the numbers. He glanced back at her with a frown. "I thought you'd gone upstairs. We're going to New Hampshire."

She closed her eyes briefly, feeling as if she'd been caught in a quagmire that would take more skill than tenacity to escape. "Why?"

He lifted his hand in a waiting gesture. "This is Stone. Is Potter still there? Yeah, I'll hold." He glanced back at Elizabeth. "Because Gordon and Naomi want you and Julianne up there for a while." He shifted his attention back to the phone. "Buzz, what's the possibility of you keeping an eye on the Healy place just till I get back? Terrific. I owe you one, buddy." He added a few comments about another investigation, then said goodbye.

To his credit, she decided while he finished his call, he at least hadn't instructed her just to do as she was told. She leaned against the doorjamb, grudgingly liking his attitude even though she didn't agree with him. "Why?"

He put the receiver back onto its cradle, seeming to think for a moment. She noted that there was no show of temper, no use of physical persuasion, such as gripping her shoulders and turning her firmly toward the stairs. She wondered if he calculated answers to cushion them, or whether, as Jim had often done, he would simply refuse to give her one.

He rested his hips against the edge of the desk and folded his arms across his chest in a weary gesture.

He's exhausted, Elizabeth realized suddenly. Mentally and physically exhausted.

Without looking at the heavy watch he wore, he confirmed her thoughts. "I haven't had any sleep for the past thirty hours, my eyes feel like someone dumped sand into them, and my mind is as cluttered as the interstate at rush hour. On a list of one to ten things I most want to do, you can be sure driving to New Hampshire is ten and answering questions is a definite nine."

He straightened, plowing both hands through his dark thick hair. It was in definite need of cutting, but she thought that on him it looked just right. Actually, Elizabeth decided, everything about him looked exactly right. His face was so rugged as to appear callused, the deep lines on his beard-stubbled cheeks testifying to years of raw experience, and his eyes had clearly seen pain and horror and atrocities.

His Celtics sweatshirt, with its sleeves pushed high up his forearms, hung carelessly over snug blue-worn-gray jeans. No, she thought distractedly, not snug jeans. Tight. The kind of tight that made women catch their breath. Sexy tight. Street-style tight. Elizabeth caught her own breath, reminding herself that his clothes only defined what an experienced undercover cop wore to work.

Her thoughts settled again, but with a shimmer of awareness lacing around the edges. "Well, at least we agree on one thing," she said casually. "I don't want you to drive me to New Hampshire, either."

"Noted," he said, making her feel as if she were part of a police report. "However, what either of us might want personally had nothing to do with what is going to happen. Just so that there is no misunderstanding. The reason is simple. Until we find out who did this and why, you can't

stay here. Certainly you haven't forgotten that we still don't
know who killed Jim.''

The mention of her husband brought back the never-
forgotten night when Zach had come to tell her Jim was
dead. He'd held her, but she couldn't recall his arms around
her, only his words against her ear.

Scream, Lizzie. Scream, he'd said with a soft, quiet rage
that was still imprinted in her mind. From those words she
had instantly learned more about Zachariah Stone than
from all the rumors and all the praise she'd ever heard.
Being the messenger of death, she recalled thinking at the
time, had appalled him as much as Jim's murder had an-
gered him.

She'd realized then, not consciously, not even logically,
but intuitively, that although he calculated moves with ra-
pier precision he had a deep core of sensitivity.

She looked directly at him now, wondering if his anger at
Jim's murder had calcified so as to bury that sensitivity even
deeper. A random thought that she knew really had no place
in what they were discussing.

In a steady voice she said, ''You know I haven't forgotten, but connecting what happened here and Jim's murder
more than a year and a half ago seems a little farfetched.''

His eyelids lowered in a long, slow blink. ''Perhaps. But
we can't rule it out.''

''Then you think it's farfetched, too.'' She wondered
briefly if vagueness and ducked answers were a job require-
ment for cops. When he didn't immediately agree or disagree, she said quickly, ''The McGanns are right next door.
The police are as close as the telephone. I could even call you
every day to assure you I was okay. It's not as if I'm out in
the middle of nowhere.''

He sighed heavily, patiently. ''And what if the McGanns
aren't home? What if the phone wires are cut? What if
whoever ransacked this place isn't all that shy about com-

ing back. And..." He moved closer to her in a predatory manner. She doubted he was aware of it, but the shiver that slid down her back couldn't be mistaken for anything but fear. "If you and Julianne happen to be here, well, hell, no sweat. After all, what's the big deal in killing a woman and a kid who happen to be in your way?"

It was the soft but defined whisper of his boots on the carpet, and the level exacting tone of his voice that frightened her more than his words. Arguing to stay sounded insane even to her; to express it to Zach would sound even more so. The mess around her was certainly evidence that someone had had no trouble getting into the house, nor had he been careful or shy about hiding the fact.

Zach stood close enough to her that she could hear his breathing. His gray-blue eyes were unsparing. "Those are the what-ifs that Gordon would drill me with if I called him and said, 'She respectfully declines your invitation.'"

"I'm not being stubborn just for the sake of being stubborn," she snapped. She was not about to be cowed.

"You're exerting your right to take care of yourself. Fine. Understandable and commendable. But also stupid."

She counted to five before answering. "Really."

"You have a baby, remember?"

"Don't patronize me, Zach. I don't like it and I won't put up with it."

He swore, shaking his head slowly as though in debate over what to say next. "Okay, I'll tell you why I, and not Gordon, want you out of here. I hope to hell a connection to Jim's death isn't farfetched. I hope it isn't a coincidence. I hope whoever trashed your house is tied in so tight the most savvy criminal lawyer in the state won't be able to plea-bargain the bastard. If any of those hopes are true, we might catch ourselves a killer."

She swallowed, letting that possibility settle in her mind. To find the person who had robbed Julianne of her father, who had robbed her of her husband, Gordon and Naomi of their only child and, yes, even Zach of his partner...

Suddenly the ransacking took on a positive hope.

He glanced at his watch. "We've spent ten minutes discussing this—"

Elizabeth interrupted. "How long will Julianne and I be gone?"

Zach relaxed as if he'd played his last card and was relieved to find it was a winner. "Knowing Gordon? Probably until whoever did this is caught."

"Which could be a long time," she added, feeling guilty for her own exasperated reaction to finding that her life was going on hold. She loved Gordon and Naomi for their concern, she appreciated Zach being here, even though she could tell by looking at him it was about the last place he wanted to be. She was grateful people cared and were concerned enough to act on that caring, but she also honestly hated the smothered feeling that now clawed along the back of her mind.

What did other people do when faced with someone lurking about and planning to do God-knew-what? They didn't have a former police chief for a father-in-law. They certainly didn't have Zachariah Stone as a personal bodyguard. No, they installed an alarm system, or had someone move in with them.

In other words, they took necessary precautions, which she, too, could do. She was about to present that possibility to him when he shook his head.

"You're reading my mind, aren't you?" she asked with a defeated sigh.

"Lizzie, I know you want there to be another way, but there isn't." This time he did take her shoulders and gently turn her toward the stairs. "I've got to make a couple more phone calls, and then I'll come up and give you a hand carrying things down."

* * *

Upstairs, Elizabeth went into the nursery. It was decorated with white wicker furnishings and yellow wallpaper printed with giraffes, balloons and tiny kittens, and Elizabeth had made white ruffled curtains for the single window. Julianne, still dressed in the red corduroy overalls and hand-knit sweater that Naomi had made, was asleep on her stomach. With her knees tucked up beneath her, and her diapered bottom high in the air, she slept with all the contentment of a safe and happy baby.

Elizabeth smoothed her hand down her daughter's back and over her bottom, then lightly clasped her fingers around Julianne's white lacy-socked feet.

"I love you, sweetheart," she whispered, thankful all over again that she hadn't left Julianne with a baby-sitter that afternoon. She gently pulled the yellow kitten-printed quilt up to the baby's neck, then tucked a favorite teddy bear close to her.

Straightening, she crossed to a white wicker trunk and opened it to check her dwindling supply of disposable diapers, which she used only in emergencies. Normally she preferred the cotton ones provided by a local diaper service. Tonight certainly qualified as an emergency, she decided, making a mental note to ask Zach to stop at a convenience store.

Quietly, she opened drawers and began to take out clothes for the baby.

Fifteen minutes later, she was contemplating how many sleepers to pack, when Zach said, "How are you doing with the packing?"

She jumped, so startled she dropped the armful of sleepers. "You scared me. Why don't you make noise when you walk? Yes, I'm just trying to decide how much to take."

They both bent at the same time to pick up the spilled items. Because she hadn't wanted to waken Julianne, she'd only put on a small lamp with a low-wattage bulb, but the dim light gave an immediate impression of soft closeness between her and Zach.

Their knees were a hand-span away from touching, and the contrast of tight-muscled thighs in almost threadbare denims with slender legs encased in sleek black and fairly new jeans brought a jolt of awareness to both of them.

Elizabeth squeezed her eyes closed and shoved the reaction away.

Zach scowled, his mind immediately listing all the reasons why he was here. Awareness of Elizabeth Healy in any way but as Gordon's daughter-in-law wasn't one of them.

"Sorry I startled you," he said in a low voice. "I didn't want to wake the baby." He picked up the seventh sleeper. Eyeing the array, he asked, "You think you have enough of these things?" He came to his feet as did Elizabeth.

"Babies go through a lot of clothes," she said, enormously grateful that the low light kept her reaction to him from being visible. Catching herself by surprise was enough to handle.

Examining a fuzzy pink sleeper with bunny-shaped faces appliquéd on each knee, he said, "How do you get her into this?"

Elizabeth showed him how the garment came apart.

He shook his head. "Amazing. If you put it back together wrong the kid could end up with her foot where her arm should be."

Elizabeth grinned. "I think she'd complain." As if on cue, Julianne squealed.

They both glanced up, and the baby grinned back at them. She'd sat up in the middle of the crib, the quilt now bunched around her. Her blond curls were tangled, her cheeks rosy from sleep, her blue eyes wide as she peered at Zach.

Elizabeth walked the few steps to the crib, and spoke softly. "This is Zach, sweetheart. You haven't seen him since you were christened. He was your daddy's partner."

Zach didn't move. Julianne didn't take her eyes off him, then her mouth broke into a grin followed by another squeal.

"Does that mean she approves or that I've scared her?" He kept his distance from the crib, staring at the baby for a long moment. Elizabeth noted the combination of wariness and wonder in his expression. She also noted that he still held the fuzzy pink sleeper cautiously, as though not quite sure what to do with it.

"Of course she approves," Elizabeth said with a laugh. "Don't you, sweetheart?" Julianne showed off new teeth. "She hadn't quite reached the wary-of-strangers stage yet. It's curiosity mostly, but if you smile at her and say 'cookie,' she's yours forever."

"She's beautiful," Zach said simply.

"I think so."

He moved closer to the crib, laying the sleeper on the changing table. "She has your eyes—not the color but the expressiveness. And the way she smiles . . ." He came to a stop, suddenly looking uneasy.

Elizabeth watched him in fascination. Seeing him standing this close to Julianne and seeming so unsure, she suddenly recalled how he'd balanced the baby in his arms the day of the christening.

He'd tried to object when Gordon, his intent clear, had directed him to sit down and then carefully laid the six-week-old infant into Zach's arms.

Elizabeth had just returned from the kitchen. She'd paused to talk to Naomi and her own mother when she'd spotted them across the room. In that moment Zach had appeared more stunned than scared. However, he'd cooperated and allowed Gordon to settle the baby against his thighs. Julianne's tiny feet, shod in satin booties, had pushed against his stomach; her white lace dress, a mass of ribbons and ruffles, spilled over his tanned hands as she slept in his lap.

Elizabeth had been captured then, as she was now, by the contrast of sweet innocence with this man who carried a gun, consorted with back-alley lowlife, and whose hands had been covered with Jim's blood.

Her fascination, she knew, stemmed from who mastered whom, and there was no doubt Zach was more leery of Julianne than she was of him.

Now Julianne put her thumb into her mouth, keeping her eyes glued on Zach. Apparently deciding she wasn't going to scream, he eased his way a little closer. Julianne worked her way to the crib bars and gripped one of the slats.

To Elizabeth they looked like two strangers trying to figure out the easiest way to get acquainted. "It's okay to touch her," she said softly.

"She might not like it."

"She liked it when you held her at the christening."

He finally dragged his eyes away from the baby and glanced at Elizabeth. The gray-blue color, usually piercing and cold, astonished her with its candid uncertainty. "Yeah? She told you, huh?"

Elizabeth grinned. "I think she's trying to tell you herself." She gestured at Julianne, who had lifted her arms to be picked up. Zach stared as if presented with a bomb wrapped in a pretty package.

"How about if you just let her grip your finger?" Elizabeth suggested.

He looked vastly relieved, but he didn't move.

Elizabeth closed her hand around his wrist and was astounded at the pounding of his pulse. His tight leanness made his veins hot with life against her palm. At first he resisted when she tried to urge his hand closer, then finally he relented. Julianne, who wasn't the least bit shy about touching him, gripped his finger with a bold naturalness.

Elizabeth felt a sudden welling of tears that she couldn't explain. Perhaps it was seeing Zach caught so completely by the exquisite and confident grip of a baby's hand. Possibly it was the contrast of his strength and Julianne's dependency and vulnerability. Or maybe, Elizabeth acknowledged finally, it was simply her own deep gratitude to Zach that he cared enough to come because Jim couldn't.

Julianne pulled on his finger, and he laughed. Elizabeth liked the sound. She wished she could tell him he should laugh more often.

Hesitating, not sure how to say it without sounding melodramatic, she touched his wrist again. "Thank you for being here."

He turned his head enough so that she saw his eyes slide from Julianne to her. "Jim would have done the same thing for me if you were my wife and Julianne were our baby."

Momentarily startled, she was glad that Julianne had picked that precise moment to test her new teeth on his finger. It wasn't what he said, but the ease with which he said it. True, Jim would have done the same thing; both men were dedicated and loyal. But what disturbed her was the image that floated into her mind and stalled.

Unbidden, certainly unwarranted and absolutely ridiculous. Zach as her husband...

She couldn't imagine even the possibility, because he didn't fit the domestic, conventional role of husband and father. As a lover... Yes, that certainly was part of being a husband, she told herself firmly, blaming the blossoming low in her stomach on nervousness. Yes, as a lover, Zach would be...

"Ouch!" Zach yelped. "Hey, she's doing serious damage here with those teeth."

Elizabeth rescued his finger, which he examined closely for damages. "Is she part cannibal?" he asked, working the knuckle and scowling.

"You shouldn't have let her put it in her mouth."

"I didn't let her."

"Then how did it get there?"

He eyed the baby, who looked back and forth from one to the other. Zach lifted an eyebrow. "Come on, princess, confess."

Julianne grinned broadly at Zach.

"She's hungry," Zach said matter-of-factly, as if he were suddenly an expert on Julianne's eating habits. He jerked a thumb toward Elizabeth. "She doesn't make you eat all that ground-up mush, does she? Not with those teeth. That stuff must taste like..." He darted a glance at Elizabeth. "Can I say the s-word?"

"Absolutely not," she said solemnly, but pleased that he'd thought to censor his language. "Tell her that baby food tastes wonderful."

Zach leaned sideways close enough to Elizabeth so that their shoulders touched. His mouth a breath away from her ear, he whispered, "Now, that is definitely a bunch of..." The explicit word that followed left no doubt as to his opinion of baby food.

"It's what babies eat."

"No wonder she liked my finger," he said, keeping his hand out of Julianne's reach but giving the baby a wink.

He glanced over at the stack of clothes and accessories that Elizabeth had been gathering to take. "You're not going to be gone for a year, you know."

"I could add the playpen," she said succinctly.

"By the time you get your own stuff, I'll have to rent a truck." He glanced at his watch, then grinned at Julianne, who had pulled herself to her feet. "Your mother is making us lose time, princess."

Elizabeth started to say something, but instead felt herself swallow hard at Julianne's obvious fascination with Zach. He, too, seemed equally taken with her. And as silly as it probably was, she very much liked the idea of the two of them getting along so well.

They worked silently and quickly. Elizabeth handed things to Zach, and he in turn carried them out to the car. After he took out the last load of Julianne's things he almost collided with Elizabeth as she came out of the guest room with a suitcase. She handed it to him.

"There are slacks and sweaters on my bed. Put them in this one. I'll get the other suitcase."

When she entered her bedroom moments later, the chintz fabrics, the wall mural of an English garden in the spring, the queen-size bed with its brass headboard, had all taken on a different feel with Zach in the room. A nebulous quickening spread through her, followed by a sudden nervousness that she told herself was ridiculous.

She wasn't nervous in any other room with him.... Well, most of the time she wasn't. Besides, telling him to leave after she'd been the one to hand him the suitcase would only call more attention to a silly feminine reaction that Zach would probably find laughable. She doubted he'd ever encountered a woman who was uneasy about being in a bedroom with him.

Ecstatic was more like it, she concluded, thinking about all those stories she'd heard about his 125-mile-per-hour marathon drives on the interstates in his black sports car and the stunning blondes who graced the passenger side.

He'd packed the slacks and sweaters she'd laid out on the bed, and stood with his head cocked to the side staring into her open closet. She had the immediate impression that the rows of clothes stunned him.

Elizabeth had never denied that she liked clothes. However, she did acknowledge that fleeting moments of guilt plagued her. Normally, she was able to dismiss them with the logic that everyone was entitled to at least one vice. She paid her bills, didn't smoke, drank very little and only overspent at sales. Which was justified, she told herself, by the money she saved.

What she purchased she wore. Most of the time. But occasionally she made an impulsive selection, like the black watered-silk dress with iridescent pearl buttons running neck to hem that Zach was pulling out of the closet.

She moved quickly to place herself between him and what suddenly loomed at her like the annex to a department store. He held up the dress, staring at the watered silk as though he'd never seen a black dress. Or maybe he couldn't imagine her wearing it.

For no logical reason, she felt shallow and frivolous. "I don't think I'll need that where we're going."

He glanced at her as though suddenly realizing she was in the room. Studying the garment again, his eyes moving slowly up the row of buttons, he asked, "Do you start at the top or the bottom when you button this? When I was a kid and had to deal with more than four buttons I always came out wrong if I started at the top." His eyes again skimmed the length of the closures. "There must be thirty or more here."

"Thirty-three," she said hurriedly and wondered why she hadn't stuffed the impulsive purchase in the back of the closet. "It doesn't matter. I shouldn't have bought it, anyway."

He frowned as if the fabric had a flaw he'd missed. "What's wrong with it?"

"Nothing. It's a beautiful dress, but I bought it on a whim and when I got it home I didn't like it."

He studied her for a long moment, not in any obvious, assessing way as if he were trying to decide how it would look on her, but as though he were more interested in what prompted the impulse. "You must have liked something about it."

In truth, she'd fallen in love with the silky creation the moment she'd seen it in the window of Monique's, which was known in Liberty for its exquisite collection. She'd debated all of ten seconds before entering and trying the dress on. In the tiny mirrored dressing room scented with French perfume and lighting that threw sultry and flattering shadows, the customer was lulled into the sensation that a purchase from Monique's would ensure fulfillment of all the most coveted desires.

Elizabeth had entered the dressing room determined not to be seduced by scents and sensations. She'd had no intention of buying, and Monique's policy that if a customer needed to know the price she should go to a department store had only reinforced that intention.

Yet when the silk had draped around her body, and she caught sight of herself in the mirror, she forgot about price and impulse. Captured by the understated simplicity of the garment and the thirty-three buttons that could determine her daring, she was defeated and she knew it.

For those few moments, she'd felt incredibly feminine and sleekly sensual. Both sensations settled over her with a languid extravagance she knew came very close to arousal.

Later at home, many dollars poorer and knowing there was not one place in Liberty where she would wear the dress, she began to have regrets. Good sense said to take it back, but she hadn't. Instead she'd put it in her closet and tried to ignore it.

Zach, still holding the dress, murmured casually, "I bet you'd look sensational in this."

It was a stunning comment—unexpected and deliberately complimentary.

Elizabeth sighed. Between thoughts of the dress and unease at Zach's presence in her bedroom, her usual calm-

ness had deserted her. Now that she considered it, she'd had
a number of undone moments since she'd walked into the
den and seen him. They would be together no more than the
time it took to get to New Hampshire, which she knew,
given Zach's reputation for sound-barrier-breaking driving, would be about two and a half hours.

She took the dress from Zach. "As I said, it was a whim.
Even if it was my favorite dress, it's hardly what I'd pack to
go to Gordon and Naomi's." She stuffed the black silk back
in the closet.

Zach said, "I think I hear the baby."

Elizabeth started toward the nursery.

"I'll close up this one suitcase and take it down to the
car."

"All right. I can get the rest."

In the nursery, Julianne had in fact gone back to sleep.
Elizabeth heard Zach go down the stairs. She tucked the
quilt around the baby, deciding he must have been hearing
things. She went back to her bedroom to finish her packing.

After she added cosmetics, underwear, her flannel night-
gowns and other items, she closed the second suitcase. She
crossed to the windows, intending to close the drapes.

Her bedroom was located above the den and looked out
across the backyard. She glanced toward where she remembered having seen the intruder run away. The late-afternoon
sun was a smoky yellow, the gray sky heavy with brooding
clouds. Beyond the neighbor's yard she could see headlights spraying white beams down the next street. A few
outside lights were on, and she could hear Prince, the
McGanns' German shepherd, barking.

She ought to get a dog, she mused thoughtfully as she
adjusted the drapes. For protection and for Julianne. Julianne loved Prince, and Prince...

Elizabeth drew in a quick gasp, her fingers clutching the drapery cord, her legs suddenly wobbly.

''Zach . . .'' She whispered his name as if he were standing mere inches away instead of downstairs loading the car. Someone stood near the maple tree, so still she had to blink twice to make sure it wasn't a shadow or an illusion of her imagination.

She backed away from the window. Suddenly all her earlier arguments and reluctance about leaving seemed silly and childish and stupid.

Taking another step back, she felt hands grip her shoulders.

Chapter 3

"Lizzie, it's me." Zach whirled her around and she sagged against him.

"Out...there. Someone..."

He steadied her, then moved her to the side, easing her down to sit on the bed. Quickly he worked his way to the window without stepping directly in front of it. The drapes were partially closed. He knifed a finger down one of the folds and looked out.

Elizabeth pressed her arms against her body to stop herself from shaking.

"I don't see anyone, Lizzie."

"By the tree."

He searched again, then backed away. "I'm going out to take a look."

She came to her feet instantly, reaching out for him. "No!"

He caught her to him, stunned by the sheer terror he could feel in her body. He made his voice low and soft and, he hoped, reassuring. "Shh, it's okay."

"Please don't go."

Her hands gripped his waist, her fingers digging into his ribs, her eyes wide and hauntingly deep and vulnerable. Momentarily, he was taken aback by her reaction, then wondered if she was thinking about Jim. About his leaving and not coming back.

He rubbed one hand down her back in a soothing motion, noting in passing the shape of each bone, the warmth of her skin, which seemed to penetrate through the layers of clothes to heat his palm. Her breasts pushed into his chest, and he wasn't sure if the pounding heart was hers or his or both. Her legs trembled against his thighs, but it was her hands gripping at his ribs almost painfully that made an indelible impression.

He gently set her away, still lightly gripping her shoulders. When she finally raised her lashes, he saw a new terror.

Her voice was barely a rasp as she clutched at handfuls of his sheepskin jacket. "He might have a gun. What if he tried to kill . . . ?" She swallowed hard, her cheeks tight and pale, as if she were trying to brace herself for the possibility that he would not return.

The unfinished sentence floundered between them. She must have asked herself that question every time Jim went out on assignment, Zach thought. He seriously doubted that whoever was out there, if there was anyone, had any intention of using a gun. He would have seen the second car in the driveway parked behind Elizabeth's. He probably knew the police had been here, and in fact were still here. But Zach knew that to make assumptions based on probabilities was both naive and stupid.

Pressing his fingers into her wrists, he felt the terror throb in her pulse. Lizzie certainly had more reason to fear than most. Jim's murder had given her that.

Finally she released her grip on his jacket.

"Stay away from the window," he ordered softly. "I'll be right back."

He hadn't taken two steps when her words stopped him.

"Aren't you going to tell me not to worry?"

Her question held a ring of startled surprise rather than fear. In Zach's opinion, the standard phrase was a patronizing insult that assumed the good guys always won, and cops feared nothing.

He knew better. The bad guys did win—too damned often. And as for fear, he'd learned that a healthy respect for the emotion was a reliable protector.

Meeting her eyes directly so that she would know he was being straight with her, he said, "No, it's impossible not to worry. I'd be concerned if you didn't worry."

She seemed to relax, looking less stressed, less terrified, as though he'd given her permission to be afraid.

Her resilience impressed him. He tucked that realization into the back of his mind, subconsciously aware that his mind was more objective than his heart.

She kept her hands lightly clasped, but her voice still rasped with the remnants of concern. "Be careful, please."

Outside, the December afternoon was gathering into twilight. Zach moved quickly and silently. His eyes searched and his ears listened until he was reasonably sure the yard was deserted.

Depending on the gut instinct that he had doggedly formed in an array of foster homes, developed in the army and honed during his years in police work, Zach was alert to any change in the air or a noise that was out of sync.

He hunkered down beside the tree, his boots making no imprint on the frozen ground. Concentrating, and moving only his eyes, he made a slow investigation of the area.

Logic told him that the obvious—a crushed and still-warm cigarette, a gum wrapper, a discarded toothpick—would be too easy. Yet if there'd been someone here, why would he deliberately stand where he could be seen? Why not hide behind the tree where he wouldn't be spotted from any of the house windows?

Perhaps he had been hiding and had hurried away when Lizzie appeared at the window. And if that were the case, it made it more than probable that the bastard would return.

He stood, his anger coming almost instantly. He needed no close self-examination to know that his reaction to the ransacker returning went beyond the knee-jerk reaction of protecting a woman and child in danger. That reaction was a given for a cop. This anger, he knew, was different. It went deeper and dragged open doors he'd closed and locked years ago.

He added annoyance to his anger. God, he thought, it didn't take any cosmic revelation to know that at some point after he walked into Lizzie's house, he'd let his guard down. But when?

When he'd seen the hellish mess? When he'd picked up the piece of sculpture she'd shaped? When he'd seen her come into the den, her expression sad, and questioning, and strained?

Or had it been Julianne and those few moments of laughter and wonder? Or Lizzie's overstuffed closet? Or her clinging to him? Frightened for herself, frightened for him.

The "whens" and the "ors" unfolded in his mind like a multitude of unwanted layers suddenly thrust upon him. The flip side of his thoughts wasn't any more reassuring, and a hell of a lot more troubling.

If the force had treated the ransacking as routine vandalism, if Gordon hadn't called him, and if while this scum was standing out here, Lizzie and Julianne had been alone in the house...

He swore raggedly, letting his head drop forward, shaking it slowly. God, he knew better than to do this. Ifs were a guaranteed road to the crazies.

He leaned against the tree. Despite the below-freezing temperature, a trickle of sweat inched its way down his back. The wind ruffled through his hair as he glanced up at her bedroom window. The drapes were still partially closed.

His thoughts, however, were centered in the nursery when she'd thanked him for being there. He'd seen the dampness in her eyes. Gratitude, even tearful gratitude, was normal given the situation. It was his own response that unsettled him.

He should have said, Jim was my partner and I don't want anything to happen to his widow and his daughter. Concerned objectivity should have been his reaction. Cool and precise and professional.

But instead—and too damn naturally, he thought in retrospect—he'd said, Jim would have done the same thing for me, if you were my wife and Julianne were our baby. Too subjective, too involved, too tough to step back from.

He turned away, his gaze as unfocused as his thoughts. Grappling with where in hell he was going rattled him as much as the fact that he'd even framed the question. He made it a point of never getting into a situation without knowing how to get out. It had been a simple, dependable philosophy that he'd applied since he was a kid, back in those days when he had allowed his feelings to box him in.

Hell, this wasn't tough, and it involved nothing but his car and his presence. Get them out of Liberty and up to New Hampshire.

Not a lot of muscle and hustle, Stone. Not even complicated. Just do it, and chalk up all this involved, introspective mush to lack of sleep and too long without some down time.

Pushing away from the tree, he sighed heavily.

He pulled up his coat collar against the chilling wind. Nothing here but his own unwieldy thoughts. His questions about the ransacking returned as he walked back to the house.

What could be in the house that suddenly had become important now? A year and a half later? Even Lizzie had wondered about any connection to Jim after so long a time.

Another question ate at him, as he closed the back door and moved through the house and up the stairs. Why hadn't the ransacker started in the master bedroom? The bedroom was the common place to hide valuables and every thief knew it. That the ransacker had not touched the bedroom pointed, as he and Gordon had already suspected, to some connection to Jim.

Outside of Lizzie's bedroom, he rubbed at his temples, his weariness making it difficult to think. Once he got Lizzie and Julianne to safety and got some sleep, then he could begin to piece this together.

Yeah, safety for Jim's family and then sleep. Once those priorities were accomplished, then he could examine the other question about Jim that lay in the back of his mind, unexplored and unwanted.

"The squad car is here," Zach said to Elizabeth. "I'm going over to give them your keys."

Half an hour had passed since he had returned from the backyard. Julianne had been snapped into a head-to-toe pink snowsuit and strapped into the car carrier, which was now anchored firmly in the back seat of Zach's car. Elizabeth had dressed in warmer clothes, exchanging her white wool coat for a more practical down jacket.

She wished the verbal exchange with Zach had been as simple. After he returned to the house, saying that whoever had been in the yard was gone, he'd been brisk and distant—the cop doing what he'd come for.

She wouldn't have called their conversation a few moments earlier an argument, because she found out quickly he didn't argue, he just stated his position and his opinion. In retrospect, she decided, his comments revealed a lot about him. But then, in the little time since she'd walked into the den and faced Zach, she'd learned that no exchange with him was simply a calm discussion of differing viewpoints.

There was this undercurrent of unspoken words and thoughts and feelings that she couldn't identify. But they were there, swirling and thick, scary and fascinating.

Yes, she thought, fascinating described the exchange that had taken place in her kitchen.

She'd had Julianne propped on one hip and her shoulder bag rested against the other one. The lights in the house were out except for the outside one. It was almost five o'clock, and the murky afternoon had finally ebbed into darkness. Elizabeth wasn't sure what had set her off—whether it was her distress at having to leave her house in shambles, or the feeling of invasion that hadn't dissipated, or the myriad reactions she'd had to Zach Stone.

He'd packed everything she'd asked him to with few questions, and stood impatiently with his hand on the doorknob, waiting. Maybe it was his stance—too tense. Or maybe his attitude—too distant and cool.

She had held her ring of keys as if her ownership of them was suddenly crucial. "I can lock my own door."

He didn't move. "You've got your hands full."

"Every time I go out the door with Julianne I have my hands full. I manage then, I can now."

"Now, you don't have to." He pulled open the door, indicating she should go out and hand him the keys on the way.

Her only emotion was to get a firmer grip on Julianne. "Do you know how sexist that sounds?"

He sighed. "Lizzie, we don't have time to debate your rights, your independence or my sexist attitude."

Her eyes widened. "So you admit you have one."

She was about to add him to a list of men that included Liberty's city council president and the truck driver who made deliveries to The Easel. She never had a chance.

"With every breath I take."

His response stunned her. The council president denied such an attitude, the truck driver laughed it off, and she knew a few men who skirted the issue altogether.

As irritated as she was with him, she couldn't fault him for laying out how he felt regardless of the way it sounded. Zach didn't flaunt pride like some macho badge. His attitude had established roots that went deeper than disagreement about male and female roles.

He lifted the keys from her fingers while she was still trying to decide whether to push the issue. When she met his eyes, the gray-blue color seemed cold and bottomless.

"Any keys on here you don't want Buzz to have?" he asked, hefting her key ring as though it exemplified a life of secrets and locks.

His question reminded her why the argument had begun. Unsure if it was his tone of voice or his implication that she didn't like she still wasn't about to let this one slide.

Glaring back at him, she snapped, "Keys to what?"

From the puzzled expression on his face, she knew she'd caught him by surprise. "I don't know. That's why I'm asking."

"Any keys I didn't want Buzz to have wouldn't be on the key ring," she said briskly.

He showed absolutely no change in his expression, but he didn't back off, either. "What about keys to the store? Or does the Foley woman have a set?"

Elizabeth had made some phone calls to let people know she would be away for a few days. She'd called her parents in Virginia, and without giving them details that would worry them, had said that Gordon and Naomi had invited her to New Hampshire. She had called her neighbor, Betsy, and finally Yvette Foley, her store manager.

To Zach she said, "Yvette has her own set of keys."

He opened the back door and ran a finger above the door ledge, checking for any spare keys.

"Really, Zach, I do know better than to be so obvious."

"Don't get defensive. You'd be amazed at how many people hide keys in obvious places as if any thief is a real dummy."

She couldn't see his eyes because of the shadows in the kitchen, but there was no doubt he was impatient to get going. Coming up to her and urging her out the door ahead of him, he said, "Now that we've managed to argue about something as inane as who locks the door, let's go."

"It wasn't an argument."

He sighed. "Ah, a debate. A brand-new experience for me—debating with a woman."

And with that he had locked the door and made sure she and Julianne were settled in the car.

Her thoughts came back to the present as she watched him talk to the officers in the police car.

The inside of Zach's car was deliciously warm with a subtle smell that she couldn't identify, but a scent she associated with Zach. Not after-shave, but an elusive male scent that lingered pleasantly around her.

As fascinating as the man, she thought as she buckled the seat belt. She noticed a spill-proof coffee mug large enough to hold three cups resting on the console. Along with the mug was a handful of change, a package of peanut butter crackers, cellophane-wrapped peppermints and the kind of small notebook that cops used to keep track of any police-business mileage accumulated in their own vehicles. Curious, and telling herself he'd have locked it in the glove compartment if it was confidential, she opened the log to the last entry.

The mileage was listed and next to it: *Elizabeth Healy— 439 Greenwood Drive—12/3-2:48 p.m.* For no reason that made any sense she was disappointed.

Really a dumb reaction, she told herself. What did she expect to see? Some personal comment? Some warmth between the lines? Something that told her she and Julianne weren't just some entry or an assignment that would soon be lost among a hundred others?

He was a professional doing his job. That was why he was here. Gordon had sent him. Period. But in her bedroom for those few terrified moments, she'd sensed something different, something beyond the cop doing his duty. The debate, as he had called it, over her keys had more to do with who was going to be in control than with who was going to lock the door.

What was going on between her and Zach?

They were barely more than casually acquainted. Their disagreements certainly overshadowed their agreements. Julianne had been the one thing they hadn't argued about.

She glanced over to where he stood by the police car. Admittedly, she liked him, and while on the surface there was certainly nothing wrong with that, the fact that she took note of the feeling puzzled her. Liking wasn't love or hate or anger or jealousy—all strong and easily identifiable emotions. No, from her own experience, she knew that liking someone was elusive and many times instinctive.

With Zach the feeling took on a different definition. Encompassing. And rushing at her from so many directions she wasn't sure of the source.

She shook her head to clear away the muddle of thoughts. What did it matter? In a few hours she and Julianne would be in New Hampshire. Allowing herself to simply like him for that short amount of time certainly wasn't going to change her life.

The two officers inside the squad car had just come on duty, and Zach envied their alert eyes and exhaustion-free faces.

A few more hours, he told himself, unsure whether his exhaustion came from lack of sleep or from fending off the shift and churn of reactions that were set in motion every time he allowed himself to think about Lizzie.

He wished to hell he didn't like Gordon so much. He'd hand off this assignment to another cop, call Kathy... He scowled. Or was it Katy? He shook his head in self-annoyance.

A lousy commentary on the women in your life, Stone, when you can't even remember their names. Or worse. You don't even care. Except Lizzie. He not only couldn't forget her name, but he'd begun to like it.

He glanced at his watch. The driving time to Gordon's was three hours. With a little luck from the weather, he could make it in two and a half. He silently sent a plea heavenward.

Reaching through the open window, he plucked a package of cigarettes off the dash and lit one, ignoring the fact he'd quit smoking six months ago. "When is Buzz coming?"

"Twenty minutes max." Don Massey, the more talkative of the two officers, was full-faced and soft-bellied from too many hours in a squad car on duty, and too many beers off duty. "He had a couple things to clear up. You really think this guy will come back?"

The smoke burned Zach's lungs. He coughed, scowling at the cigarette. He wasn't sure whether to blame Elizabeth for distracting him, or himself for allowing it.

He dropped the cigarette to the ground and stepped on it. "Yeah, I think he'll be back, and I have a gut feeling he isn't gonna be real nice about it."

"Probably that depends on what he was looking for. Any theories?"

"Yeah, but none that I'm ready to talk about. I'd just feel better if the house wasn't vacant. No sense in sending him an invitation." He tossed Elizabeth's keys to Massey.

The officer threw the keys on the dash. "How's Elizabeth handlin' all this?"

"Like we all are. Cautiously."

"You look beat-up, Zach."

"Nothing some sleep won't cure." He glanced up at the brooding clouds, wondering if his no-snow plea had made it through. The air bit sharply at his cheeks. "Heard any weather forecasts?"

"You don't want to know."

He swore, then clamped a hand down on Massey's shoulder. "Tell Buzz thanks, and I'll be in touch."

Massey wished him luck, as did the other officer, Lippincott.

"Hey, Zach," Massey called as he walked away.

He turned back.

"It's a good thing she ain't a blonde, huh?"

Zach arched an eyebrow. "It wouldn't matter. She's Gordon's daughter-in-law."

"Yeah, come to think of it, that's about as off-limits as a woman can be. I bet on a clear day a guy could see the warning signs all the way into New Hampshire." Massey nodded knowingly. "Which is why you got the transportation job."

Zach frowned as he walked back to join Elizabeth. It wasn't the off-limits or the warning-sign comments, not even the implication that Gordon trusted Zach more than another cop. No, it was his own comment that she was Gordon's daughter-in-law, rather than Jim's widow.

His mind was as beat as his body felt and, no doubt, looked. Bad choice of words, he told himself. Not worth thinking about.

He climbed into the car. "All set."

"Everything okay? You look concerned about something."

"Just about getting going before the snow."

Zach backed out of the drive, beeped at the men in the squad car, who honked in return, and headed down Greenwood Drive. He made a few turns, coming to a stop at a light in downtown Liberty.

Christmas lights were strung in festive loops that spanned the street like a bower. The traffic was steady, a combination of rush hour and shoppers. When she saw a station wagon turn in to a convenience store, Elizabeth remembered the diapers.

Zach glanced over at her. "Correct me if I'm wrong, but didn't I carry out a box of diapers?"

"Not enough."

Zach put on his turn signal. "Now, why didn't I know that?" he muttered beneath his breath. He double-parked, but didn't turn the engine off. She already had the door open when he said, "Here, you'll need some money."

"I have money."

He hesitated a moment, frowned, and then said, "Sexist, huh?"

She grinned, liking the way he puzzled over his own words. "Perhaps."

"Am I going to have to watch every word I say? I can't swear in front of Julianne and I'm suppose to treat you like..." He paused, then gave her a measured look. "I'm not even sure."

Elizabeth swung her legs out of the car. "How about equal?" She gave him her most dazzling smile. "It should be an interesting trip."

She bought diapers and two coffees, putting cream in his because she used cream and she didn't want to lose her place in line to go out and ask him whether he did.

After she returned to the car, she found herself inordinately pleased when he thanked her and said he hated black coffee.

Fifteen minutes later, Zach parked in front of an apartment building, beside a gleaming black sports car with tinted windows and the kind of grillwork that tended to growl rather than smile.

"So it's really true," Elizabeth commented as she sipped her coffee.

He put the cap back on his to keep it hot for the few minutes it would take him to get some clothes. "What's true?"

"The black sports car. I've heard all sorts of stories."

"Uh-oh. Should I take the fifth?"

She grinned. "They're all true, aren't they? The speed, the state police not stopping you, the blondes you're often seen with."

"I like to drive fast, and yeah, the cops indulge me. We have this deal that they won't stop me if I behave at rush hour."

"Somehow, you behaving doesn't quite fit."

"Ah, you've been listening to all those stories, but no one rides with me at 125 miles per hour."

She shivered. Sixty-five was about as fast as she ever drove. It made her dizzy just thinking about 125. "Why do you do it?"

"Relax, I'm not suicidal. Mostly, to ease job stress. Every time I go to work, whenever I draw a gun to go around the next corner, I'm expecting some bastard to come at me with no intention of walking away until I'm dead. I live with it, and I deal with it, but sometimes the strain…" He shrugged, tossing it off as a job hazard. "It takes the edge off."

"It shouldn't be that way. The strain and pressure, I mean."

"No. It should always be the good guys winning and amen to happy endings."

"So you drive and for those moments you forget."

"Yeah. It doesn't change anything, but it drains me out so completely that the stress and the strain are gone. In a lot of ways it's like good sex."

The correlation between men, sports cars and sex certainly wasn't an original comparison, but his matter-of-fact statement left her mouth a little dry.

He opened his door and the dome light came on. She blinked at the sudden brightness.

"I'll just be a few minutes. You want to wait here or come up with me?"

"We'll wait. Julianne is almost asleep."

He turned around and playfully tugged Julianne's foot. "Keep an eye on your mother, Princess."

After Zach had gone into his apartment, Elizabeth frowned. It had been a night of chance and different feelings.

He and Julianne had certainly become friends quickly.

Between herself and Zach, other feelings tugged. Feelings that intrigued her. Feelings she liked. Feelings she'd promised herself she would never have again for a man with a dangerous job.

Then with a clarity that made her catch her breath she realized she'd broken her own promise when she saw the figure by the tree in her backyard.

Her fear had rushed at her, and she'd reacted automatically. She hadn't wanted some sweet man in a safe job, who would hold her hand and tell her everything would be fine.

She'd wanted Zach Stone.

Chapter 4

He simply liked her and that bothered him.

Zach knew little about liking women unless they were fringe acquaintances such as his landlady or the waitress at the coffee shop around the corner from his apartment. But there was a comfortable distance to his relationship with his landlady or the waitress. Nothing beyond polite conversation, some friendly teasing on occasion or, at the most, his talk with the waitress's son—at her request—about his occasional drug use.

Yet with Lizzie he felt as though he were facing an unexplored territory. And territory stumbled through without preparation, he knew from experience, tended to get complicated, emotional and messy.

He snapped on his directional signal and took the ramp onto the interstate. They were about an hour out of Liberty and the snow he'd hoped wouldn't happen had arrived and was getting heavier. The wipers worked tirelessly, but the white stuff was building up so that the windshield appeared imprinted with side-by-side spread-open fans. The car wasn't overly warm, although Zach had turned the heat higher for Julianne. The baby was asleep and he could hear her soft, even breathing behind him.

Lizzie was buckled in and sitting as far away from him as she could get. Body language, he'd learned over the years, rarely was faked, and no doubt her distance had more to do with her experiencing a loss of independence in doing as Gordon had requested than with her feelings about him personally. At least that was what he assured himself.

She had turned her head enough that he could just make out the details of her profile. He noted again, as he had at her house, that she had a strong face, not in the sense of being tough or rigid, or foolishly stubborn, but expressively determined.

Since they obviously couldn't continue this silence all the way to New Hampshire, he decided to break it. Taking a thoughtful breath, he considered asking her an innocuous question such as, "Are you all right?" Or an even more useless comment such as, "This is quite a snowstorm."

He did neither. "You're still angry, aren't you?"

When she didn't answer right away, he wondered if she'd fallen asleep or had decided to ignore him. Perhaps it was just as well, he decided, given the range of feelings that had passed between them. Anger, fear, some laughter—thank God for Julianne—but beyond any of those emotions he'd felt the underlying tension.

The question of when the strain had first occurred didn't disturb him as much as why. He wanted to ignore the why only because *why* scared the hell out of him. Had she, too, felt the expectation? He suspected so, which could account for her silence since they'd left Liberty.

She sighed heavily. "I just wish there'd been another way."

What an understatement that was, he thought ruefully. "You cooperated extremely well, given the sudden circumstances." He wondered if he sounded as patronizing to her as he did to himself.

"Did I have a choice?"

"Of course."

She straightened up, her eyes wide. Despite the dimness of the car's interior he could see the sudden interest in her expression. "You mean there was a way I could have stayed in Liberty?"

Zach slowed down and eased his way past a van fishtailing along as though the driver had never encountered snow before. When he was safely beyond him, he glanced in the rearview mirror. "Damn fool," he muttered under his breath. Then to Lizzie he said, "I thought we settled that. No, I meant you had a choice in how you'd come with me. Either the sensible way that you did or being carried kicking and screaming."

For a moment she said nothing, as though she thought she had heard wrong or that he was being facetious. When he didn't explain or pass it off as a joke, she gave him a dark and annoyed response. "Not very likely."

He shrugged and flexed his fingers, then repositioned his left hand on the top of the steering wheel. He rubbed his other hand along his thigh where he could feel the beginning of a leg cramp. It was a sure sign of his exhaustion, combined, he was positive, with the difficult driving because of the snow and these not very welcome reactions to Jim's widow.

She turned in the seat, drawing one leg up and angling it for balance while at the same time loosening her seat belt. He was glad it wasn't summer, when she'd probably be wearing shorts and one of those flimsy cotton tops. Yeah, winter was definitely better. Coats and boots and multilayered clothes didn't coax interest quite so obviously.

She tipped her head to the side and asked, "Is that what you usually do when you don't get your way? Use force? Or is that a particular trait you only use with women?"

Calm yet confrontational, he noted, adding another interesting facet to his knowledge of Elizabeth Healy. He liked these changing tones in her voice; the variety enhanced the depth he suspected she possessed. He'd heard stubbornness when he first mentioned New Hampshire, nurturing softness when she spoke of Julianne, fear when she'd seen someone in the backyard and even the occasional flash of humor.

With a mental shift that came so quickly and automatically he didn't have time to kill his thoughts, he allowed himself to consider what scared him about her: Lizzie, the woman, not Elizabeth Healy, Jim's widow and Gordon's daughter-in-law.

Then as though acutely attuned, his body stirred, reminding him of the dangerous potential in his first thought.

Despite the fact he had no intention of turning thoughts or fantasies into reality, he imagined the feel of her sleek body wrapped around his, her eyes heavy and liquid, her mouth a little swollen, her breathing too quick as though her passion outpaced her need for air. How would she sound when aroused? Breathless? Aching? Perhaps husky, tantalizing him with love words?

Enticing thoughts that would remain just that, he reminded himself. He concentrated instead on the tone of her questions. What he'd heard now had a kind of biting sweetness, with more dark impact than a screech of outrage. If he were so inclined he could have answered in such a way as to keep an argument going all the way to Gordon's. But he rarely argued with women. He maintained that the energy needed for a fight could be put to better use.

"I never use force with a woman."

"How chivalrous of you," she said, the sarcasm in her voice so dry it smoked.

"It's called mutual agreement."

"What happens when they don't agree?"

Given the direction of his previous thoughts, he allowed himself a touch of amusement to filter his words. "That's never happened."

She slumped back in the seat. "Including this time," she said, sounding dejected and disappointed in herself.

Zach winced as the cramp in his leg worked its way higher. "Lizzie, don't read more into it than there is."

"Read more into it! Carrying me out kicking and screaming hardly needs a lot of translation."

"Why are we arguing about this? You're here. You co-operated and therefore I didn't have to be too persuasive."

"In other words you got your way."

He deliberately ignored the challenge in her voice. He didn't want to sound arrogant, but he had gotten his way and he had no intention of apologizing for it. "And you didn't fight me. At least not too much."

She shivered and folded her arms against her body. Zach nudged the temperature up despite his own preference for a cool car. Not only did it keep him more alert, but by nature he was rarely cold. He was dressed now in jeans and a black turtleneck sweater, having shed his jacket when he returned to the car with the charcoal-gray nylon bag containing his clothes, and a garment bag. The latter hadn't exactly been a last-minute thought, but he was leaving himself plenty of room to change his mind. He didn't intend to stay long at Gordon's, but if nothing had broken in Liberty and Buzz wasn't having any problems, he might stay overnight. But then again he might not.

Elizabeth turned around to check on Julianne, and then settled back and rebuckled the seat belt. She reached for one of the peppermint candies on the console.

"Do you mind?" she asked suddenly, as though she had touched something personal.

"Help yourself. If you're hungry we can stop," he said, deciding that walking around would definitely loosen his cramp.

"Maybe some more coffee." The cellophane crackled and she put the candy into her mouth. "Do you want one?"

"Yeah." But before he could reach for one, she had one in her hand and was opening it. He knew what she was going to do as surely as he knew there was absolutely nothing seductive or flirtatious in the act. He also knew he wanted her to do it.

A state trooper passed him and honked twice. Zach jumped at the sudden intrusion, damning himself for his inattention. He honked back and scowled. "On second thought—" he began, but she was talking, too.

"...something in common. She loves peppermint ice cream."

"What?" he asked.

"You and Julianne have something in common."

He didn't dare look at her, but he sensed the motion toward him. It's a lousy piece of candy, for God's sake, hardly worthy of a passing thought. And yet he anticipated the confection on her fingers, headed toward his mouth, with a deep gut-pulling ache usually aroused by tasting and exploring the textures of a woman's breast.

She moved her hand closer, distracting him far more dangerously than a honking horn when she braced a hand on his cramped thigh. He wasn't sure who jumped, she or he.

At that moment a car pulled onto the highway to his right. Zach reacted as though the road surface were as dry as an August afternoon and changed lanes. Despite the four-wheel drive, the car lurched dangerously, tossing Lizzie against him.

Zach swore and wrestled with the wheel, while at the same time resisting the instinctive urge to jam his foot down on the brake. That would guarantee an accident. He let the car slide. They spun sideways with the grace of an ice skater. Lizzie's fingers gripped his thigh through the denim of his jeans. He felt their baggage in the back shift and slide.

"Hell," he growled, wishing for a handy line of Jersey barriers to slide into. Lizzie reached behind him and gripped the side of Julianne's car sleeper. That action pressed her up against him. If the car flipped, at least he'd be able to cushion her, but he had no intention of this trip ending with them upside down in a snowdrift on the side of the road. He damned his inattention, his exhaustion and his distracted thoughts.

The spin finally slowed. They came to a stop. Zach gripped the wheel and sighed in relief. He could feel the beads of sweat on his forehead. Lizzie was still frozen against him, although he felt her sag as if she'd been holding her breath the entire time.

They were catty-corner across the road. Her fingers felt permanently attached to his leg. Softly he said, "Lizzie, could you loosen your hand?"

"Oh, God," she murmured in a dry raspy voice.

"It's all right." He squeezed her fingers and then let them go. "Now I know where Julianne gets her grip." He eased the car around, taking note of an oncoming car across the median so they didn't end up going in the wrong direction.

"Zach, I'm sorry."

"It wasn't your fault. I should have seen the car coming."

"The visibility is terrible and me arguing with you probably didn't help your concentration."

"We weren't arguing, and even if we were, that's not an excuse. I should have seen him."

Then, before she settled back on her side of the car, she again leaned toward him and deftly tucked the piece of candy into his mouth. And against his tongue. It happened so quickly that he barely tasted the gentleness and the smoothness of her fingers before the cool sharpness of the candy. The entire episode, from the moment she had asked him if he wanted the peppermint to her settling back, buckling up and tucking the wrappers into the litter bag, had taken less time than a deliberate seduction. Yet he'd been seduced. Maybe not in a literal sense, but he wasn't sure if that might not have been safer. This nerve-ending sizzle had nearly gotten them in a nasty accident.

Zach scowled, not at what she'd done, but at his reaction. Whether its cause was the naturalness of the gesture, the unexpected contact or his own interpretation, he wasn't sure.

However, he was grateful for the distance, the darkness and the silence. He sucked the candy down to a wafer-thin disk, trying to dispel the taste of her. When the candy melted away he could still taste her.

He eased up on the gas and gently braked when they came up behind a snowplow. Sand sprayed out in a wide sweeping motion from behind the truck as the driver moved the drifting snow ahead of him. The road surface had long since become invisible. The green reflective signs were crusty-white, their letters partially covered with snow. Zach knew that if the roads had been dry, they would be outside of Boston right now. But because of the slow travel, they'd barely crossed the state line into Massachusetts.

He recalled the plea he'd sent skyward while still at Lizzie's. "I'd hoped this would hold off for a few hours. Instead, the damn snow is getting worse."

"At least we're not on a side road where they don't plow."

"The way this stuff is coming down, plowing is almost futile." A sign appeared advertising gas and food two miles ahead. "I think I'll give Gordon another call and tell him what we've run into. Knowing him, if we're too late he'll send the state police to find us."

The two miles took six minutes. In the parking lot there were only three cars but a lot of trucks parked with their engines running and their lights dimmed. Zach stopped close to the entrance of the restaurant.

Elizabeth undid her seat belt and got onto her knees to lean over the seat. She spoke softly as she bundled up Julianne, who wasn't too happy at being awakened. Zach unlocked the doors, turned the engine off and got out of the car. His boots sank into four inches of dry powder. The wind bit with a snapping cold, but what concerned him was the combination of snow and wind. That meant drifts. So far the plows were handling the accumulation, but he wondered if it would have been wiser to stay in Liberty for the night. Depending on how far north the snow line extended, they could have many hours of exhausting driving yet to go.

But then again, staying in Liberty would have meant spending the night at her house. He certainly wouldn't have allowed her to stay there alone, nor would he have gone home and left her with Buzz. No, he would have slept in her guest room, or on the couch in Jim's study. He would have been a cop doing his job. As he was now.

He pulled open the back door, grabbed his jacket and shrugged into it. Then he reached for Julianne.

The baby seemed lost in the snowsuit. She scrunched her face up at having been awakened and taken from a warm car. Snow swirled and she sucked in her breath, blinking into the wind.

"I don't blame you, princess." Zach turned her away from the blowing snow, and tucked her snugly inside his open jacket.

Lizzie came around the car, the snow clinging to her lashes. Zach reached out and steadied her when her foot slid.

She looked up at him. "I think we have a full-blown New England blizzard."

"A royal pain in the ass." He cupped Julianne's head and murmured, "You didn't hear that, did you, princess?"

Lizzie laughed softly and he felt himself relax. The baby burrowed deeper into him, and Zach shook his head when Lizzie reached for her. "Better let me carry her."

Elizabeth didn't object, and in fact slipped her hand around his arm as they ducked their heads against the wind and made their way the short distance into the restaurant.

They both blinked at the bright lighting. Puddles of melted snow spread dirty tracks across the floor. An arcade of computer games stood blinking in a side room. To the right was the eating area, the rest rooms were straight ahead, and three phone booths stood beside a magazine and candy counter.

A dark-haired woman with thick layers of red lipstick sat on a stool behind the counter and watched an old sitcom on a small TV screen. She glanced up when they came in and gave them a look of disinterest.

Zach handed Julianne to Elizabeth. "I'm going to call Gordon."

"I'll order some coffee." She juggled Julianne, who was beginning to complain from being shifted around.

He reached for his wallet. Then, remembering her reaction when he'd wanted to give her money for the diapers, he changed his mind.

She noticed his interrupted motion and said, "You're funny, you know that?"

"How so?"

"It's as though you're trying to adjust the way you think."

"Yeah, well, I'm not used to women with babies, who have their own ideas about doing things."

"It's okay, you know. You don't have to change anything for me. I can handle macho and sexism for a few hours." She smiled. "As long as you watch your language around Julianne."

"I didn't say anything close to what I wanted to say when that car pulled onto the road in front of us."

"I know. Jim wouldn't have minced words, either."

Zach wasn't sure if her comparison was positive or negative. Probably neither, he reminded himself, nor did it matter one way or the other. "Yeah, he could be succinct and creative with the expletives."

She shifted Julianne once more, this time pushing back the hood of her snowsuit and loosening the neck. "If it's any consolation to you, I wouldn't have allowed Jim to swear around the baby, either."

A few minutes later in the phone booth, he dug his telephone credit card out of his wallet and cursed the way his memory had latched onto the word *consolation*. It was a lousy word and he disliked it as much now as when he first understood its meaning.

He'd been thirteen and passed over by an adoptive family for a kid everyone called Mushroom. The woman at the Family Service Center had patted him on the head and said if it was any consolation, there was a nice foster home that wanted him. Foster home number ten.

For years after, Zach had thought of himself as second-best. Not good enough.

He rested his head against the booth wall, and closed his eyes. It was a long time ago and it had nothing to do with who he was now. He'd overcome it. He'd worked and driven himself until he'd made something from his life. It wasn't ego or even arrogant pride, but a fact. Zachariah Stone had worked like hell to be one of the best cops in the Northeast.

And it was enough. Dammit, it had to be enough.

He yanked the receiver off the hook. The memories were behind him, shut off and forgotten. He knew better than to muck around in the past, raking up things he couldn't change, yet he felt the unwanted litter of them as though he'd let down his guard.

Like that near-miss accident. Inattention and distraction, Stone. He knew better. He never went into any situation without knowing how he was going to get out. That was a self-imposed rule he never deviated from. It had served him well. In fact, he thought now with a twist of amusement, the rule had become a consolation of sorts. Yeah. That was why the word rushed at him. It wasn't his past, it was now. He wanted the present to be as he intended his future. Set, settled and content.

The cramp began again in his thigh, but what he felt was different from the usual knot. This time the cramp was consoled by the memory of the imprint of her fingers.

When Zach finished the phone call, he expected her to be waiting by the magazine counter. She wasn't. Then he remembered that she was getting coffee. Terrific. He'd made a big deal about her locking her own door, and here he'd let her try to juggle coffee, her purse and a baby.

Annoyed with himself, he crossed the front area and glanced along the row of tables. Julianne was out of her snowsuit and seated in a high chair. Elizabeth had taken her coat off and glanced up as he approached.

"I thought you were just getting coffee."

"The smell of food made me hungry." She gave Julianne a teething toy that she promptly put into her mouth. "You don't mind, do you?"

In truth he did mind. Beating the storm was no longer possible, but waiting around while it worsened would make the driving that much more hazardous.

He slid into the booth opposite her.

"Was Gordon worried?"

"About the snow or getting you out of Liberty?"

"I don't think he was worried about you getting me out of Liberty. He sent *you,* didn't he? Gordon never just sends someone to a job, he sends the best."

"Sounds as if you know him pretty well."

"Yes, I guess I do. Jim told me that when his father was the chief of police he used to double-check all the shift assignments to make sure an experienced cop was always with a rookie, or in your case—"

"I was an imported untried commodity."

"From Providence. But Jim told me you were recognized by the governor's crime commission as having done some of the most professional and coolly calculated police work since the state started keeping track of such things."

He looked at her in surprise. "You could do public relations for the department."

"Jim had great admiration for you, Zach, as Gordon obviously does."

"Yeah, the little matter of losing two partners in as many years is just a minor blip in an otherwise flawless record." He knew he sounded sarcastic, but somehow sarcasm made it easier to not vent his rage over either Chuck's or Jim's death.

"Two partners?"

"Yeah, Chuck Tarlarski left a wife and two toddlers. Karen moved back to Ohio so the kids would be near their grandparents. She wanted to get them away from any reminder of their father's death. I knew Chuck was a PTSD victim—" He paused, glancing at her.

"Posttraumatic stress disorder, right?"

"Right. They okayed him to go back on duty, but that first night he—" Zach stopped himself, feeling a cold shiver climb up his spine.

She waited, watching him.

"You sure you want to hear this?"

"Only if you want to tell me."

He nodded. "Most of the women I know get all jittery or change the subject, but then I don't know any widows of cops."

"Except me."

"Except you."

It was a poignant moment, one that needed no words and no explanations.

Zach leaned back, his eyes staring for a moment as he sorted his thoughts. He hadn't really talked about it to anyone, and he wasn't sure how he'd gotten into it now, but he wanted to tell her.

"Chuck and I went on a call for a drug overdose at an address in a nice neighborhood. The house was a lot like yours, and I remember there was a red convertible in the drive. It was summer and busy as hell, and both Chuck and I were beat. The woman who opened the door was as white as the snow is tonight." He lifted the tumbler of water and drank, and Elizabeth felt herself tense up at what he was about to say.

"Chuck and I went upstairs and found the daughter at about the same time. She was sixteen. Her father had come up to her bedroom to find out why she hadn't answered a phone call. He found her on the floor with the coke and some syringes."

"Oh, Zach, how horrible."

"We knew she was dead, but the father refused to believe it. He just came apart." Zach took a deep breath. "It was the kind of scene a cop never gets used to seeing. No matter how you prepare yourself, and try to stay objective—" He closed his eyes for a moment. Finally, he said, "Chuck just couldn't deal with it. In retrospect he never should have gone on the call. That night he had a heart attack and died a few hours later.''

She watched his hands as they turned the glass around and around. Softly, she said, ''I don't know what to say.''

He took a deep breath. ''Yeah. There isn't much left to say.''

''How awful for his wife. Did you have to tell her?''

''No. I was off duty. She took it real bad. Blamed the department and initiated a lawsuit that never went anywhere. Chuck had been okayed, and no one was forcing him to do any more than he was ready for.'' Zach drained the tumbler of water. ''It was shortly afterward that I requested to be transferred to Liberty.''

They sat for a few minutes in silence while Julianne added an occasional squeal of delight. Neither Zach or Elizabeth felt there was anything more to say on a painful subject.

''You're an unusual woman, Elizabeth Healy.''

She smiled. ''And you're an unusual man, Zachariah Stone.''

He lifted both eyebrows. ''Gordon is the only one who calls me that.''

''Really? I like the name. It has a sense of majesty and old-fashioned honor.''

''I think you're reaching.''

''No. I think I'm right.''

The waitress came with the order, and after she left Zach scowled at the steak, baked potato and salad. He then glanced at Elizabeth's hamburger and French fries. Julianne was busy picking up tiny *O*'s of dry cereal out of a bowl.

''Did I look starved? Never mind, don't answer that. I am starved.'' The steak was done just the way he liked it, the potato hot and soft and the coffee bracing. He skipped the salad. Lizzie ate most of her hamburger, and the fries she didn't eat, Julianne did. After the dishes were cleared away and refills of coffee set in front of them, Elizabeth brought up the ransacking.

"The whole thing bothers me," Zach said grimly. "From Jim's unsolved death to what happened at your house."

"But surely you don't blame yourself for Jim."

"Not blame as much as frustration. Especially now. I have a lot of unanswered questions, such as, is the ransacking tied into Jim's death? And if so, why did it take them so long?"

"Could it be a coincidence? Like you said before, I wasn't home and maybe someone just randomly decided to see if he could find some money or something valuable."

"Do you keep money in the house?"

"Change in an old sugar bowl and some bills in my dressing-table drawer, but they weren't missing. Nor was the change."

"Then he wasn't looking for money. Those are both common places for cash."

"You think he was looking for something that belonged to Jim?"

"The den was pulled completely apart. And your bedroom wasn't searched at all. If it had been a random housebreaking, that would have been the first place they went. Since most of the damage was done in the den, whoever it was must have assumed either correctly or incorrectly that whatever he was looking for was in that room." He pushed his mug of coffee aside and started to slide out of the booth.

She reached across the table, and circled her hand around his wrist. Her eyes were bright and curious. "You think Jim hid something?"

"Maybe. For all I know, the ransacker might have found what he came for, although I doubt it. If he had, he wouldn't have been in your backyard watching the house. He would have been miles away. I think you probably came home before he had a chance to search everywhere. It's unlikely that if Jim hid something it was that obvious. You would have found it if it was out in the open.''

''Or if it was something out of the ordinary.''

''Exactly.''

Zach glanced at his watch and reached for his wallet. ''We'd better get moving.''

He slid out of the booth as did Elizabeth. Julianne was once again bundled up. Elizabeth put on her coat while Zach went over to pay the bill.

When they were once again on the interstate, Elizabeth asked, ''Zach, do you think Jim was somehow involved in all this?''

He'd hoped she wouldn't even have considered that possibility. The fact that he already had, plus this attraction he felt to Lizzie, made him uneasy and a little scared. He wanted to say no way, not a chance, but she was neither stupid nor the sort of woman whose attention could be easily diverted.

He glanced over at her. ''I don't know, sweetheart. Jim Healy, the cop I worked with, was straight and honest, and so far there is no reason to doubt that.''

The conversation came to an abrupt halt when Zach scowled at the assortment of red lights up ahead. ''Oh, hell,'' he muttered in disgust as he applied the brakes.

Elizabeth sat forward. ''Looks like an accident.''

''More than one,'' he replied. ''It looks like a damn parking lot.''

Chapter 5

As they approached the accident, Elizabeth caught her breath in a gasp when she saw the tangle of cars. It did look like a parking lot, but one where a giant hand had spilled the vehicles, making no attempt to arrange or park them. Headlights threw tunnels of light that reflected the falling snow. Some of the cars faced the opposite direction as though they'd been suddenly halted while going the wrong way.

A pickup truck was tipped perilously into a snowdrift as if it had veered sharply in an attempt to avoid crashing into something. Two cars squared off in the median, inches from a head-on collision.

The van that Zach had cursed earlier for fishtailing had flipped onto its roof, and its underside was already dusty with snow. Travelers milled around, huddled against the snow and wind. A siren wailed behind them and Zach pulled over to let the police car pass.

"I hope no one is hurt," Elizabeth said as Zach drove another few feet and stopped. "Especially in the van."

Zach shut off the engine, and leaned across her to open the glove compartment. The motion pressed his body against her for only a few seconds, yet long enough for her to feel its weight and lean tenseness. She found herself staring at the heavy texture of his dark hair as it lay over the turtleneck of his sweater. She'd seen him drag his hands through its thickness, and remembered the way it had brushed softly against her temple when he held her in the bedroom only a few hours ago.

He extracted gloves and a flashlight. Then he stuffed a notebook and some other papers back inside, closed the compartment and reached around to the rear seat for his jacket.

He pulled on the gloves and glanced at Elizabeth. "Stay here. I'm going to go take a closer look."

With those words he was out of the car before she had a chance to raise an objection. But then again, she wouldn't have done so. He was a cop, and although they were in Massachusetts and he had no authority, she imagined his instinct to help would kick in automatically.

Elizabeth watched him shrug into the jacket, pull the collar up around his neck, flip on the flashlight and walk toward the parked state police car. She studied him openly now that there was no chance of his glancing at her and wondering about her curiosity.

She really knew very little about him, but from all Jim had said, Zach was a private man and a loner. However, she remembered clearly two things her husband had said. Zach wouldn't cave in when things got rough and he'd risk his life for a principle he believed in.

Funny, she mused now as she recalled how many times Jim had praised Zach. At times she'd had a sense that Jim was envious. But of what? They'd been partners, both exceptionally good at what they did. And yet she couldn't ignore a nebulous feeling that Jim had wanted to be like Zach. Unless she was looking in the wrong direction. He might have felt a nostalgic envy of Zach's freewheeling life-style from a perspective of marriage and more and more responsibilities.

And yet here was Zach with a widow, a baby and more responsibility than most men would want willingly, never mind taking it on as a favor for his partner's father.

Oh, she knew Gordon had asked Zach, but she was aware that Buzz or two or three of the other officers could have driven her and Julianne to New Hampshire. Was it simply because Zach and Jim had been partners? Or perhaps Gordon knew how responsible Zach had felt about Jim's death. If that were the case, then it was plausible Gordon was doing this as much for Zach as for Julianne and herself.

She smiled in the chilly silence of the car. He hadn't been able to prevent Jim's death, but he could remove his partner's family from danger. He was certainly like no other man in her experience, despite his overly macho, well . . . maybe macho was too strong a word. Male right to decide fit him better.

She watched the wind lift his hair, and reminded herself that she shouldn't be interested in the way the heavy texture would feel against her fingers.

Up ahead a uniformed officer had just gotten out of his car and closed the door. Zach joined him as they hunched their shoulders into the blowing snow and made their way toward the overturned van, the vehicle that seemed to have sustained the most obvious damage.

Zach squatted, trying to see into the van. Elizabeth would have liked to get out and see if she could help, but she didn't want to leave Julianne alone in the car. Zach stood and walked back to the police car, ducked inside for a moment, then once again disappeared into the snowy night.

Elizabeth sat and absorbed the scene. No one was rushing frantically from any cars, nor did there seem to be any sign of hysteria. But with the snow coming down and the windshield wipers off, the glass soon became snow-covered, and within a few minutes she felt isolated. She turned and checked on Julianne. The baby wasn't asleep, but was curled on her side playing with a toy. Elizabeth tucked the down quilt tighter around her and felt her cheek. She wasn't fussing and seemed warm enough, but with the heater off Elizabeth felt cold. She slid across the seat and started the car. The wipers strained and groaned, but she soon had a fan-shaped opening. She saw nothing of Zach.

Another police car passed her, stopped and backed up. The officer got out and approached. She rolled the window down. The wind sliced against her cheeks.

"Everything okay?" His eyes were alert and probing as he leaned down to speak. The strong smell of after-shave indicated he must have just come on duty.

"Yes. I'm waiting for someone. He walked up to see how bad it was."

The officer shone his light on her and then flashed it around the interior in what she assumed was probably a routine procedure. She expected him to nod with satisfaction when he saw that nothing seemed out of order. Instead, he asked, "This is Zach Stone's car, isn't it?"

She couldn't help but wonder if this was one of the troopers who glanced the other way when Zach went on one of his speeding ventures across Massachusetts. "Yes, it is."

"Thought so when I saw the license plate." He stared at her as if he were trying to put her and Zach together. He again flashed the light from her to Julianne to the packed luggage and the huge box of diapers, then back again to the baby carrier. Julianne gurgled and for a moment the trooper kept the light on her as though he couldn't comprehend a baby in Zach's car.

Then with a chuckle and a too-knowing smile as though he'd put some missing puzzle pieces into place, he said, "Well, I'll be damned. If I hadn't seen this for myself, I wouldn't have believed it. The guy who swore he'd never get married went and did it."

His conclusion was logical, what with Julianne and all their stuff, and Elizabeth sitting alone in the car, waiting like a good wife. There certainly was nothing seductive about the scene. Given Zach's reputation, the officer must have encountered Zach other times when he'd been with a woman. No doubt a blond one, and more than likely his destination a motel or some hideaway.

"He didn't get married," she said in a breezy voice, telling herself that marriage to Zach Stone was as remote a possibility as the sudden disappearance of the accident-littered interstate. "We're just friends."

His eyebrows lifted as though he were considering a foreign concept. "Friends?"

Elizabeth met his look. "Friends."

Zach seemed to appear out of nowhere. The officer straightened and backed away from the car as though Zach were about to accuse him of something. Elizabeth frowned, glancing from one to the other.

Zach's voice was cold and measured each word. "O'Reilly is looking for you."

The cop moved another few inches, and Zach placed himself in front of the window, his back to Elizabeth. He said something, but in such a low voice she couldn't catch it. The other man's reaction was an uneasy grumble and a shrug. Zach waited until he got back into the police car and drove toward the accident.

Zach muttered something else and opened the door. Elizabeth scooted over, but before she'd gone more than a few inches he was in the car and gripping her arm to stop her from moving.

He'd brushed off the snow, but a light dusting clung to his hair. Despite the layers of clothes between them, she could have sworn she felt the hard line of his thigh against hers.

The interior was lit only by the distant lights reflected off the snow. Elizabeth swallowed, trying to clear her throat of its sudden tightness. When that didn't work, she coughed. Keeping her eyes straight ahead, she tried not to think about his thigh pressed next to hers, his hand on her arm. The physical contact was unnerving enough, but she'd caught a glimpse of his eyes when he got into the car. They had seemed to bore deep into her as though searching beyond what he could see on the surface.

"Is everyone all right up there?" she asked, feeling nervous and not sure why.

His hand loosened slightly, added a final squeeze that said don't move away, and then let her go. She didn't move.

"The guy in the van is banged up. EMT's will probably have to use the jaws of life to get him out. A couple of tow trucks are on the way. This side of the interstate is closed, and traffic is being routed around."

His voice was even, calm, carrying none of the intensity she'd seen in his eyes. she turned her head and looked at him as closely as he was looking at her. His body felt permanently sealed against hers and yet unthreatening. That in itself evoked an unusual feeling. She'd always found it off-putting when someone used his physical strength to make a point. Usually it was nothing more than raw intimidation. Zach no longer gripped her arm. She was free to move, but she hadn't....

Zach pulled off his gloves, his voice low, his words clipped. "What did he say to you?"

She didn't miss the anger in his voice nor the set line of his jaw, and yet she knew the anger was directed at the police officer and not at her.

"He recognized your car," she said.

"That's not what I meant."

"He didn't say much. Just asked if I was okay and shone his light in the car."

Zach turned slightly and she felt as though he were erecting some invisible wall that couldn't be penetrated.

"Did he say anything about us?"

The question sounded as ominous as his reaction to the trooper's talking to her. Her curiosity about Zach expanded. Why was he so incensed over an unimportant conversation?

When she didn't answer, he reached over and cupped her chin, bringing her face inches from his. "Connolly is noted for his off-color cracks and sleazy comments. I want to know if he insulted you."

Elizabeth blinked and tried to equate his fury with his concern. The comment was so old-fashioned, she wasn't sure how to respond. Most of the sexist insults she'd encountered in the past had come from men who held to the theory that men were smarter than women.

But it was obvious Zach wasn't talking about female versus male intelligence, but about a moral question that at another time in history would have called for a challenge to a duel in defense of her honor. While every facet of her independence should have dismissed his concern as archaic, a deep part of her was quite touched by it.

And independent or not, she couldn't resist probing to see how far he would go. "What would you do if he did?"

"Never mind. Just tell me what he said."

She wanted to know. Her mind conjured up images of white knights and dragon slayers. The mental leap to a modern hero who set his own standards of honor that were impeccable and noncompromising fit Zach perfectly. Sort of the emotional side of how Jim had described him, she realized.

There were too few modern heroes, and what exactly he would do intrigued her.

Elizabeth felt her sympathies go to poor Connolly. If the fierceness in Zach's reaction—and fierce seemed like a mild description—was any indication, the wrong answer would no doubt get the trooper, at the very least, an angry confrontation with Zach. What struck her, however, was Zach's determination to know what had been said, as though it were his responsibility to right some wrong.

It was one thing for him to protect her from an unknown ransacker, but quite another to think she couldn't handle a few exchanged words, whatever Zach thought they were.

"Zach, he didn't say anything offensive."

"I don't believe you."

"Are you calling me a liar?"

"Are you lying?"

"No!"

"Then what did he say?"

When she tried to pull away from him, he let go of her chin and slipped his hand around her neck. She tried to relax as though his touching her meant nothing, but his hand felt hot and to her chagrin she knew the pulse in the side of her neck was pounding.

"I know Connolly, Lizzie. He gets off trying to be a smart guy, so whatever you're trying to cook up to save his butt is wasting time."

"I'm not trying to save his butt," she snapped back, incensed at herself that a simple question had so undone her. "Has it occurred to you that what he said is none of your business?"

"No."

"Then maybe it's time it did."

"What did he say to you?"

"You're not going to quit, are you?" He continued to look at her, his face uncompromising. Finally, she sighed. "All right. I'll tell you."

But he didn't let go of her. Sometime during the exchange his thumb had moved down her throat, pausing at the pulse point.

She felt the flutter change to a race. "Now I know what it must be like for some guy you're interrogating."

"You got lucky. I kept my language clean. I'm waiting, Lizzie."

"He thought we were married." She blurted it out, thinking that after all that had been said he was going to be disappointed. The comment sounded as harmless now as it had when Connolly said it. Zach moved, and she expected a shrug followed by an apology that he'd blown the conversation all out of proportion.

However, his motion wasn't away from her, but toward her. His silence intensified the feel of his hand against her throat.

In one smooth motion, he pulled her into his arms and burst into laughter.

The switch from anger to laughter so stunned her, she was barely aware that he was holding her as if relieved, as if her answer had removed some great barrier. She didn't know whether to be pleased that poor Connolly wouldn't get a punch in the mouth or furious that the idea of their being married struck him as so funny. She pushed back from him, scowling.

"I think I've just been insulted," she said stiffly, telling herself she didn't care because he would be the last man she'd want to be married to, anyway.

He slid one hand up her back and with his other hand gently positioned her face so that he could see her. She felt a shimmer of tears and lowered her lashes. Damn, she thought miserably, where had the tears come from and why?

She should be glad he wasn't angry, pleased that poor Connolly wouldn't be confronted with Zach's fury. To her astonishment she felt his breath at her ear as though he had a secret to tell.

"Ah, Lizzie, your being with me probably added more respectability to my reputation than I'll ever deserve."

His comment so stunned her that she turned to him and at the same time tossed her head back. He, too, moved. They sat hip to hip, their mouths as close together as they could get and not be poised for a kiss.

"What an incredible comment," she whispered.

"Considering who you are? It's the truth."

"But I didn't tell him my name."

"I told O'Reilly. He wanted me to stick around and help, and I said I couldn't because you and Julianne were in the car. The crazy thing is that this sort of thing usually works the other way. You know, the woman usually gets her reputation ruined by running around with the guy with the bad rep."

"And you don't think that happened this time?"

"Not a chance."

"Why?"

"You're Jim's widow and Gordon's daughter-in-law. As far as the cops are concerned, you're above reproach."

"Sort of like a porcelain doll," she muttered, feeling too much as she had as a child. Shielded and smothered and trapped.

What she found so curious was her sense that despite all the attempts women had made in the past twenty years to gain independence, credibility and certainly the right to do as they pleased, with this group they might just as well have saved their energy. Was it the macho image of cops in general, or just these ones in particular? Zach, she knew, had strong opinions, as did her father-in-law. Gordon's abrupt orders for her to come to New Hampshire were certainly those of a man from another era. Jim, too, had shown a tendency to be overly concerned about her at times, but she'd never really examined that concern as anything more than a husband's natural reaction to his wife.

In truth, in that brief exchange with Connolly, she'd discovered a whole group of men who still thought in terms of a woman being above reproach and of preserving her reputation.

And then there was Zach. His reaction to Connolly had been more territorial than Jim's had ever been. And to her that was the most puzzling part of this entire conversation.

Zach released her, and she shivered from the lack of warmth. He got out of the car, scraped the accumulated snow off the windows and took off his coat before climbing back into the car.

"Aren't you ever cold?" Elizabeth asked, glad for the chance to change the subject. She grabbed his jacket before he tossed it into the back seat and tucked it around her legs, relishing the warmth that remained from his body. Somehow in the time during which he'd let go of her, gotten out of the car and climbed back in, she'd neglected to move all the way to the passenger side. She sat now with his coat wrapped around her legs as though the middle of the seat was where she intended to stay.

Zach turned the car around and headed in the opposite direction.

At her short gasp he said, "Relax. I told you they closed the interstate from the last exit to the next one until they get this mess cleared out. According to O'Reilly, there have been scattered accidents all night. He suggested we get off rather than take a chance we might be in one. I agree."

"So we're stuck with the side roads." She started easing her way toward the passenger door, thinking she could curl up tighter if she had more room.

"The unplowed side roads," he reminded her, glancing over at the distance she was putting between them. "You don't have to move."

"I'm crowding you, and besides—"

"Besides what?"

"I'm freezing."

"Now I'm insulted if you think the passenger door is warmer than I am."

The way she wanted to respond would open up areas best not discussed. Especially after his impromptu hug. And most especially because she *would* much prefer to snuggle against his body than a cold door.

"Just a habit. Jim always liked lots of room when he drove."

"I'm not Jim." He didn't add anything else, nor did she allow herself to think about the implications involved in the three words. He eased the car down a very slippery off ramp and stopped to read a sign.

She'd almost completed her unobtrusive slide across the seat when he glanced over at her with a touch of wary indecision in his eyes.

"I have a suggestion." When she stopped moving he shook his head. "Not about where you sit, but where we sleep tonight."

One long look at him made it very clear he didn't mean "we" as in together in the same bed, but then why in heaven's name would he? Of course she'd felt some tension between them, but that was to be expected. They were confined together, and a man and a woman alone together always had the potential for—

"What's your suggestion?" she asked.

"O'Reilly said there's a motel about three miles west of here."

When he didn't say anything more, Elizabeth wondered if he wanted her to nix the idea. Realistically, she thought getting off the road for the night was the best idea. Zach had been exhausted before they began the trip, and the snow, rather than slowing down, seemed to be getting worse. Besides, staying in a motel meant nothing more than what it was. Shelter, warmth, sleep and an escape from the storm. They would have separate rooms and it would be no different than if they were strangers who happened to have stopped for the night at the same motel.

"I think that's a good idea. You could call Gordon and tell him we decided to wait out the storm."

He let out a long breath. "Now all we have to do is get there."

Getting there proved to be frustrating, tense and exhausting. Apparently the town they were in didn't use snowplows. Nor was there a vacancy at the motel O'Reilly had referred them to.

"Damn," Zach muttered when he saw the sign.

Elizabeth peered through the windshield, trying to see a distant sign. "Are we anywhere near Walcott?"

"Hell, I don't know," he growled. "What is Walcott?"

"It's a lovely small town with the most spectacular summer art festival."

"Just what I needed to know in twenty inches of snow."

"It has a lovely inn, also."

"How convenient. Is it filled with all the velvet paintings they couldn't give away at the festival?"

"Don't be such a grouch."

He brought the car to an abrupt halt, got out and walked over to a sign. Elizabeth grinned as he brushed the snow off to reveal the name of the town they were in. Back in the car, Zach said, "Well? Are we near Walcott?"

"My guess is about ten miles east."

"Thank God. This has got to be the longest, most convoluted trip I've ever made to New Hampshire."

"Think of it this way," Elizabeth said, already thinking about the Wisteria Inn, Greta's hospitality and a warm bed. "When we get there you can take a hot shower and fall into bed."

"And what if they don't have any vacancy?"

"Such a cynic. Think positive. Besides, other travelers probably didn't get that far off the highway."

When they finally arrived in Walcott, it was nearly midnight. Elizabeth felt as drained as though she'd walked through the storm rather than ridden. Zach had said little, his mood darkening with every snow-clogged mile.

There'd been a near collision when another car slid through a stop sign, and the visibility remained almost zero. Her trips to Walcott when she was regional manager for Evans Art Supply had been in the summer, when landmarks were clear and distinguishable. The darkness and the snow made the town barely recognizable.

By the time they located the Wisteria Inn, the ten miles felt more like a hundred.

Elizabeth had purposefully ignored Zach's frustration and snappiness, deciding that in many ways it was probably justified. Besides, there was nothing she could say that would change the strain or the blinding snow. Zach cursed the storm, the roads, the ransacker and his own stupidity for not leaving Liberty much sooner than they had.

The lights at the inn were few, and Zach shook his head ominously. "Why do I feel like this was a wasted trip?"

Her own annoyance and weariness suddenly rushed to the surface. The storm wasn't her fault, nor were the accidents. And a no-vacancy motel that close to the interstate shouldn't have been a surprise. She took his coat off her legs and reached for the door handle.

He grabbed her arm. "What are you doing?"

"Going in to check if they have rooms. With the foul mood you're in, Greta probably won't open the door. She has little use for men who yell and demand."

"I do not yell and demand."

"You're very intimidating, Zach."

"I'll be sweet as sugar."

One glance at the chill in his eyes told her not to argue. She sighed and let go of the door handle.

Before he got out of the car he turned to her. "You want a crib, right?"

She must be tired, she thought. She hadn't even thought about a bed for Julianne. "Yes. But if Greta doesn't have one, I'll figure out something."

He opened his door to get out of the car.

"Wait a minute." She took her wallet from her purse and held out her credit card for him.

He looked at the plastic as if it was on fire. "What the hell is that?"

"What the hell does it look like?" she snapped back, angry and cold and tired and not in the mood to deal with his male ego.

"Put it away." He tried to slide out when she grabbed his arm.

"Dammit, Zach!"

"Don't swear in front of the baby."

"You should talk. You've done nothing else for the past two hours. Take my credit card."

"You're not paying for this."

"And you aren't paying for my room."

"If you think I'm going in there and handing Greta two credit cards, you're nuts."

"What's the big deal? It's two rooms, two rates, two bills. If we came in here as strangers and happened to be standing next to each other at the counter, you wouldn't feel that way."

"Look, if you're offended by this, you can reimburse me in cash when I get my bill, fair enough?"

Elizabeth took a long breath, telling herself she wasn't going to win the argument. He was too tired, too ornery. But dammit, so was she.

She mentally counted to three. "Zach, I'm not trying to be difficult, but you're doing more than you should have to do just taking us north. I don't want you to have to pay for everything along the way. And besides, I didn't put up a ruckus when you paid for dinner."

"But you ordered it for me, didn't you?"

For a moment she thought she'd heard wrong. "Don't tell me you resent that? I was just trying to save us some time. You were hungry, at least from the looks of the empty plate you were."

"I'm not used to women taking over."

"Ordering dinner is taking over?" She shook her head in amazement. Glaring at him and not caring now if they argued so badly they didn't speak from here to New Hampshire, she said in a breezy clipped tone, "But then I keep forgetting that you don't like a woman to make a decision without consulting you. After all, you're Zach Stone. Your encounters with women are when they're on their backs and sighing with pleasure." Too late she realized what she'd said.

He stared at her, saying nothing, his face so unreadable she had no idea what he was thinking.

She turned away, damning herself for her crudeness. Silently she prayed he'd ignore her. What had her insistence gotten her? Just embarrassment. At this point she didn't even care if he paid for the rooms. There was no sound of the door opening, little movement apart from a slight crushed-seat sound of his body settling back.

Elizabeth chanced a sideways glimpse of him. He was leaning his head against the headrest, his eyes closed, one knee drawn up and braced against the right side of the steering wheel.

The night cocooned them in silence, the snow whispering across the windshield. Julianne slept behind them, blissfully unaware of the tension and frustration in the front seat.

"Zach . . ."

"Don't apologize."

"I didn't have any right to say that."

"I'm not much good at this sort of thing. This being friends with a woman."

"You don't have to explain."

He rolled his head to the side, his eyes frank with honesty. "I would explain if I knew how. I might even deny it if I thought you'd believe me." He swore then, low and explicit. She thought the curse was more self-directed than aimed at the direction their conversation had taken.

Finally, he said, "You're right. I'm used to them on their backs and sighing with pleasure."

To Elizabeth his words sounded like the final pronouncement of his life, a verification that there was no hope he would ever change. She felt a wrenching sense of pity at the thought that he had undoubtedly passed up many opportunities for a relationship with a woman that moved beyond her expertise in bed. Or perhaps he hadn't.

"Look, you'll have to come in with me to sign the credit card receipt." He glanced in the back seat. "Julianne is asleep. Will she be okay?"

"Probably, but I never leave her in a car alone. You go ahead. We'll do as you suggested. I'll give you the cash when you get your bill."

He nodded and was almost out of the car when she called, "Wait!" She tried to hand his coat to him, but he shook his head, slamming the door before she had a chance to protest.

He tramped through the snow and up the steps. His shoulders hunched against the wind, he rang the bell, and in a few moments Elizabeth saw Greta peer out of the side window. She disappeared and a few seconds later she opened the door. Zach said something, and she invited him in.

Elizabeth felt a huge measure of relief. Greta did have rooms. She must have, otherwise she would have told him no when she opened the door.

A few minutes later he came out, but he certainly didn't look like a man anticipating a hot shower and a comfortable bed.

She opened the car door to get out. "All set?"

"Not quite." He came around the car and got back inside.

"If Greta doesn't have a crib, it's okay," she said when he closed the door.

"Oh, she's got a crib."

"Then what is it?"

"She's only got one room with one bed."

Chapter 6

Elizabeth let her eyes close slowly, feeling a sudden daunting weight of exhaustion. If she believed in such silliness as the fates being against her, then this was the inevitable conclusion to what had become an incredible day. What unsettled her was a distant part of her that considered the feasibility of actually saying, "Fine, let's take the room and get some sleep," as though she made it a habit of waiting out snowstorms in bed with men she barely knew.

She wasted no time reminding herself there would be a definite difference between ordinary sleep and sleeping with Zach. Allowing her thoughts to dwell on the latter didn't make her uneasy or embarrassed as much as very curious.

And that, she knew, was dangerous.

In theory, sharing a bed for the purpose of sleep sounded practical and unavoidable given the alternative, which was finding another vacancy at this late hour. But she knew the natural progression of her thoughts had nothing to do with the storm, but with getting into bed with Zach and *not* calmly falling asleep.

Elizabeth gave herself a mental shake. She'd always avoided the obvious sexual situations, from her first encounters in college to the more veiled hints she'd received in the guise of friendship since Jim had died. And this situation, while not planned, was still about as obvious as one got. They not only barely knew each other, but seemed to be having major difficulties trying to form a simple friendship.

"I have a feeling all this silence means we're either sleeping in the car or driving until we drop." He'd folded his arms and propped his shoulder against the driver's door as though resigned to her decision.

She glanced down at his jacket, which was still covering her lap, and wished that sharing a room was as simple. "I'm thinking."

He muttered, "Yeah, that's what I'm afraid of."

"Surely Greta must have something else. I'll go in and talk to her. Even if I have to sleep on the couch in the welcoming room, that would be better..."

"Than sleeping with a man who's used to women on their backs and sighing their pleasure?" he asked so calmly he might have been talking about couch-sleeping experiences rather than sex.

Elizabeth had reached for the door handle, then let it go to turn and stare at him. He'd changed positions and was leaning flat against his door, one leg drawn up, his faded jeans and black shirt making him look even more mysterious. It occurred to her that if she were a woman who wanted Zach Stone, this blizzard and one room at the inn was a made-for-pleasure opportunity.

The car, which had gotten chilly with the engine and heat off, suddenly felt too close and too warm.

"That has nothing to do with it and you know it," Elizabeth said evenly.

"Doesn't it?"

She sagged back in the seat, finding his question more probing than the issue of sex. "Are you asking me if I trust you?"

"No."

"No?" Now she really was curious. Most men would be eager to say they could be trusted even when all the signs pointed to mistrust. She studied his expression for some kind of emotion and found none. The man, she decided, could give lessons on cold objectivity.

He hadn't moved nor did he say anything more. Feeling as though she'd been unintentionally handed a challenge, she asked, "Does that mean you don't care if I trust you or that you can't be trusted?"

"Trust isn't the issue," he replied blandly. "You already trust me. You wouldn't be here if you didn't."

"You're very sure of yourself, aren't you?"

"Let's put it this way. I wouldn't be here if I thought this involved more than an official escort to New Hampshire."

She scowled. It was one of those answers that could mean any one of a dozen things. Stop being so curious, she told herself. But perhaps fascination better defined her thoughts. There was a difference; fascination wasn't objective. Truthfully she was better off being neither. At face value she knew that Gordon had arranged this, and she recalled Zach saying earlier that going to New Hampshire was not high on a list of things he wanted to do.

Saying nothing more was probably wise. Changing the subject was probably even wiser. But whether from curiosity or fascination, she couldn't let it go. "Is that the Zach Stone, professional cop, answer?"

He expelled a long breath followed by a short expletive.

She'd turned completely now, meeting his eyes. "Is that your answer?"

"Lizzie..." he said in a warning tone.

The nickname, which in the past few hours had come to mean easiness and warmth, now seemed to hang in the cold air between them.

"I'm not trying to be difficult. I just—"

"Let's drop it, huh?"

It had to be his eyes, she told herself, unable to look away. The question lay in her mind, and she knew that if she asked it, she would immediately want to snatch it back, and yet she couldn't resist. "Why?"

The intensity level thickened and climbed. Zach never blinked. He never allowed his gaze to drift from her mouth. "You know why."

She moved her head in a slow, shaking motion, feeling as if it weighed a thousand pounds. The gesture was automatic rather than truthful. She did know. She'd known from the beginning. The trip was official because he was doing it as a cop, not as a friend. And his telling her he wouldn't be here otherwise meant just that. Why shouldn't it? He was Zach Stone, the man with the endless supply of blondes, who drove a sports car at the speed of sound and liked women who did as they were told. Yet here he sat with a widow, her baby, a sense of obligation and a snowstorm that wouldn't quit.

Yes, she knew why. It might not be very flattering but sometimes the truth wasn't. She pushed aside the sense of disappointment that slipped over her.

They sat for a few silent moments, not looking at each other, being very careful not to move, to breathe too erratically, but mostly not to talk about it anymore. The snow swept across the windshield, building a layer of fresh powder now that the wipers were still.

Finally Zach straightened. "We're both tired. By tomorrow we'll be okay."

Elizabeth relaxed a little. Of course, he was right. By this time tomorrow night they would be at Gordon and Naomi's. In the meantime they'd just have to be more aware of conversations that got too personal.

She started to pick up his jacket from her lap. "Will you keep an eye on Julianne? I'll be right back. Once Greta knows it's me—"

"She already knows it's you."

"Oh." She frowned. "Then why would she even mention the single room?"

He sighed, drawing his hand down his face wearily. "After she opened the door and ushered me inside, she started talking about her guests being trapped by the storm and therefore having to stay longer than anticipated. I was about to say we needed two rooms, but before I got the words out she said she was glad I was alone, because she only had one room."

Elizabeth slumped back in the seat. Zach was obviously no happier about the limited accommodations than she was. "So what did you tell her?"

"I considered saying thank-you and leaving, but I figured we were better off with one guaranteed room than finding nothing at the next place."

"I agree." Elizabeth shivered as a burst of snow blew across the windshield. She was curious as to what Zach had said to Greta. "You said that she knows I'm with you. How—?"

He cut her off with a dark look. "I told her, but before I had a chance to explain anything, her immediate response was to ask why didn't I say so in the first place, and that she couldn't wait to see our baby."

"*Our* baby?" When she realized what Greta's assumption had been, Elizabeth sighed a resigned "Oh my God."

"Yeah, you got it. She assumed we were married."

"And you didn't tell her we weren't," she said, deciding there was little more tonight that could astonish her.

"No, I did not." He certainly didn't sound very happy about it, but then neither was she.

She couldn't help but remember their earlier conversation about being married. "Should I take this opportunity to laugh as hard as you did when I said Connolly thought we were married?"

"Look, if we're going to have another argument let's not do it in this deep freeze." He gave her a level look. "To say we weren't married raised a whole hell of a lot of questions that are none of her business. Plus you know her. I didn't think I had the right to say you were going to sleep with a man you weren't married to. For all I know this Greta might be a prude, or think sex outside of marriage is what's wrong with the world, or have some policy against unmarried guests sharing a room. I wasn't taking any chances."

She leaned over and placed her finger against his mouth. "You really are very sweet, you know that? Despite all that hard professional attitude, you're concerned about what people might think about me. Just like you were with Connolly."

Zach lifted her hand away and studied her palm as though it might hold untold secrets. He glided his thumb around her palm. Then he drew it forward to touch his mouth, once again as though the texture and taste of her skin were a brand-new sensation. Elizabeth felt the heat from his breath shimmer in her hand. He pressed his mouth in the exact center and when he drew away she felt the clinging dampness. Slowly he folded her fingers inward to clasp his moistness as though he was hiding something of himself there. Then carefully he moved her hand back to her lap.

"Julianne doesn't need a mother who is whispered about. I know what that's like, and it isn't the kind of thing any kid should have to deal with."

The unexpected dip into his past touched her because it had come so easily. He'd obviously had to deal with some nasty talk as a child. How different their childhoods had been, she suddenly realized. With a touch of insight she felt a rush of gratitude toward her own parents. They had smothered, but they had never embarrassed her or made her ashamed.

"You're right," she said in a voice that sounded too husky. "I don't think Greta is the judgmental type, but I admit I'm not sure."

"At last we found something we agree on," he growled. "So here's the deal. I let Greta think the obvious and I took the room. Incidentally, I paid cash. I didn't want her to question my name on the credit card since it is obviously not Healy."

"Oh. I never thought of that."

"You're not a cop. She probably wouldn't have noticed, but since I thought of it I figured there was no need to raise any questions. As to the room, it's only one night and both of us need to get some rest. I can sleep on the floor. I've done it before, and right now I'm so tired that even the floor will feel good."

Fifteen minutes later, Elizabeth stood holding a bundled and slightly cranky Julianne in the welcoming room of the Wisteria Inn. The nineteenth-century structure had been named for the purple wisteria that bloomed in the late spring along the columns on the front porch. Originally a private guest house, it had been converted into an inn around the turn of the century.

A flagstone fireplace with a wide hearth had been built as one entire wall. The embers still glowed red from an evening fire. Reproductions of Revolutionary War and period furniture gave the room a cozy ambience that was beautifully illustrated by a hand-rubbed hooded cradle that stood near Elizabeth.

She knelt so that Julianne could see the huge gray cat with a squirrel-like tail that had commandeered the cradle. Obviously accustomed to being admired, the cat lifted its head to be petted.

Julianne wasn't quite sure, her only experience with a cat being a kitten that had scratched her when she yanked its tail. As though the cat understood her reluctance, it began to purr.

"Be gentle," Elizabeth said to Julianne when she reached for the cat's head. "They like to be petted but not pulled." Julianne giggled when the animal nuzzled her hand.

"Why, Elizabeth, I do declare I wouldn't have known you." Greta Creighton, wrapped in a floor-length wine-colored velour robe, glided across the braided rug to greet her. In her late fifties, she'd never married, having once confided to Elizabeth that the only man she'd ever loved had gone to the drugstore one evening and never returned.

Elizabeth stood and shifted Julianne, who strained to get back down to pet the cat. The two women exchanged an awkward hug with the baby fussing between them.

"How wonderful to see you," Elizabeth said.

"You're as charming as you always were." Greta stroked her hand over Julianne's curls. "What a beautiful baby. Time certainly does fly. It's had to believe you're a mother. Why the last time I saw you was, let's see...."

"Four years ago when I stayed here during the summer festival."

"That's right. That wasn't too long after you were married."

"Just about a year. It was my last trip as regional manager for Evans." Wanting to avoid the subject of marriage, since it would invariably lead to Zach, she asked, "Is the art store still here in Walcott?"

Greta nodded. "As a matter of fact, Penny Kingston just finished relocating it in a new shopping plaza a few blocks from here."

Elizabeth remembered Penny Kingston as an enthusiastic young manager who had been in the process of trying to secure financing to buy the art store from its owners, who had wanted to move to California. "Penny owns the business now, then."

"Yes. And I know she'd love to see you while you're here." She glanced out at the accumulating snow. "If this storm ever stops. You are planning on staying a while, aren't you?" Greta brushed her knuckles across Julianne's cheek.

"I'm afraid not. We're on our way north."

Greta glanced over to where Zach had carried in the last of their luggage. He stepped back outside to stamp the snow off his boots, removing his jacket as he returned. He hung it on a brass coat tree, and Elizabeth was suddenly struck with the reality of what she was doing. She wasn't having second thoughts about sleeping in the same room with him; it was her first thoughts that disturbed her.

She liked the idea a little too much.

He came toward them, his movements precise. She'd heard Gordon tell Jim once that Zach was a cautious man who made decisions based on logic, fact and necessity. His decision to let Greta think they were married had been based on none of those, but made because he cared about Julianne and her.

"A policeman, isn't he?" Greta asked.

"Why, yes, he is."

He came to a stop beside her. Elizabeth tried to recall if she'd ever mentioned Jim by name to Greta. She didn't think she had.

"We already introduced ourselves," Zach said, as though he had already realized that possible complication and taken care of it.

"Yes, we did. You certainly picked a terrible night for traveling."

Elizabeth concurred, mentioning they were going to New Hampshire, but not why. Instead she related the problems they'd encountered because of the snow. Amazingly, she managed to recount the details and at the same time sound more like Zach's wife than like a woman who was going to her in-laws' house with a police escort.

Julianne began a squirm once more, reaching out for Zach.

"Come on, princess, you ready for bed?" He lifted her from Elizabeth's arms into his as though he did it nightly. She curled into him, peeking shyly at Greta and putting her thumb into her mouth.

"Isn't that sweet," Greta said on a long maternal sigh. "We need more of that in the world, you know. Babies and daddies and families."

Elizabeth nodded. She certainly couldn't disagree, and found herself relieved that Zach had allowed Greta to assume they were married.

Elizabeth walked over and picked up the diapers and a huge carryall that held what Julianne would need for the night.

Greta stood still, seemingly mesmerized by the sight of Julianne tucked warmly in Zach's arms.

Zach glanced over at Elizabeth and then said gently to Greta, "If you could show us to our room, Lizzie wants to get the baby settled."

"Oh, of course. What kind of an innkeeper am I, keeping my guests down here gabbing when they're obviously exhausted?" She moved over to a long maple trestle table where the registration book lay open, and pulled out a drawer to take two brass keys.

Elizabeth picked up another bag, and Zach said, "Leave them. I'll come back and carry them up."

She started to say she could help, but didn't. She didn't want another argument, at least not tonight. Greta motioned them to follow her.

The other guests were apparently all asleep, and as they climbed the stairs to the second floor, Elizabeth could hear the wind howl along the eaves. They moved down a hall wallpapered in a red-and-gold design that depicted inns during the Revolutionary War. Wall lights gave out an inviting glow. Greta stopped at the last door.

"This room is a little drafty when the wind whips around from the north. If we make sure the crib is away from the windows, you all should be fine. I'll get some extra blankets just in case."

"Julianne has heavy sleepers," Elizabeth said as Greta put the key in the lock.

Zach shifted the baby. "Lizzie gets colder than I do."

Elizabeth nodded, "Yes, I can't get him to wear a coat half the time."

They stared at each other, realizing how they sounded, like an average married couple beset with the usual problem of one partner needing more warmth than the other. After a few poignant seconds Elizabeth lowered her head and adjusted the carryall. Zach frowned.

Greta turned the key and the door swung open. The scent of a rose potpourri drifted out at them. The lights were flipped on and Zach followed Elizabeth into the room.

Of average size, it had a high ceiling and an overhead summer fan. Wallpaper with a soft-green background and a tiny garden print gave it a feel of spring despite the blizzard outside. The cushioned window seat, scattered with plump pillows and framed by blue drapes, made Elizabeth long for a down quilt, a good book and a cup of hot cocoa. For a few moments she regretted that they would be leaving first thing in the morning.

There were two dressers, a pair of wingback light-blue-and-cream upholstered chairs, and a king-size bed covered with a patchwork quilt. Zach and Elizabeth glanced at the bed and then at each other almost simultaneously.

Elizabeth thought, *You won't have to sleep on the floor. There's plenty of room.*

Zach responded, *I'll take the floor.*

That's silly. It would be no different than if we slept in the car.

He simply stared at her a moment as though he no more believed that than she did.

Elizabeth shook her head to clear it. My God, she thought, we're arguing silently as if we know each other so well we don't need words. That's ridiculous, she reminded herself as she turned away from him and put her purse and Julianne's carryall on the bed. It's only these crazy circumstances, which are even more unnerving because of our argument in the car.

"I'll get the crib if you tell me where it is," Zach said to Greta as he handed the baby to Elizabeth.

"It's in a large store room on the first floor. Unfortunately, it will require some assembly. I have to take it partially apart to store it. I'll turn on the lights for you."

While they were gone, Elizabeth went about changing Julianne into a clean diaper and a heavy sleeper. The room felt comfortable but, as Greta had said, a bit drafty near the windows. The crib would fit nicely between the bed and the bathroom, which meant that if Zach was insistent on sleeping on the floor, it would have to be by the windows. She glanced once more at the bed as she lifted Julianne into her arms.

If she asked Greta for a whole bunch of pillows to stuff between them, then there was no reason why they couldn't share the bed.

She sat down in the wing chair and tucked the baby close to her, singing softly. Zach returned with the crib, and Greta excused herself to find a crib sheet and extra towels and blankets.

"Are you cold?" Zach asked after Greta left the room. Without waiting for Elizabeth to answer, he lifted a green-and-blue cross-stitched quilt from the bottom of the bed and tucked it around her.

"I'm not cold," she said, glancing up at him when he wrapped the quilt around her hips.

"The room is chilly. Is she warm enough?"

"She's almost asleep. And the draft near the windows is all the more reason why you can't sleep on the floor."

He'd hunkered down in front of her and let his hands stay at her hips. Although her clothes and the quilt made it impossible for either to feel the other, Elizabeth could have sworn she did. Julianne's eyes were drifting closed as she nestled between them.

"You are making this very difficult, Lizzie Healy."

"And you are very stubborn, Zach Stone. And later you'll be very cold."

"But definitely safer."

He watched Julianne breathe, her head against Elizabeth's breast. "Did you feed her?"

"She ate at the restaurant, remember?"

"I meant when she was tiny."

"Oh, you mean did I nurse her?"

"Yeah." He touched Julianne's cheek and his finger lightly feathered Elizabeth's breast. She felt a deep curl low in her stomach and a tightening in her breasts. She wore a sweater over a blouse and beneath that a bra, yet still she felt that whisper touch of his finger.

"I nursed her, yes."

"No wonder she's so healthy and beautiful."

She smiled. "I'll take credit for the healthy, but the beautiful didn't have anything to do with how she was fed."

Zach's finger lay lightly at the corner of Julianne's mouth, but just a breath away from Elizabeth's nipple. She didn't dare move or breathe, but felt as if every nerve ending in her body had centered on that tiny spot between them.

"Perhaps it did," he said softly.

Elizabeth tried to swallow the dryness in her throat. How was it possible that she was having this kind of conversation with a virtual stranger? He wasn't her husband, and he had admitted he didn't know how to be friends with a woman, yet there was something very profound going on between them.

She let her gaze follow him as he rose to his feet—from his face, to his chest, to his waist, the snug jeans, the slight swell of the zipper, his muscled legs.

He cupped her chin and tipped her head up so that she had to look at him. His thumb touched one corner of her mouth and then the other.

"Your lipstick is worn off," he whispered.

Never had her lips ached, but they did now. "I know. I must look pale."

"Very young and very innocent."

"No."

"And exceptionally desirable."

"Zach . . ."

"And very hard to resist."

She wanted to say, *Don't resist me, please indulge me, please kiss me.* But she said nothing. She did work one hand out from the quilt and reached up to curl her fingers around his wrist.

"Your pulse is racing," she murmured, pleased that he was as affected by her as she was by him.

He rubbed his thumb along her bottom lip as though tracing the texture. In a low husky voice, he said, "I should tell you to open your mouth so I can kiss you. Then perhaps..."

"What?" The word grew and expanded between them.

"Perhaps both of us will be satisfied."

She shook her head and again whispered, *"No."*

He let her go, his eyes too thoughtful, too probing, too hot. "That's what I'm afraid of."

Greta returned with an arm load of blankets, towels and extra bars of soap. "I brought some tools, too."

Zach relieved Greta of the items and made sure the tools were the ones he needed. He then went back downstairs for the things he'd brought in from the car for the night. Greta separated the towels from the blankets and took them and the soap into the bathroom.

Julianne had fallen asleep. Shifting her, Elizabeth got to her feet, then tucked the baby and the quilt into the deep chair. She moved another chair in front to act as a barrier just in case Julianne should awaken and try to sit up.

"I just need to get the mattress and a crib sheet," Greta said. "Can you think of anything else?"

Elizabeth wanted to ask for a cot or rollaway bed for Zach since he'd insisted upon sleeping on the floor, but she didn't want to call attention to the sleeping arrangements. Since Greta assumed they were married, she decided to leave well enough alone. "I would like some extra pillows if you have them."

"Sure, how many?"

Elizabeth calculated the length of the bed just in case she could talk him into occupying one side. Not sharing with her, or sleeping with her, but just occupying. "Maybe five?"

"Five! My word, I don't think I've ever been asked for five pillows."

Think, Elizabeth, think. "Uh, Zach's back gives him trouble sometimes, so he puts pillows under his spine," she said, coming up with the first thing she could think of.

"The poor man, and here I let him carry that crib and he's downstairs getting luggage. Elizabeth, you should have said something earlier, I could have awakened Fred to help."

"Who's Fred?" Zach asked as he came into the room.

"He's my maintenance man." Greta sped forward to relieve him of Elizabeth's suitcase. "I know you men like to handle everything and not complain, but a bad back is nothing to play around with."

Zach glanced at Elizabeth, lifting his chin a fraction in a silent what-is-she-talking-about gesture.

Elizabeth gave a slight shake of her head, indicating she'd tell him later. "I think we're all set, Greta. Thank you for everything."

"I'll get the extra pillows."

Elizabeth groaned. She had been hoping Greta might just forget.

Zach set down his nylon bag, propped his hands low on his hips and looked from one woman to the other. "Pillows for what?"

"Just extra for sleeping," Elizabeth said hurriedly.

"Why, for your back, of course," Greta added.

Now Zach turned all his attention to Elizabeth. "What about my back?"

It was clear from the curtness of his question that he didn't like being the topic of conversation, especially one that made him sound at a disadvantage.

Greta, of course, caught none of the tense but silent exchange. Elizabeth took a deep breath, crossed the room and slipped her arm around his waist. She felt him stiffen. "I told Greta you sometimes have trouble with your back because of that time you strained it skiing. The extra pillows will make it feel better."

Zach put his arm around her and held her firm against him when she tried to step away. He gave Greta his best smile, but Elizabeth could tell from the grip he had on her that the smile had nothing to do with being happy.

"As long as you're going to get pillows, could you spare a bottle of whiskey?"

"Certainly. I even have some hot buttered rum left over from earlier tonight. Elizabeth?"

"Yes, that would be fine." She tried for the third time to pull away, but he gripped her tight.

"I'll be right back." Greta hurried out, closing the door, and before the sound died, Zach whirled her around to face him.

"Now, Zach, I can explain."

"If you're going to make up stories about me, baby, you better find out what I like and what I don't like. I hate skiing."

"It was the first thing I could think of. Since snow and New Hampshire and skiing all go together, it seemed very logical."

"Logical because of a bad back that I don't have? What am I about to get? Some insight into the inner workings of the independent female mind?"

"I said I could explain."

"Yeah, I'll bet."

"Then maybe I won't," she snapped. She pushed at his chest, which had all the effect of trying to move a wall.

"I'll tell you what," he murmured in the softest of words. "You've got about one minute until Greta gets back. You can either explain, or I'll follow my earlier impulse and kiss you."

She was tempted to test him, so tempted she stopped pushing on his chest and let her hands rest against the soft cotton. She could feel the heat of his body seep into her fingers. He moved closer and placed his hands on the side of her neck, his thumbs riding along her jaw.

"Come on, Lizzie." He watched her mouth, but made no move to touch the corners as he had done when she was seated with Julianne.

She, in turn, watched his, aware of where she could go with this, and at the same time knowing that whatever she did, it wouldn't change the truth. They were together because of Gordon, a worse than normal blizzard and her ransacked house.

And yet there was that curious fascination. "Maybe I'd rather you kiss me."

"No, you wouldn't."

"Zach..."

"I can hear Greta coming up the stairs." He lowered his head and for a moment she stopped breathing, but he didn't allow his mouth to touch hers. "When I kiss you I want it long and wet and hot."

She felt as though her stomach had plummeted to the floor. He'd said *when*, not *if*. The words spun around in her mind even as she mechanically explained, without taking one breath, about how her request for pillows had led to telling Greta he had a bad back.

Half an hour later Elizabeth was sitting in the middle of the bed watching Zach put the last of the screws into the crib. After Greta returned with the hot buttered rum for Elizabeth and a decanter of whiskey for Zach, she gathered pillows from a nearby linen closet in the hall and wished them good-night, saying that breakfast would be at eight.

Elizabeth was feeling comfortably warm and drowsy, and just a little reckless. Tipping her head after a long sip from her mug of hot buttered rum, she said, "There doesn't seem to be any end to your talents. Rescuing damsels and their babies, fighting blizzards, assisting at accidents, guarding my reputation and assembling a crib that must be about forty years old.''

He straightened and tested his handiwork by shaking the crib. ''Seems sturdy enough.'' He put the mattress in and stretched the clean sheet over each of the four corners.

Elizabeth took another long sip. ''I'm impressed.''

He gave her a wary look, his gaze moving from her slightly glazed eyes to her hair, which was tangled and brushing her shoulders as though she'd combed it with her fingers. He noted the way she sat tucked among the pillows and blankets that Greta had left. The innkeeper had brought an insulated carafe with the rest of the hot buttered rum. Zach had barely touched the whiskey, preferring to wait until Elizabeth was asleep before he indulged. He had no intention of getting drunk, but he had no intention of allowing any inhibitions he held concerning one Elizabeth Healy to get out of control.

''If putting a sheet on a crib mattress impresses you, you must be a little tipsy.''

''Relaxed,'' she said, lifting the mug to her mouth once more, finding it empty and reaching for the carafe.

He put his hands low on his hips. ''You know, a smart woman stuck in a bedroom all night with a strange man wouldn't be quite so... relaxed.''

''I trust you.''

''Yeah, I know.''

''Well, you won't sleep with me,'' she said as though there were no logical reasons why he should be refusing, ''you don't want to kiss me, and you've made it very clear you would rather do anything than take me to New Hampshire. So I've decided you are very trustworthy.'' She toasted him, giggled and lifted the mug to her lips.

He came over to the bed and in one smooth motion lifted the drink from her hand. He took a sip. ''God, how much rum did Greta put in this?''

"I thought it was just right."

"Because you're on your way to being too drunk to notice."

"I am not drunk. I never get..." She paused a minute, scowling. "In college once at a keg party. Then once with Jim, but that was on bourbon and soda. It didn't taste anywhere near as good as this."

She came up on her knees to reach for the mug. He held it away from her, while at the same time taking her arm to steady her. "Look," he said, "why don't you use the bathroom and get ready for bed. I'll get Julianne settled."

"I don't want you to sleep on the floor."

"It's already decided." He put down the mug on the night table, thinking he just might have a bad back after a night on the floor. But better that than the alternative.

"No. I want you to sleep in the bed. That's why I wanted the pillows. I want you to be warm. I want—"

He gripped her shoulders, pulling her to her feet. She let her head fall back, and with the motion her lashes fluttered and her mouth opened enough for him to see just the tip of her tongue. If she had been cold sober, it would have been the most blatant of invitations.

But she wasn't, and while fourteen different reasons he shouldn't methodically marched through his mind, he kissed her anyway.

He tasted rum and readiness and was sure he heard a throaty sigh of relief. Had she wanted the kiss as much as he had? Her mouth responded as if her thirst could be quenched and he were the source.

Somehow her hands had climbed up and around his neck, her fingers gliding into his hair. He knew she was tipsy enough not to realize what in hell she was doing. Otherwise, she wouldn't be opening her mouth wider and pressing her body closer. He cupped her hips, his fingers pressing through her clothes and into her bottom. He wanted to lift her against him, to let her know how dangerous it would be for them to share a bed. He wanted to let her feel how thick and full and hot he was. He wanted to allow himself the sweet agony of kissing her breasts, sliding his fingers deep....

He almost lost it when he heard her sweet moan of satisfaction. If he didn't untangle himself from her now, he knew he wouldn't be sleeping on the floor.

He thought of his threat of a long, wet and hot kiss. There was just one problem.

It was only supposed to be sexual.

The kiss wasn't supposed to reach his heart.

Chapter 7

The storm continued throughout the night.

Zach woke at the first break of light, not because of any desire to watch the snow get deeper, but to get up from the uncomfortable bed he'd fashioned on the floor. Pillows and blankets didn't even come close to making an adequate mattress. He felt as though he'd tossed more than he slept, but then again, he would have done the same sleeping with Lizzie. Admittedly, for different reasons, but ones no less painful.

The room was startlingly light, although more a threatening gray than the reflective white he would have expected. He rolled out from under a quilt, bumped his hip on the hardwood floor and shivered at the sudden change in temperature.

Searching around, he found his jeans where he'd tossed them across a chair. He pulled them on after silently coming to his feet. The zipper hissed in the quiet room and he winced painfully. The ache surrounded his lower back, and he rubbed his hand across his spine, trying to ease the spasm. Lower-back pain, he thought grimly. Lizzie had invented his back trouble to justify the five pillows to Greta, but now he had it.

He stretched and twisted his body from side to side, turning slightly at the rustling sound that came from across the room. Lizzie was still asleep, but Julianne was peering at him through the crib bars as if she'd been awake for hours waiting for someone to notice her.

The baby squealed, and Zach shook his head. "Shh, you'll wake your mother." He crossed over to the crib, and grinned at her. "You're quite the bright-eyed young lady for—" he peered at his watch "—ten after six, princess. Greta said breakfast isn't until eight. Think you can hold out?" She seemed to consider that for a moment, then reached for his finger. When he said, "Oh, no you don't," she promptly put her thumb in her mouth. Zach smoothed her mussed hair and urged her to lie back down. He took her teddy bear from where it had managed to get wedged in the crib's corner and tucked it under the quilt with her.

Making sure she was adequately covered and warm, he rested his forearms on the top of the crib railing.

She stared back at him, grinning around her thumb.

"Are you trying to charm me?" he asked, raising an eyebrow. Her grin widened. "Ah, you want me to smuggle you some good food and not that—" He stopped himself. "Can't say the s-word, your mother will kill me, but you know what I mean, don't you?" Julianne watched him as though fascinated by every word. "Tell you what, we'll let your mother sleep. When it's time, you and I'll go down and see what Greta is serving."

He reached down and touched the baby's cheek. Her eyes drifted closed and he stood for a few moments, watching her sleep. He made sure again that she was warm enough, then went into the bathroom.

After a quick shower, he came out, dug around in the jumble of clothes he'd tossed into the nylon bag and pulled out a heavy cotton shirt. While he pulled it over his head he walked to the window seat and looked out.

"Damn snow," he muttered. He watched it swirl and blow, the visibility as limited as in a whiteout. A snowdrift just below the window rose and curled like a surfer's perfect wave that had been magically captured in a gigantic snow sculpture. And then, as though the thought were the most natural progression, he knew that since Lizzie sculpted, she would appreciate the shape and grace of the drift. For a fragmentary moment he considered waking her, and then just as quickly decided not to. After that kiss the previous night, he felt a lot safer with her asleep.

Damn.

In one breath he'd both cursed the delay and admired snowdrifts. He puzzled over why he was finding he liked the idea of being snowed in with Lizzie and Julianne. He reminded himself that the three of them could have been in that accident on the interstate, or another one. They could have been trapped in the car and risked dying of exposure. All those reasons were valid and grim possibilities, but they were the kind of things one said to Greta or the Healys or the cops at the accident scene; they had nothing to do with his puzzled thoughts.

Perhaps it was the coziness of being with her. Sharing this room while she worried about him sleeping on the floor. Doing the domestic stuff like putting the crib together. Kissing her.

He scowled at how quickly his mind had leaped upon the real excuse. Now you've got it, Stone. You liked kissing her. You liked the mutual need. That need had not only surprised him, but for a poignant moment had made him forget why he was with her.

He drew in a breath, letting it out slowly. Whom was he trying to kid? She'd had a little too much hot buttered rum. Maybe not enough to call her drunk, but enough to break down any inhibitions she had. And yet, while he had been the one who initiated the kiss, her mouth had been soft and eager, opening as quickly as her hands had slid up and around his neck.

He could have had her and yet he'd broken away. He'd lifted her to her feet and urged her into the bathroom to get ready for bed.

Now he dragged his hand through his hair as though to settle all the strands back the way they were before she touched them.

He had propped one foot up on the window seat when he heard her move in the bed with a soft blanket-settling sound. Determined as he was not to turn around, he found he was wondering if that flannel nightie with lacy ruffles that he'd caught a brief glimpse of before she climbed into bed the night before was up around her waist. The next question followed hard on the first one's heels. Did she wear panties to bed?

Shivering again, he blamed the reaction on the draft from the windows. He wished he had some coffee. He wished he was at Gordon's right now and getting ready to return to Liberty. He wished he was anywhere but here.

To his annoyance, he realized he was giving little thought to the ransacker, or to why there'd been such a time lapse if it was connected to Jim's murder or even to Jim himself. That last thought was unsettling, but he had a gut feeling that there was a connection. Some of the stray pieces in the unsolved investigation were falling into place. Once he returned to Liberty, he intended to read the reports Jim had filed just before he died.

In truth he would like to ignore the entire issue. He didn't want to think about what a revelation of Jim's involvement, if it existed, would do to Lizzie and the Healys.

But be that as it might, he'd spent little time turning it over in his mind. No, he thought, not as disgusted with himself as he should have been, he'd been thinking mostly about how to get it on with Jim's wife.

Aw, hell, he thought with a resigned shake of his head. The truth jarred him, but he couldn't deny it. He did know, and he knew it as sure as there were more than twenty inches of snow and counting. But in all honesty, he'd never thought of Lizzie in an intimate way until that fleeting moment in Jim's den when their eyes had met and something had sprung to life between them.

What he needed to do was reduce it all to a common man-to-woman sexual reaction. Never mind all that heart stuff that had gripped him in the throes of kissing her. Wanting sex was so much simpler. It required only bodies, passion and mutual satisfaction. It began and it ended. No hassle, no regrets, no worrying about reputations and deep feelings.

And when had he become so concerned about a woman's reputation? About what an innkeeper would think? The irony that he'd succumbed to such concerns was indeed incredible.

Although all the reasons he'd given Lizzie were valid, and the last thing he wanted to do was put her in an awkward position, there could have been another way. The truth, for starters. This wasn't television drama. Nor were they being followed. Certainly secrecy about who they were wasn't crucial. If he'd explained their situation, Greta would probably not only have understood the situation, but have moved another bed in for him.

Then he wouldn't have a backache now, nor would he be wondering why their mutual decision that he should be Lizzie's husband for one night had made him edgy. Not scared, he thought, which would have been a hell of a lot easier to deal with. If he'd been scared he would have bluntly told Greta why they were together, and insisted on a rollaway bed. No, he had wanted to test the tension, to push the invisible boundaries between them. That edginess had made him want to hope.

It was nothing but a fantasy, he reminded himself. It was make-believe, just like the family he'd tried to recreate every time he was moved from one foster home to another. Believing that he wasn't wanted had hurt too much, so he'd made up a family who did want him.

This family fantasy with Lizzie was different, however. He was an adult now; he knew what he was doing. Getting out of it was not going to be any kind of problem. No one really trusted in make-believe.

He could play the part of Lizzie's husband, of Julianne's father, for Greta and the other guests at the inn because he had created the fantasy. In this situation with Lizzie, he'd gone into it knowing exactly how he was going to get out.

Getting them to Gordon's was the getting-out part. Now all he had to do was get there.

He turned away from the window and saw that Julianne was still asleep. Lizzie had turned over so that she was no longer in the middle of the bed. He watched her a few minutes, shivering again. Hell, why not? He was dressed, the bed was large enough, and he had no intention of touching her.

Again, he glanced at his watch. 6:25. He could watch the snow fall, or go back to the makeshift bed. Why was he hesitating? She'd point-blank told him last night she wanted him to sleep with her. It had been thanks partly to her over-indulgence in hot buttered rum, but nevertheless, hadn't he been noble and said no despite his mind screaming, "You're a damn fool, Stone"? Hadn't he flat-out refused, no matter how many pillows she said they could put between them?

But this morning he'd figured it all out. Maybe he was playing some make-believe-family game, but as long as he knew that, as long as he was prepared for the ending, he was all right.

Carefully he pulled back the covers and slipped into the warmth of the bed. He stretched out, unable to recall when any bed had felt so good. She shifted and rolled toward him, but he didn't move until she was once again still. He let out a long breath, feeling as if he'd passed a crucial test.

"Well, I have to tell you, this looks like one of those famous New England blizzards we used to have years ago. Didn't have all this fancy-dancy weather radar then to tell you how bad it was going to be. In those days you stuck your head out the window and sniffed." George Bishop tucked his napkin under his chin, carefully covering a paisley silk tie. He had a sweep of silver hair that looked as though baldness would never be his problem. He took the platter of steaming pancakes that was being passed, forked four, and after a moment's hesitation added a fifth.

His wife, Muriel, to his right, wore a blue suit and a pink blouse with a stand-up ruffled collar that she'd closed with a cameo. She wore large pearl clip-on earrings, and her silver hair looked so perfectly styled, Zach wondered if she'd slept sitting up.

She sat with her back straight, watching Zach settle Julianne into the high chair. "You can smell snow, you know," she said as though one's nose was more reliable than the weather bureau. She put three pancakes on her plate and passed the dish to Zach. Reaching for the butter and syrup, she added, "You must have arrived late last night."

Zach considered ignoring her. Her comment wasn't a question, but more of a statement to elicit confirmation of what she already knew.

The dining room of the Wisteria Inn was set up with small groupings of tables that sat no more than four to give a homey feel. When he'd come in with Julianne, the other guests were already seated. They included a young newly-wed couple seated alone and oblivious to everyone else, four women who were on a bus tour of historic places and a middle-aged couple who were discussing the price of real estate in the area. The high chair had been placed at the Bishop's table, so he had made the logical assumption.

Resigned to Greta's arrangement and answering Muriel Bishop's comment, Zach put a pancake on a small plate for Julianne. "We came in around midnight."

"And you let your wife sleep. Isn't that nice, George? Doesn't he remind you of our Donnie? Taking care of the baby and being a sweet husband." She concluded with an indulgent smile, her pride in Donnie obvious.

George said, "I wish you'd call him Don, Muriel. At twenty-five he's not a kid anymore." He peered at Zach curiously.

"To me he'll always be Donnie," she said with a passion that said a lot about still-connected umbilical cords. "I'll bet your mother still feels very close to you, Zach."

No emotion showed on Zach's face, but his cut into Julianne's pancake was deeper than necessary. "I wouldn't know."

"Of course she does. Mothers never really let go of their children," she said with confidence. "Just as I'm sure your wife thinks you are very sweet to be taking such good care of little Julianne. Greta just raved about you when we all came down this morning."

Despite Muriel Bishop's conclusion that he was sweet, Zach knew he probably didn't look very sweet, and the term *husband,* with all its connotations of domestic and family relationships, was even farther off the mark. Although he smiled, he knew he resembled a man who had had little sleep and didn't know zip about dressing a baby. He would have preferred a table with just him and Julianne. He wasn't used to morning conversation. But then again, little that had happened in the past twenty-four hours was routine. Such as getting into bed with Lizzie this morning.

Just when he'd thought he had it all under control, she'd drawn even closer. Even though he'd known she was still sleeping, he'd wanted to pull her beneath him, to find out exactly where her nightie had risen to, and if she wore panties to bed.

He refused to think about the possibilities that even now, more than two hours later, still waved like steam and smoke through his mind and other less cerebral places. Instead, he made himself concentrate on getting through breakfast. Later he wanted to get the car repacked and find out which roads had been plowed. He didn't want to spend another night in the same room with Lizzie.

George had been studying him and finally asked, "You one of those house husbands?"

There was no doubt about George's definition. Wimp. Given Muriel's assessment of their son, Donnie no doubt fit that term in his father's eyes.

Zach added syrup to Julianne's pancake and put the plate on the high-chair tray. She had her mouth open before he got the first bite onto the spoon.

Zach winked at her and she giggled and opened her mouth wider. He gently tucked the full spoon into her mouth.

Glancing briefly at Bishop, he said, "I'm a police officer."

Muriel rolled her eyes and sighed.

George beamed. "Hey, a man after my own heart. You here to arrest someone? Oh, hell, Muriel, do we have another tape for the camcorder?"

Muriel ignored his question and took a plate of sausage away from him. "You know you can't have those." She smiled over at Zach. "Too much fat and cholesterol. Don't mind George. He listens to a police scanner all the time and knows all the jargon."

What jargon? Zach wondered, but he didn't comment except to say, "I'm not here to arrest anyone. We're on our way north." He grinned at Julianne, who was on her second pancake. "You were hungry, weren't you, princess?"

"Sure not going to be traveling today," George said, and speared Zach with a look that was both confidential and serious. "Maybe we can trade some stories later."

"Stories."

"Police stories. I read a lot of books about cops. You guys lead pretty exciting lives."

"A thrill a minute," Zach muttered, signaling for Greta when she came into the dining room to refill the coffee carafes. She hurried over.

"Greta, could I get some coffee to take up to Elizabeth? And also I need to use your phone."

"Of course. There's jacks in all the bedrooms. Would you like to take a phone up with you?" She patted his shoulder. "How's your back this morning?"

"Oh, dear, did you hurt your back?" Muriel asked, immediately concerned. "I have a heating pad."

Zach shook his head at both women, privately thinking that Lizzie's little story to account for so many pillows was turning into a real pain.

"Greta, I'd really appreciate a phone." He started to take the plate of pancakes from Julianne, but she reached out for it, her lower lip trembling.

"She looks as if she's not finished," Greta said. "Why don't you let me finish feeding her while you take the coffee and make your phone calls?"

"You're sure you don't mind?" Zach asked, a little dubiously.

It wasn't that he didn't trust Greta, but he didn't know how Lizzie would feel. Then he looked at Julianne with syrup all over her mouth and thought of the discussion they'd had about baby food in Julianne's bedroom.

"Actually, she should be eating baby food," he said, doubting that Greta kept that stored in a closet as she had the crib.

Greta chuckled. "I don't think she'll be too thrilled after pancakes and syrup."

Zach made one more attempt to remove the plate, but this time Julianne let out a howl that turned every head in the dining room. He'd never heard her cry; in fact, now that he thought about it, the baby had barely whimpered since they left Liberty. In her eyes he could see tears glistening, and he knew there was no way he would do anything to make her unhappy. "You win, princess. I just hope your mother understands."

Greta patted Zach's arm. "Elizabeth will, and besides, my pancakes wouldn't hurt a baby."

A few minutes later, she brought him a tray with a pot of coffee, cream and sugar, two cups and a white telephone. Muriel was chattering to Julianne about how much she reminded her of her own granddaughter. George excused himself to go into the welcoming room to smoke a cigar. Zach thanked Greta, dropped a quick kiss on Julianne's curly head and left the dining room.

Elizabeth was still asleep when he eased the bedroom door open. He put down the tray and hunted around for the telephone jack. Finally locating it behind the night table, he carefully moved Lizzie's hoop earrings and the carafe holding what was left of the buttered rum. He plugged the phone in the jack and sat down on the edge of the bed. Behind him, he felt her move. Quickly he punched Gordon's number.

When Gordon answered, Zach said, "Good morning. If New Hampshire has a shortage of snow for the ski season, I've got a deal they won't want to pass up."

Gordon chuckled. "Naomi was hoping it was you. How is it down there?"

"They've stopped measuring it in inches."

"I'm glad you haven't lost your dry wit, Zachariah."

"Yeah, well, it's hanging by a goddamn thread. I meant to call you last night, but it was near midnight when we stopped."

"We figured you pulled in somewhere. The snow is bad up here, too. Might be a good idea to wait until tomorrow after they get the plows moving."

"I'd like to get out of here today."

"Look, I know this wasn't what you wanted to do." Gordon sighed. "I sure didn't expect it to get this complicated."

Neither did I, Zach thought, glancing at Elizabeth.

Gordon continued, "I know you were due for time off, but, hell, I didn't know how else to do it quickly. I didn't want Elizabeth and my granddaughter in a house with some loony ransacker on the loose."

"It's all right, Gordon. In fact, I agree with you. She's better off somewhere safe. I just wasn't planning on the worst blizzard in thirty years happening at precisely this time."

Elizabeth stirred behind him, and he turned to look at her. She was still buried under the blankets, but he could see enough to know she was facing in his direction.

"Buzz called a little while ago," Gordon was saying. "He thought you were here and he wanted to fill you in on a few things. You probably should give him a call."

"They got a lead on the ransacker?"

Lizzie moved again. This time when he glanced at her, she was awake and watching him. He put his hand over the mouthpiece and whispered to her. "Want some coffee?"

"Mmm, sounds wonderful. Is it still snowing?" Her voice was low and husky. She turned toward the windows. The flannel-and-lace nightie he'd thought about more than any silky satin confection looked even more appealing in the bright morning light. He knew it was billowy and shapeless and had a quaint ruffle around the bottom. He knew it should be a turnoff, but it wasn't. And no way could he blame her for that.

She blinked into the gray light that streamed in the windows. "It looks like a 'winter in New England' Christmas card."

"It looks like fifteen inches more than they predicted. Yeah, Gordon, I'm still here. They're fine." He watched her as she pushed the covers back. She used his shoulder to steady herself as she climbed slowly out of bed. "Gordon, could you hang on a minute?"

Again he covered the mouthpiece. The flannel nightie swirled down to her bare toes, and Zach thought she looked deliciously tousled.

"You feeling a little hung over?"

"Don't be silly," she replied evenly. "I'm just a little groggy."

"You remember what happened last night?"

She let go of him, facing him, and every trace of huskiness left her voice. "What happened?"

Never had he heard two words that managed to combine "tell me" and "don't tell me."

"Let me finish this call and then we'll talk."

"Zach, oh God, I didn't do anything that, uh, that—"
She stood straight, her eyes so wide that he knew he should level with her, but he didn't.

Suddenly it seemed very important to know how she would feel. "That you should regret this morning?"

He had to give her credit. She stared him down and she didn't try to duck the question.

"Yes."

"Do you regret the kiss?"

She closed her eyes briefly as though trying to recall whether the kiss had been only the beginning. She shook her head. "I wanted to kiss you," she said quietly.

He'd expected another yes, not such honesty. He could do no less with her. "Nothing happened but the kiss, Lizzie. Nothing."

She stared at him for a long moment, and he felt an instant of regret that this trip with her was just a job, that he was here because he was a cop. He was about to say something about another time, that maybe when this was all over, they could get together.

Then she saw the empty crib. "My God, where's Julianne?"

"Take it easy. She's fine. She's with Greta."

She sank down on the bed beside him, and as though it were the most natural thing in the world, he put his arm around her. She leaned against him and he could feel her heart racing.

"Gordon?" Zach said. "Sorry for the long interruption. Look, I'll call Buzz and get the details. I'll call you back later this afternoon and maybe I can give you a time when we can get out of here."

He hung up the phone and gathered Elizabeth into his arms. "You didn't think I'd let anything happen to her, did you?"

She shook her head, curling into him as though she were suddenly cold. "I was just startled. I'd expected to see her there and she wasn't."

With his other hand, he poured her some coffee. "I want you to promise not to laugh when you see her."

She took the cup, her eyes suddenly wide. "Why?"

"Well, I had some problems getting her diaper to stay up, and I don't think she wanted to wear another sleeper. But I figured I was safer putting her back into the same kind of thing I took off her instead of trying to figure out the other stuff."

Elizabeth quickly rebalanced the cup she had almost spilled. "You changed her diaper?"

"I wasn't supposed to do that? She was wet and uncomfortable."

"She hates a wet diaper."

"Then what's wrong with me putting her in a dry one?"

"It's terrific. A lot of men refuse to change diapers, and just yesterday you were afraid to even get close to her. This morning you got her up, changed and dressed her, and took her downstairs for breakfast. That's amazing."

He grinned, feeling a deep swell of pride. "Yeah, it is, isn't it?"

A knock came on the bedroom door. He called, "Come in," not even thinking of the picture he and Lizzie made of natural marital closeness. She was tucked in close to him, and his arm was even more firmly around her.

Greta came into the room with a very unhappy Julianne. The baby's hair was damp, her face flushed and her cheeks wet. Her small body shook with shuddering sobs as she held out her arms to Elizabeth.

"I'm sorry to interrupt, but she hasn't been happy since you left, Zach."

Elizabeth handed the cup to Zach and took the unhappy baby into her arms, talking to her, soothing her.

"It's okay, Greta. I was about to come down and get her, anyway."

"Oh, before I forget, Zach, George Bishop said to tell you he remembered reading a story about you in some police magazine. He wants to ask you some questions about it."

He considered telling Greta to inform Bishop that he could take his questions and shove—

"Zach." Elizabeth lifted her eyebrows with just a touch of amusement in her eyes.

"I didn't say it, did I?"

"You came very close."

Greta glanced from one to the other, now totally confused.

"What did I miss?"

"Lizzie doesn't like me to swear in front of the baby."

"He's usually very good about it, but sometimes he forgets."

"And you knew he was going to swear?"

"Hmm. He gets this fierce look and his face gets hard. Most of the time he catches himself, but on occasion he forgets."

Greta shook her head in amazement. Zach was no less amazed. How had he become so readable? He'd always been the cop who presented an unfazed stare no matter how much what he saw bothered him. It was a trick learned early as a defensive measure and it had served him well.

He closed the door after Greta left, folded his arms and leaned against it. Elizabeth changed Julianne and put her into the crib. She walked over, poured herself another cup of coffee, turned to him and said cordially, "Who's George Bishop? His name sounds like he should make men's hats."

"Mostly he makes useless conversation. How did you know?"

"Know what?"

"I was about to swear."

"You heard me tell Greta."

"I don't give fierce looks and my face doesn't get hard."

She walked over closer to him, peered at him intently and said, "Yes you do, and yes it does."

"I don't like you reading my mind."

"You mean you don't like anyone to get close enough to you to know what you're thinking."

"There. You're doing it again."

Sometime during their conversation, her hand had come to rest on the center of his chest. His hand had slipped around her neck and his thumb gave light support to her upturned chin. Julianne sat in the middle of her crib with her thumb in her mouth, watching them.

"She's watching us, Lizzie."

Elizabeth turned slightly, and when she once again looked up at Zach, she said, "if I were to read your mind, I would bet that the reason—"

He pressed his thumb to her lips. "You'd be wrong."

She brought up her hand and circled his wrist, brushing her mouth across his palm in the lightest of kisses. "I'm not wrong. The reason you're so careful is because of Julianne. You don't want to do anything in front of her."

He scowled and tried to draw away, but she wouldn't let go of him.

"And you know what else I think?" But she didn't let him answer. "I think you are an incredibly honorable man. No wonder Jim said you were the best partner he ever had. No wonder Gordon insisted on you bringing us to New Hampshire."

He gave her a guarded look. "Stop thinking that I'm some kind of hero filled with noble intentions."

"Real heroes never think they are."

He pulled her closer and whispered in a very low voice, "You want to know what kind of hero I am?" He pushed her hair away from her ear, and in very explicit words he deliberately didn't censor, he told her exactly why he wasn't any kind of hero.

To his utter amazement, she didn't flinch. Instead she brushed her mouth across his cheek, which he knew throbbed with a hard pulse.

"Julianne and I think you are quite wonderful; no matter how many nasty words you know, don't we, Julianne?"

The baby grinned and clapped her hands. Zach felt as though he'd been run over by a truck.

Elizabeth picked up the cup of coffee, finished it and said, "Now if you two will excuse me, I'm going to take a shower and get dressed. I know you want to call Buzz, and we should think about how soon we can leave." She went over to the dresser where she had put her clothes and Julianne's and from a drawer she took a pair of wool slacks, a heavy sweater and underwear. She picked up her travel case and sailed into the bathroom as if she had faced an impossible enemy and come away the victor.

Zach stared at the closed bathroom door.

"You know what, princess?" He glanced over at Julianne. "Your mother is not only messing up my thoughts, but I'm beginning to like it."

Julianne simply clapped her hands again.

Chapter 8

In the living room of the Wisteria Inn, a crackling fire and the arrival of after-dinner brandy made the storm outside feel like an excuse to be lazy, and a chance to make new friends. The conversation throughout the day had moved from the topic of the storm to charming anecdotes about family and personal experiences. Dinner had been a hearty beef and barley soup with hot crusty bread, accompanied by wine; dessert had been a date and raisin cake with a cream cheese and walnut frosting that Greta said had been served at the Wisteria since it welcomed its first guests.

Greta had just cleared away the coffee cups and finished serving brandy when someone flipped on the television for the weather forecast.

The weatherman smiled broadly and enthusiastically. "We can expect another five to six inches of snow, but I feel confident in predicting that it should taper off to flurries by tomorrow. The major roads are still clogged with drifts, so the public works department and the state police ask that you remain at home. If it's any consolation, this storm should go into the record books as one of the great New England blizzards." He was obviously pleased to think that since the snow had most of the Northeast grumbling and suffering from cabin fever, his raising the status of the storm to greatness would ease the pain and frustration.

Elizabeth sipped her brandy gingerly. Her experience with the rum drink the night before was one she definitely didn't want to repeat. Or perhaps her recollection of both Zach kissing her and her own welcoming response—no, not welcoming, she told herself, refusing to sidestep the way she'd acted.

She set the glass down at the realization that she'd not only welcomed his mouth, but had been eager and willing. She almost wished she were beset by guilt or shame, for, in fact, either would have been easier to explain. No, the plain truth was that she'd been drawn by need and want and a deep desire to know him.

Need and want weren't unusual feelings. It was the deep desire to know him that made them complicated. She allowed the words to settled into her mind. Knowing him held many more facets than a desire to make love. And he wasn't an easy man to know. He'd proved that conclusively whenever he felt that she might intrude. Their disagreement this morning about his supposition that she was trying to read his mind was an excellent example. Ironically, she'd accused him of the same thing when she was trying to think of ways to stay in Liberty. Perhaps they were more in tune with each other than either had thought.

Glancing over at him now, she needed little insight to know he was wired just about as tight as she'd ever seen any man.

She tried to concentrate on the Scrabble game she was playing with Muriel Bishop. Elizabeth had learned after they began that Muriel was the undefeated champion at her church; the woman tried to prove that with every arrangement of letters, including Elizabeth's.

The four ladies who were traveling together were working on a thousand-piece jigsaw puzzle that Greta had set up. Ken and Lisa, the newlyweds, had been outside and had come in a short while ago, giggling and laughing about playing angels in the snow. Instead of joining the others by the fire, they had gone to their room and hadn't returned. George Bishop, swirling the contents of his brandy glass, had pulled a chair up beside Zach and launched into a detailed story about drug kingpins and some money-laundering scheme.

Zach was sprawled in a recliner. He was wearing jeans and a heavy shirt, which, considering the warmth from the fire, surprised her. But when she asked about it, he'd scowled at her, as though she wasn't supposed to notice that this was the same man who rarely wore a coat when he went outside. Julianne, dressed in pink overalls and a white blouse with tiny ruffles trimmed with pink ribbons, had been perched in his lap for most of the day.

Zach's eyes were mere slits, and anyone simply looking in his direction would have thought he was concentrating on what George was telling him. Elizabeth knew better. He was restless, tense and annoyed with George Bishop. He'd ducked him numerous times, including one foray outside to shovel snow.

Now he was apparently resigned, or as Elizabeth suspected, counting on George to run down soon like an overwound clock.

Toward Julianne, Zach had been endlessly patient and endearingly gentle. Toward Elizabeth, he'd been either totally silent or so guarded that she weighed his mood before she spoke to him. She had tried to keep her own mood upbeat, although truthfully, she felt lousy. Facing what she knew couldn't happen and contrasting that with what she wanted to happen were playing havoc with her nerves. She'd never been one to duck her feelings, or to close her mind and pretend they weren't there.

She recognized that she was very much attracted to Zachariah Stone, and that attraction was not only disturbing, but unrealistic. She could think of a ton of reasons why she shouldn't be. His job, since she didn't want to care about another man who lived daily in life-threatening situations. His hard-edged attitude about women, which sat in direct opposition to her fear of being suffocated. She'd worked too hard to break away from an overprotective family and to make herself independent enough to support herself. From the time she'd left her Virginia home for college to her short career as a business consultant for a chain of art stores on the east coast, even through her marriage to Jim, she'd maintained her sense of identity. Jim had always encouraged her independence, and when they decided to have a family her decision to open her own art store in Liberty had been a decision such as many young families made, a combination of work and home. It had all been so perfect until Jim's death.

And she'd worked hard to make it perfect again. Until the ransacker turned her life over to Zach for safekeeping, which ironically didn't feel very safe—at least not emotionally.

Then there were his feelings toward her. This trip, he'd reminded her bluntly, was not what he'd planned to do with his time off. He was doing a favor for Gordon, and since she was Jim's widow, Zach could do no less than help her. Based on those two facts, he no doubt assumed that any feelings she might have toward him would stem from pure gratitude.

Oh, Zach, she thought, how I wish they were gratitude.

"It's your turn, Elizabeth," Muriel said as she added up the score she'd gotten by using a Q on a triple-word square.

The highest-value letter Elizabeth had was a K. When her fingers rearranged the letters on her stand, she found herself staring at the word Zach had used as an adjective to describe the snow. At midafternoon he'd gone to shovel out the car, in the hope that they might be able to leave. Elizabeth had known it was a futile exercise, but she had kept quiet. One didn't need to be a snowstorm expert to see that the continuing storm and the unplowed roads aborted any hope of travel.

One glance at Zach, however, and she wasn't so sure. If the man could have literally shoveled his way to New Hampshire, he would have done so.

Julianne had curled down in the crook on his arm now, fascinated with his wristwatch. Zach adjusted his body to make sure she was comfortable. His glass of brandy sat untouched. Elizabeth stared again at the four-letter word spelled out in front of her. It was as short and blunt as had been their conversation earlier that afternoon.

After shoveling for about a half an hour, he'd stamped the snow off his boots and come in the front door. Elizabeth had been supervising Julianne and Foggy, Greta's large gray cat, who'd emerged from the hooded cradle and was cautiously allowing Julianne to pet him.

She'd lifted up the baby into her arms and walked over to where Zach was pulling off his gloves and blowing on his hands. His hair was windblown and flecked with snow, his cheeks red from the cold. Bracing Julianne on her left hip, she'd waited for him to look at her. Their conversation had been mostly one-sided. Mostly hers.

"Should I ask how bad it is?"

"No," he growled, shrugging out of his jacket.

"That's what I thought."

Julianne reached for him, but he shook his head. "I'll make her cold if I hold her." He started around Elizabeth.

"Zach," she whispered to keep their conversation unnoticed by the others gathered by the fireplace, while at the same time she reached for his arm. He was cold. In fact she could feel him shiver. "You're chilled to the bone."

As if on cue he sneezed. "I've been colder."

She drew closer, her voice more exasperated than annoyed. "What is it with you and all these endurance tests? Sleeping on the floor when there is a perfectly good—and very large, I might add—bed. Most of the time refusing to wear a coat. And now shoveling all that snow when you're not only tired, but probably getting a cold."

He muttered in a low, raspy voice, "Hey, listen. I've managed to get along for thirty-eight years without anyone giving a damn whether I'm sick, cold, tired or dead. I don't need a nursemaid at this late date."

"What about a friend who cares? Would that be so terrible?" She fired back the questions, her whisper rising just a shade more slowly than her annoyance at his determination not even to like her. "I didn't ask for the snow, nor, I might remind you, was I the one who told Greta we were married."

"I never told her we were married."

"You didn't tell her we weren't, either."

"And if I'd known then that we'd be stuck here for God knows how long, then—" He dragged a hand through his hair. The moisture from the melted snow he flicked off grazed across her cheek. "Never mind." He sneezed again. "I'm going to take a shower." He started toward the stairs, but turned back to her. "We're leaving tomorrow if I have to hire a snowplow to escort us." He stomped up the stairs, and Elizabeth saw the disappointment in Julianne's face.

"He's tired and cold, sweetheart. He'll hold you later, I promise."

Well, this was later, she thought now as she watched the two of them settling deeper into the chair as though destined to sleep there for the night. She laid her letters on the Scrabble board and arranged them to spell f-o-l-k-s.

Muriel said, "You're wasting that S, Elizabeth."

"That's all right. I think I'd better get my daughter upstairs and into bed before she falls asleep."

"She certainly does love her daddy, doesn't she? I don't know when I've seen a baby so taken with her father. Was he there when she was born?"

Elizabeth thought of the difficult birth, of her pregnancy and her terror that she would lose Jim's baby. She rarely talked about it, although often when she held Julianne, she relived those tense nine months. Losing Jim and then almost losing Julianne had tested Elizabeth in ways she hoped never to repeat. Glancing over at Zach, she agreed that he did indeed look the part of an ideal father. But he wasn't, nor would he ever be. She didn't doubt that he cared for Julianne, but she knew that a lot of that caring was imposed upon him by his own sense of obligation to protect her and Elizabeth.

Incredibly, that overprotective attitude that she had fought against all her own growing-up years was exactly what she felt toward Julianne. She knew now it was a natural parental instinct, but Zach's feelings could hardly be that. And yet, she didn't believe that Julianne was just a job to him, or an official order from Gordon. Herself? Yes. He'd made that undeniably clear and left no room for misunderstanding.

"Elizabeth?"

"Oh, uh, no, Muriel. He wasn't there when she was born." She pushed her chair back. "Will you excuse me?"

"I can wait until you come back down."

"Why don't you ask George to take my place?"

"George cheats," she said with a sniff. "He tries to use all those police words he knows that aren't in the dictionary.

You go on and attend to Julianne. I'll see if Greta wants to play."

Elizabeth walked over to where Zach was sprawled. He glanced up, his eyes a little glazed and definitely fatigued. She reached down to lift the baby, which meant sliding her hands into the concave warmth of Zach's stomach. She tried to do it as though the motion were normal, ordinary and meaningless.

But she knew it wasn't when he flinched so that her hand jumped and brushed too low, resting for a taut, wild moment on the zipper placket of his jeans. It had happened so fast, and with Julianne between them, Elizabeth could almost convince herself it had been her imagination. However, their eyes met briefly and truthfully. Oh yes, she had indeed touched him, and from his muttered oath, he very definitely knew where and for how long. For that thick instant their gazes confirmed the array of scattered emotions that ran from naked desire to total frustration.

Gathering up Julianne, Elizabeth hoped her reaction wasn't too noticeable. Her cheeks felt hot, and she knew she'd be more embarrassed if she blushed. That particular reaction seemed a little silly since they had shared the intimacy of a kiss, and had even shared a bed that morning.

George had pulled over another chair for her. "Elizabeth, sit down here with us. I was just starting to tell Zach about an arrest right down the street from our house in Trenton. Did Muriel tell you we're from New Jersey? Anyway, I had the camcorder loaded and ready to capture all the action in case the police needed extra evidence."

"It sounds fascinating, George, and I'd love to hear the story, but perhaps tomorrow. The baby is tired, and I need Zach to help me with something upstairs."

She immediately glanced fully at Zach with a don't-you-dare-make-one-comment look. He didn't grin or wink or make any flirtatious gesture, yet his dark eyes conveyed his thoughts as distinctly as if he'd said the words. *I don't want to want you!*

There was no mistaking his frustration and maybe even his pain, and if Elizabeth had been feeling generous about the way she felt about him, she might have allowed her thoughts to mirror his and show in her eyes. But she wasn't, or perhaps she had taken a no-turning-back step and now faced how she really felt. She lowered her head and silently prayed he wouldn't cup her chin and lift it so that she would have to look at him. She tried to concentrate on getting a grip on Julianne.

It worked only marginally. She wanted him. She very definitely wanted to want him. Perhaps if she could convince herself it was only physical, a sexual reaction, a chemistry that couldn't be denied, then maybe she wouldn't hurt after he was gone. For there was one undeniable fact, which only in the most fanciful fantasy wouldn't come true. As soon as they reached New Hampshire, he would leave and return to Liberty alone. And even if the process of finding and arresting the ransacker brought them into contact later, it would be as the cop doing his job.

She settled Julianne on her hip, and the baby immediately reached for one of her earrings.

Zach adjusted the chair to an upright position and got to his feet. He said good-night to George and placed a very warm hand on Elizabeth's back. It was the first time he'd touched her since he'd put his arm around her that morning.

"Thanks for rescuing me," he murmured after they said good-night to the other guests.

"I don't think George has too many people who sit and listen to his stories."

"They wouldn't be so bad if there weren't so many of them. I think he reads police reports instead of newspapers."

"You were very tolerant and patient."

"Since my other choices were shoveling more snow or sitting in the bedroom with you, George won out."

His hand had slipped up her back to cup her neck. Their bodies brushed as they walked toward the stairs.

"The weatherman said only flurries tomorrow. We can probably leave," she said, feeling a sudden sadness.

"God, I hope so."

At the stairs, Greta asked if they needed anything. They both shook their heads and climbed the stairs without speaking.

When they opened the door, they found the china bedside lamp on. Greta had turned down the bed, fluffed the pillows invitingly and drawn the drapes closed. Since the wind outside wasn't as furious as the night before, the room felt pleasantly cozy.

"The only thing missing is candles and wine," Zach muttered as he followed her inside.

Elizabeth swung around, suddenly angry. "She thinks we're married, and given your scowls and bad mood all day, she probably thinks we had a fight and wanted to be helpful."

"She should have done it for Ken and Lisa," he growled, snapping on the lights. "They're the romantics in this group."

"They also went to their room a long time ago. No one needs to be too aware to realize why." Elizabeth put Julianne in her crib, and she promptly began to cry.

Zach turned around, but didn't move toward her. "Do you want me to leave so you can get her settled?"

"Then she'll really scream." Elizabeth opened a dresser drawer and took out a heavy sleeper. "I think you've spoiled her with all the attention."

He sat down in the chair, his legs stretched out in front of him. "Babies should be spoiled."

"It depends on what you mean by spoiled. They should be loved, certainly, but not given everything they ask for."

"Like what?" he asked, and she could feel him watching her as she moved from the dresser.

With Julianne's sleeper and a fresh diaper in hand, she glanced toward him. Sprawled low in the chair, he'd propped his elbows on its arms and watched her over fisted hands.

"For example, tonight when she wanted the cake. It was too rich for her, and the nuts in the cream cheese frosting aren't good for a baby."

"Your baby-food theory isn't shared by Julianne."

"Nor by you. After these few days, I'll probably never get her to eat it again."

"I take full responsibility for corrupting your daughter," he said in a low voice.

Elizabeth glanced back at him. She didn't want to argue with him, and given his mood all day, she knew it would take very little disagreement for them to get into a shouting match.

In truth she thoroughly approved of all the special attention Zach had paid to Julianne. "By giving her pancakes, and holding her until I know you would have preferred doing six other things, by giving her attention and caring about her? I'd hardly call that corrupting her." She quickly snapped Julianne into the heavy sleeper.

Zach didn't say anything, but instead glanced at a sketchbook that Elizabeth had left on the window seat. "You draw, too?"

"Yes, but only as a preliminary. This afternoon while I was watching the snow, I saw this perfect drift, and I thought it would make a wonderful contemporary piece."

"The one near the bush?" At her nod, he said, "I saw it this morning."

"You did?" She was frankly amazed. Since his reaction to the snow had been mostly negative, his awareness of a particular drift as anything other than an obstruction in need of a snowplow struck her as quite remarkable.

"Yeah, I was going to wake you up."

"You should have. I would have loved to see it in the dawn light."

She lifted Julianne and was about to set her in the crib when the baby squirmed to the side, holding out her arms for Zach.

"After this is all over, I'm going to have to hire you to come and hold her every day," Elizabeth said with amusement as he came and took Julianne.

"I'd do it for free," he said, winking at the baby.

"You would, wouldn't you?"

"Absolutely. We'd have a chance to talk, wouldn't we, princess?"

Elizabeth watched as he cradled the baby, walking with her from one end of the room to the other, whispering; an occasional laugh came from Zach, a giggle from Julianne, as though they shared a joke. It was a warm relationship, the kind she'd wanted Jim to have with Julianne, the kind a baby needed from a father and one that Julianne and Zach seemed to have fallen into without any effort.

Zach settled down in the chair with Julianne on the verge of sleep. His head was lowered, and Julianne was tucked into his arm as though he was sheltering her. Elizabeth stared at the picture they made for only a few seconds before she realized how it captured an exquisite bond between the man and the child. Quickly, she went over to the sketch pad, opened it to a new page and hunted for the pencil, which had fallen between the cushions.

Drawing the necessary outlines, her fingers raced, eager to add details and make notes about how she would work and mold the clay when she got home. She watched the two for a long time, memorizing details. She knew she could never have captured the impression in a planned pose. The image of the man and the baby, wariness and absolute trust, and the bond of father and child all blended in a poignant picture she knew would never quite leave her mind.

Finally Zach whispered, "I think she's asleep."

Elizabeth put the sketch pad aside and went over to where he sat. "Maybe you should carry her. I don't want her to wake up."

Awkwardly and carefully Zach got to his feet. He eased Julianne down into the crib and tucked the teddy bear in beside her. Elizabeth covered her with the down quilt. She started to turn away, but Zach remained.

He stared down at the baby. His voice sounded heavy with frustration when he said, "She's so innocent, Lizzie, and it's a hell of a lousy world out there."

Elizabeth touched his arm, somewhat taken aback by the unmistakable fierceness beneath his words. "But she's not out there. She's here with us."

As though he didn't hear her, he said, "Drugs, death, irrational jerks who get off hurting other people, punk kids looking for action who will try to use her, take advantage of her."

She was aware of all the awful things in the world, but she also knew that a family that supported and cared and educated children could go a long way to diffuse all the negatives. And yet no guarantees could be given. Elizabeth knew of families in Liberty who, despite the most ideal conditions, had seen tragedy occur. Certainly the family Zach had talked about, the one that had lost the daughter to drugs, had held great hopes for her when she was a baby.

Elizabeth folded her arms to stop the ominous tremble as she, too, watched Julianne sleep. Suddenly she wished she could wrap her in cotton batting, infuse her with all the experience and wisdom she would need, or perhaps seal her safely away. As her own parents had tried to do with her, she thought. The nature of a parent was to shelter, just as the nature of a child was to rebel and struggle for independence.

Softly she said, "Zach, she won't be defenseless. Now she's just a baby, but by the time she's grown she'll know. I'm not about to send her out into the world without making sure she knows what to expect. Education, preparation, responsibility—I intend to teach her all those things."

Zach was silent for a moment, then asked, "What about a father for her?"

For an instant she wanted to say that he would make a perfect father, but she doubted that was what he wanted to hear. "I haven't really thought about that. I'm certainly not going to marry a man just to give her one."

He cleared his throat, reached down and smoothed his hand over the quilt, making sure it was tucked around Julianne.

Elizabeth said, "I was serious about you coming over to see her and hold her."

"Maybe after this is all over..." He let the sentence trail off as though not at all sure what he was getting into. Or perhaps he was leery of what wasn't said but could be implied. A continuing concern for Julianne might be misunderstood, as might a continuing relationship with Elizabeth. Yet despite his leeriness, she found his hesitation said more about his feelings in a profound and meaningful way than a gushy promise of devotion to Julianne.

She assumed the subject was closed and began to gather up her nightie and robe.

Zach stood staring down at Julianne, his voice so low she almost didn't hear him. "He didn't know me. For four years I searched for him, and when I found him he said he didn't even remember my mother."

Elizabeth's eyes widened. His words had come out of nowhere, and yet she knew Zach didn't talk about himself easily. Perhaps in those moments when she was sketching and he was holding the baby, he had been remembering and comparing. "You mean your father?"

"Yeah. A real symbol of the American family," he said with a potent sarcasm.

Elizabeth laid down her things on the bed and moved over beside him. She didn't want to leap in with a hundred dumb or nosy-sounding questions. At the same time she knew she couldn't let this moment of openness on his part get away. So instead of saying anything, she slipped her arm around his waist. For a moment, he stiffened and then winced, but he didn't push her away.

"I don't like to talk about him. After Jim was killed, I went to the stress counselor at the station for a while, and he immediately zeroed in on when I was a kid. Emotional poverty, he called it, when I told him I spent my first fifteen years going from one foster home to another. Many of the families were okay, but it was so transient, so rootless. I always knew that I'd leave. I used to tell people when they asked me where I was from that I grew up between somewhere and somewhere else." He moved away from her. "You don't want to hear all this crap."

"Zach, yes. I do want to hear it," she said, not wanting to sound pushy, but also wanting him to share it with her.

"My mother was about sixteen and unmarried. Back in the fifties that was a big deal. There was a lot of talk about her because she wouldn't say who my father was. She got accused of sleeping with a lot of guys, and I ended up a ward of the court. Later, she told me my father's name and I went looking for him. After I found him, I decided that maybe she knew he wouldn't remember her and was trying to protect herself."

"And perhaps you."

"Me?" He seemed startled at her question.

"She probably wanted you to have some stability even though she couldn't keep you. Maybe she saw your father as a threat to that."

"Like he might come and claim me and threaten to love me and want me?" The cynicism couldn't have been clearer. "She needn't have worried. He wasn't interested."

Elizabeth felt as though she'd discovered pieces to a puzzle. This was why he was so caring of Julianne. He not only saw her as a child who had no father, but he saw himself in the role he'd wanted his own father to play toward him.

"When I told him who I was, I expected him to deny I was his son or give me some money and tell me to get lost. But, yeah, I also harbored some deep hope he'd say, 'I'm glad you found me, and more than anything I want to be your old man.' He took care of that when he said he hadn't the least memory of my mother. I had a picture of her and I watched his eyes when I showed it to him, but there was absolutely no response."

He paused for a moment, and then said in one of the deadest voices she'd ever heard, "I was fifteen, and I stood there and bawled like a baby when he slammed the door in my face."

Elizabeth blinked to stop the threat of tears. She refused to insult him by saying she understood. She didn't. Her own childhood had been spent with parents who were more than willing to comfort, protect and sometimes smother. How odd that the smothering effect would probably have been welcomed by Zach.

"You sound so . . . I don't know . . . passionless? Unemotional? Certainly you couldn't have felt that way then."

"No. I was both passionate and emotional. And both went from hope to hate with the slam of a door. I hated him with an obsessive passion." He hesitated as though unsure whether to go further, then added, "I decided I would kill him."

Elizabeth stared, certain that she had heard him wrong.

He moved over to the windows and stared out into the blackness. "For weeks I planned. I had the gun and the opportunity, and God knows I had the hate."

"But you changed your mind." It wasn't a question as much as a desperate hope.

"I chickened out," he said flatly. "I told myself he deserved to die for what he did to my mother and probably to other women. I had a thousand reasons why I was doing the world a favor, but when the moment came I couldn't do it."

She let out the long breath she hadn't been aware she was holding. "Thank God."

"Yeah. I found out that hate is as dangerous an emotion as love, so I learned how to not do either."

Learning not to hate was indeed commendable, but learning not to love had a tragic and cold aloneness she simply couldn't comprehend. The miracle was that despite his background and his father's denial of him, he still had moments of vulnerability. Especially with Julianne.

She guessed that he wouldn't like her question, but she asked it just the same. "What did you do after you, uh, changed your mind about your father?"

He met her eyes directly. "After I chickened out and didn't kill him? That's what it was, Lizzie. Don't soften it up as though I'd had a momentary lapse in judgment or was suddenly struck by a strong sense of right and wrong. If I learned anything out of that experience it was that motives aren't always idealistic. I didn't kill him because I lost my nerve."

After a long silence, she said, "Now you wouldn't lose your nerve."

"If you're asking me if I would kill him today, the answer is no." He shrugged. "Growing up tended to harden the passion into a kind of cold disconnection. I heard a few years afterward that he'd moved out west somewhere.''

"And your mother?"

"She died when I was in the army.''

Listening to the emotion in his voice, she knew he was wrong about learning not to love. Maybe it was buried deep and maybe he never wanted it to show for fear of the pain and the memories it caused him, but it was there. She'd seen it and she'd felt it the day he came and told her Jim was dead. *Scream, Lizzie. Scream* had been as much for him as for her.

She walked across the room to stand beside him. The snow had almost stopped and she knew that tomorrow they would leave. "I've never forgotten what you said to me when Jim died. It was strange to me because my parents had always been so concerned with keeping the awful things out of my life. With protecting me against tragedy. When there was bad news I was always told gently or prepared by someone, usually my mom. She always worked into it so carefully that I had the feeling they thought I was too weak to handle anything stronger than a literal dose of bad medicine. When you told me about Jim, you didn't try to protect me, but simply supported me. It was as if you were telling me that I could handle this in whatever way was natural, including screaming.''

He pulled her into his arms, tucking her head beneath his chin in much the same way as he had done that day. "You were incredible.''

She wrapped her arms around his waist. "And you were an incredibly good friend.'' She paused and then glanced up at him. "And you still are.''

He laid his hands on her cheeks, his thumbs tipping her face up as he allowed his eyes to search hers. She thought he was going to kiss her, and indeed his mouth was so close that if she had stood on tiptoe she could have kissed him, but instead he murmured, "On that note, I think we should both get some sleep."

Later she came out of the bathroom in her flannel nightie and her robe. He'd put together the makeshift bed, and had already crawled into it. She stood for a moment contemplating what she was thinking—the potential awkwardness of sleeping together. However, she was frankly more concerned about Zach spending another night on the floor. She knelt beside the pile of covers and distinctly saw him shiver.

"Zach . . ."

"Go to bed, Lizzie."

"You're cold and uncomfortable." To prove her words, she touched his cheek. It was indeed chilled. "Please don't be so stubborn. You've already proved that when you make up your mind about something, nothing is going to change it."

He swore, and then said, "I'm not trying to prove anything. We're almost through this. Tomorrow we'll be in New Hampshire and it will be all over."

"How can it be all over when nothing has begun?"

"There's no hot buttered rum tonight that we can blame."

"No, there's just one very stubborn man who slept with me this morning—yes, I realized you were there and that you didn't want me to know."

"I had an hour to kill before breakfast."

"You could have killed it on the floor."

He rolled over and stared up at her. "And so because I crawled into bed with you for one damn hour, you're going to read all sorts of things into it."

"All I'm reading into it is that you were tired, sore and probably cold. All very valid reasons to want to be in a comfortable bed. All three of those reasons are just as valid tonight."

"Hell, don't give me logical excuses." He closed his eyes briefly and wearily rolled his head from side to side. "I just want to get through this, get you and Julianne up to Gordon's and—"

"Forget that we've interrupted your life and been an inconvenience and a pain you didn't need." She tried to stand, feeling hurt. He was welcome to the damn floor.

He clamped his hand around her ankle. "I didn't say that."

"Yes, you did say it. Maybe not in so many words, but I know you're here because of Gordon. Dammit, we are, too. I'm not any happier about being snowed in together than you are, but we're both adults and you're acting as if I'm some great threat to you."

He swore and tightened his hand so that for an instant she thought he might pull her down with him, but then he released her completely.

Immediately she got to her feet. Then, determined to prove nothing would happen between them, she said, "Look at me. I'm hardly dressed in anything even remotely appealing to a man."

"Oh, God."

"I'm not going to beg you, Zach. If you want to sleep on the cold floor, catch pneumonia or the flu, hurt your back—oh, I saw you favor it today just as I felt you wince when I put my arm around you—then fine, you do just that." She swung away and crossed to the bed, throwing back the covers. She jerked off her robe and tossed it aside before climbing under the blankets.

Three minutes later, she felt him crawl in beside her.

"Zach . . ."

"Shut up."

She smiled to herself, but when she felt his arm around her waist, drawing her to him, her eyes snapped open. "I can get the pillows."

"If I'm sleeping with you, I'll be damned if I'm going to curl around a bunch of pillows."

"Is this another endurance test?"

He moved her and settled her bottom into the cove of his thighs. She knew immediately that he was wearing his jeans, and wondered if he'd had them on when he was on the floor or whether he had pulled them on before getting into bed with her. His arm was clamped around her waist, no more than an inch below her breasts. She could feel his breath in her hair.

"No. More a test of my motives."

"You mean I might not be safe?" Incredibly she'd never felt safer, more secure and more sweetly content.

"I mean that I've never in my life crawled into **be**d with a woman just to sleep."

"Then this will be a first."

"It will also be a hell of a miracle."

Chapter 9

As miracles go, Zach decided two hours later, this one might just go down in history. To his surprise, he had fallen asleep, although his dreams had been occupied with exploring beneath the flannel nightie she wore. He had awakened and almost decided that he might pull this off—that he might manage just to sleep with her, not kiss her, not let his hand slide into the soft warmth between her thighs, not cradle her breast while his thumb prepared her nipple for his mouth. But then she moved, turning so that she was facing him, her nose nuzzled into his neck.

She breathed with a soft sigh of contentment that made him ache, because it was exactly the same sound of completion that she'd made when he slid in bed beside her the previous morning.

But now when her mouth began to explore the texture of his throat, he tangled one fist in her hair and tried to ease her gently back. She wasn't having any of it, and in fact snuggled closer. "Lizzie..."

"You're warm," she muttered against his skin, her breath feathery and moist. His mouth went dry and raw with the need to taste her. "Not cold anymore." She stretched out along the length of him, tangling her legs around his, kissing his throat again before sighing. "I made you warm."

"And you're in danger of making me hot," he growled, trying to tell himself to push her away and get out of the bed. As though reading his true thoughts, she moved still closer. How in hell was closer possible?

He felt her shake her head, her mouth damp against his skin. "No danger with you, never with you."

Trying to not like the way her lips rubbed against his throat, he muttered, "This is a hell of a time to trust me, Lizzie."

He felt as if his entire body teetered on the edge of exploding. A too-pleasant explosion that he didn't want to miss. The hell of it was, he wanted her body aligned with his, her mouth against his throat, her softness pressing into his thigh. From somewhere he managed to zero in on his reason for being with her, and it had not one damn thing to do with a get-intimately-involved situation. As though it might cool things down, he concentrated on the fact that she wasn't a woman he wanted to make love to, she was a job.

Then her leg brushed him, not hard, not even with the deliberateness of a tease or a seductive promise, but his body reacted as though an experienced hand had slipped around him for the single purpose of bringing him pleasure.

His thoughts as to why they were together melted as though they had been no more substantial than a wispy snowflake. He didn't try to catch them back, and in fact welcomed their departure.

He moved instantly, pulling her beneath him. Before he had a chance to think too much about what he was doing, he covered her mouth and found her returning kiss so intimately charged, it hardened him instantly. His leg nudged between hers, his arousal solid into her softness. Even through the denim of his jeans he felt her warmth. Her nightie had worked its way up her thighs, and the question he'd wondered about the previous morning was answered. She didn't wear panties to bed.

She was fully awake now, her mouth as hungry as his. Her hands tracked around the waist of his jeans to the button.

When he felt her fingers coax at the closure, he easily conjured up all the ways her hands would feel. Soft, curious, eager, a little experienced. A whole lot of trouble for both of them.

In a hazy fantasy he heard himself saying: Do it, baby. Slide your hands around me. Hold me. Let me make it good for you.

The button slipped from its hole. When the zipper began to hiss down, he went very still.

"Don't open my jeans," he muttered, wondering if he'd lost his mind. She moved her hands instantly, and he framed her face and felt the hot burn of her cheeks. His thumbs made soft rubbing strokes beneath her eyes. "I'm not angry."

"I didn't mean to be so bold . . ." She swallowed.

Zach brushed her mouth with his. "I wasn't complaining, sweetheart. But opening my jeans would be a real problem."

She nodded, and he knew she hadn't missed exactly what he meant.

"One more kiss, and then we'll both go back to sleep, okay?" She stared up at him, her lips slightly parted, her breasts suddenly too close to his bare chest. His unbuttoned, but still zipped, jeans felt achingly tight. "Baby, don't go independent on me, not now."

She took a deep resigned breath. "Please kiss me."

He could have handled feeling hunger, but it was the driving necessity to drown as though she were some sweet nectar of life that changed the direction of the kiss.

He slid his hands to her breasts, telling himself that as soon as he touched her he would stop.

He mentally thanked his foresight in pulling on his jeans and the strength he'd garnered to tell her not to open them, while at the same time he damned himself for indulging himself as much as he was. Her legs fell open as if the two of them had spent a hell of a lot of time in this position.

"We fit together too damn well," he muttered.

"I like the way you feel against me."

"Oh God, don't tell me that."

The light from the moon threw shadows and streaks of light into the room and across the bed. She smiled, and when he tried to pull back she locked her arms around his neck.

Zach mentally prayed for an interruption—Julianne waking up, a knock on the door, Lizzie protesting and saying no. Where was a good, old-fashioned, leave-me-alone, don't-touch-me, I-don't-want-to-do-this excuse? She wiggled again.

"We can't do this, Lizzie."

He saw her eyes widen in disbelief. He wasn't sure he believed his refusal himself. Zach Stone saying no was as much of a surprise to him as it was a miracle that he was going to be able to roll away and stay sane in the process.

"Why?"

Good question, he thought grimly. "How about you'll regret it in the morning?"

She laughed. "Don't be ridiculous."

Think, dammit, think. But it was becoming incredibly difficult to do so, because he wanted to tug his jeans down and off and fill her completely. Ah, that was it. He heaved a deep sigh of reprieve. It was better than an excuse; it was a necessity.

"Birth control," he said flatly.

She was quiet and, thank God, still for a few moments. *Ahh, Lizzie, tell me you're on the Pill. I don't know if I even much care why.*

Her eyes were luminous in the shadows. She licked her lips before whispering, "I could be on the Pill."

God, how I wish you were. "But you're not."

She slowly shook her head, and he didn't miss the disappointment in her eyes. "You don't have anything? I thought all men carried foil packets."

"Contrary to my supposed reputation, I'm very selective about who I have sex with."

"Oh."

She was pulling away with all the speed of an offended woman when he hauled her back. "Don't conclude I meant you."

"You just said it."

"I was referring to not carrying a drugstore full of condoms in my pocket."

She sagged down, but she also slid farther away from him. "This was quite insane, wasn't it? Thinking we could sleep in the same bed and nothing would happen."

"Nothing did happen," he grumbled, filled with regret that should have been relief.

She turned completely away now. "No. Nothing did."

"Now, Elizabeth, if you and Zach and Julianne are ever down Trenton way, we want you to stop for a visit." Muriel Bishop patted Julianne's cheek as they stood in the welcoming room of the inn. The car was packed and Zach had gone back upstairs to make sure they hadn't forgotten anything.

The weather had cleared and turned cold, the snow making the afternoon a blinding white. Zach had called the state police to get a highway report and had been told the interstate into New Hampshire had been plowed.

Greta insisted that they stay for lunch, and although Elizabeth was anxious to be on their way, she wasn't looking forward to the long trip alone with Zach. After the debacle of the night before Zach had returned to the makeshift bed on the floor, and Elizabeth had spent the remaining hours until daybreak wondering how she would have allowed herself to get in a position to be so thoroughly rejected.

Zach hadn't argued about staying for lunch, but then she hadn't consulted him. He'd nodded briefly and used the time in the morning to help Fred, Greta's maintenance man, to shovel the sidewalk, the steps and the porch.

Elizabeth had spent the extra hours with Greta and Muriel and the other women. Everyone exchanged addresses to remember one another with Christmas cards. Elizabeth was struck by how the inn's guests, and Greta, too, had become friends she and Zach had made as though they were married, not two people who were barely speaking this morning.

Now Greta smiled, holding Foggy so that Julianne could pet him. She did it gently, and the gray cat nudged at her for more attention. Greta said, "I think she's made a friend."

"I think so, too. She learned to pet and not pull tails." Elizabeth kissed her daughter's cheek as she watched Zach come down the stairs. She wished her own friendship with Zach could have been as uncomplicated. She wasn't even sure the word *friendship* applied. This morning it felt more as if they were two combatants waiting for something to set them off. But she'd been careful to keep the strain well hidden under a smile. Greta, the Bishops and the other guests didn't need to be embarrassed by what would soon be a finished relationship. As soon as they got to Gordon's she could escape for some much needed privacy.

Perhaps lack of privacy was part of her problem, she concluded as Zach drew closer. She wasn't used to continual company and certainly not with a man who—What? she thought distractedly, hunting her mind for a way to describe him apart from the battered boots, the snug jeans and the fatigue sweater he wore. She had no slot to put him in, simply because he was unlike any man she'd known.

Her father was urbane and polished, her brothers were sophisticated yuppies. Craig, her college boyfriend, the few men she'd dated since Jim's death, none—not even Jim— came close to being like Zach.

Not that it mattered, she uselessly tried to tell herself, for Zach did indeed matter to her. More than he should.

Zach stopped beside her.

"Did we leave anything?" she asked. Greta asked to hold Julianne, and Elizabeth handed the baby to her.

"You did," he said in a low growl.

He shook hands with Ken and wished the newlyweds much happiness. Elizabeth frowned, but since he carried nothing in his hand, whatever it was couldn't have been that important. She drew him aside.

"I couldn't have left anything. I checked all the drawers."

"Let's go," he murmured.

"What did I leave, Zach?"

He took her by the shoulders and closed the tiny space between their bodies. "A pair of panties." He leaned closer, his breath drifting across her ear. "Light blue satin with white lace. Very nice."

Elizabeth only marginally reacted with a quick intake of breath. She had no intention of rising to whatever bait he was dangling. The panties must have gotten caught with

Julianne's clean sleepers when she was packing and then became tangled in the covers of the bed.

"You're enjoying this, aren't you?" She hissed the question so that no one overheard her.

"Not particularly." He set her away with an abruptness that seemed to substantiate his words. "After last night, the one item I didn't need to find was your panties. And since coming downstairs and handing them to you would have upset you more than you already are, I decided to be a gentleman. Not a role I'm too adept at, but I thought I'd give it a shot. They're tucked securely in my pocket, and raising all kinds of hell with my—"

"Zach!" George Bishop called. "You weren't going to leave without saying goodbye, were you?"

Zach stepped around her and shook hands. "Wouldn't think of it, George. Make sure you keep on top of the crime scene in Trenton," he said sagely. He lifted his jacket and Elizabeth's coat off the clothes tree.

She put on her coat. Don't think about it, she told herself firmly as Greta approached with Julianne. Just pretend the entire conversation didn't take place.

George said, "Hey, I have a great idea. What about celebrating the New Year here at the Wisteria? Kind of a snowstorm reunion. I can bring that video I shot to show you, Zach."

She felt him move behind her to ease her out the door.

"Sorry, I have duty on New Year's." His hand rested on her back with an indifferent feel, as though the previous night had no significance.

But hadn't they both agreed that nothing happened? In the extreme nothing had—they hadn't made love—but Elizabeth felt different. Shaken, edgy and incomplete. She tried to rally reality. She and Julianne were a duty, a favor he was doing because Gordon had asked him. Perhaps instead of feeling awful she should feel relieved that he hadn't taken what she offered. How would she have felt if they had made love and now he was treating her as though all he wanted was to get away from her?

Yes, she decided, this was better. She'd rather he felt obligated to do his job than trapped into making love as though it were an obligation because she'd been so willing.

More goodbyes were said, and within another fifteen minutes they were in the car and on their way.

The roads had indeed been plowed, but the driving was slow. Zach kept his attention on the highway, glancing at Elizabeth only once to ask if she wanted the heat on. She made attempts at conversation, and when all she got for twenty miles was one-word answers, she felt a kind of slow dying of even the fragile friendship he had warily allowed.

Since she doubted anything she did mattered to him, she had no intention of acting as though it did. Scowling into the bright sun, she realized that her independence was her best shield.

She began with his jacket, which he'd insisted earlier she tuck around her legs. She wore heavy corduroy slacks and a wool sweater, but she had to admit his coat felt wonderful. Ignoring the sudden chill when she tossed it into the back seat, she unbuckled her seat belt.

"What in hell are you doing?" he growled, taking his eyes off the road a moment to give her a sweeping glance.

"What I want to do. Do you mind?"

"Do it with your seat belt buckled."

"No."

"Don't push, Lizzie."

"Why not? What have I got to lose? You getting mad and ordering me around? You refusing to talk to me as if I'd done the worst thing in the world because I asked you to sleep with me?"

He swore, which she ignored, not even caring if Julianne heard him.

She poked her finger into his arm. "You know what, Zachariah Stone? I don't care. I lived a whole life before you arrived, and after this is all over I will manage quite nicely."

"Are you finished?"

"No!"

The single word seemed to echo around the car. She should have left it there, and taken her comfort from her outburst. However, the edginess that had consumed her since the night before hadn't softened. When the question reeled through her mind, her first instinct was to ignore it, but...

"Tell me about the blondes you date?"

He glanced at her, his eyes steady and dark and effectively revealing nothing of his reaction to her question.

However, his voice held more than a little annoyance. "You're nothing like them."

"Obviously."

"No, not obviously. It's not a comparison."

"Because I'm doing something wrong. I doubt you're cold and indifferent to them. I doubt you go hours without talking to them. And I doubt—"

"That I refuse to make love to them?"

"Yes." The word slipped out on the softest of breaths. She sat rigid in the seat, waiting for some kind of flip remark, and deciding that whatever he said, she would not cry. If her throat closed up and she couldn't breathe, she wouldn't shed one tear.

Finally, she heard him take a long breath and let it out slowly, as though wanting to delay answering as long as possible. "I don't know what to do with you, Lizzie."

Her relief felt like the sweet wind of summer. His words sounded both defeated and frustrated, but she realized that they more than mirrored her own feelings. She didn't know what to do about him, either.

Feeling a slight lessening of the tension, she asked, "Why are you being this way, since nothing happened? All right, I admit it was a mistake to sleep together. I shouldn't have insisted on it, but I didn't want you to spend another night on the cold floor."

She turned away from him and damned the sudden rush of tears that came regardless of her vow. Why did she feel so hurt, so turned upon, so desperate to make things right between them? Did it matter, or had their few days of confinement simply blown everything out of proportion?

When he slipped his hand around her neck, beneath her hair and under her coat collar, she jumped. His fingers were gentle, soothing and evocative as they worked the tendons of her neck.

She didn't want to look at him, for if she saw kindness or pity she would surely fall into his arms as though she belonged there. Her emotions felt jumbled and raw, and she wished she were back in Liberty in her own room where she could be miserable alone.

"I didn't want to hurt you, Lizzie. None of this was supposed to happen. The damn snowstorm, not getting to Gordon's when we should have." He sighed. "Slide over here beside me."

"I don't want anything to happen."

"Nothing will happen. Come over here."

She peered around at him, then shook her head. "No, I mean we've already created a lot of strain between us. I really would like us to be friends, and if we continue to snap at each other we're going to destroy that, also."

While they talked, he coaxed, and she slowly moved closer. He felt so good when she finally settled against him. Their thighs touched and she searched frantically for something to say. Something that wouldn't lead anywhere dangerous.

"Are you going to stay at Gordon's?"

"For a little while. I want to call Buzz and see if there are any more developments beyond the last one, and—"

She tipped her head sideways. "What last one?"

"Didn't I tell you about the informant?"

"No. What informant?"

"Jim used one named Gizzo Gates. He's a slimy bastard who used to rat to the cops about his buddies for a price. Jim always suspected he might be playing both sides, but he could never prove it. He disappeared a few days before Jim was killed, which didn't eliminate him as the killer, but we had nothing to tie him to the murder. Anyway, when I talked to Buzz yesterday, he said Gates is back in town and word on the street is that he's scraping for cash and trying to do what he does best—selling information."

"You think he's connected to the ransacking?"

"We're not ruling it out. So far it's just a loose fact, but important because he did work with Jim." He laid his hand on her thigh in a natural gesture, and it felt as if it belonged there.

"I've been thinking..." she began after she relaxed against him.

"Uh-oh. Am I in trouble again?"

Without thinking, she slipped her hand around his arm and squeezed. "You *are* trouble."

He grinned. "And here I thought I was doing a great job keeping that a secret. What were you thinking about?"

"Jim's things. I packed away all his personal stuff so that I would have it for Julianne when she grows up. If the ransacker was looking for something that belonged to Jim, it might be in that stuff. In other words, what he wanted couldn't have been very obvious. Otherwise, I would have noticed it."

"A good theory, Lizzie. I suspect that whatever it is, it has to do with value of some sort, either to the ransacker or whoever he's working for."

"Whoever he's working for? Then you think more people are involved."

"Buzz and I haven't ruled it out."

She was quiet and still before she asked, "Is Jim one of them?"

He shifted slightly.

"I have a right to know, Zach."

"We don't know yet." He shook his head when she started to protest, then squeezed her hand. "Random speculation is as dangerous as accusation."

She sagged against him, not wanting to think it possible, while at the same time sure that if Jim was involved it wasn't for the wrong reasons.

"You're going to go back and stay on this until you know, aren't you?" Part of her wanted to commend his determination to get to the truth, and another part of her wanted him to say that since Jim was dead, it didn't matter how he was involved.

"Yeah. I'll keep in touch with you so you know what's going on." He squeezed her leg. "Besides, I promised to come and see Julianne, didn't I?"

"Yes, you did. Julianne would miss you if you just walked out of her life."

Like you're about to walk out of mine. Definitely out of my life, she thought with no small amount of regret. Suddenly she wished the snow had delayed them another day, and despite what had happened at the inn, she wanted a little more time with him. "Can we stop?"

He glanced over at her. "What's wrong?"

"Nothing, but you need to get gas, don't you?" She hesitated over her next thought. All she would be doing was delaying the inevitable, but she liked being with him and since they were getting along so well, she wanted to hold on to those feelings for a little while.

"I've got enough gas. I'll fill up before I start back."

"But if you got it now, it would save you time later."

"Sweetheart, it takes about five minutes to pump gas."

She studied her leg where his hand had rested and wished she had the guts to slide her fingers around his thigh and say something suggestive. It certainly would get his attention. But she was afraid—of rejection, or worse, of him reminding her of her boldness the night before. In the most sexual of circumstances he had said no. How much easier it would be here. She had no intention of saying or doing anything risky.

"I thought we might get something to eat."

"After Greta's lunch, you're hungry?"

"Yes."

Behind them, Julianne gurgled.

Zach said, "You, too, princess?" The baby squealed and pushed against the car seat's harness. "Who am I to argue with two starving females."

He detested head games, and yet he was playing them with himself. He'd known it earlier in the afternoon when he'd found the panties and tucked them in his pocket. He knew it now as he called Gordon from the pay phone and said they'd be there in the morning. He knew it when he walked from the phone into the motel office while Lizzie was in the small gift shop. He didn't like what he was feeling for her. It wasn't clear and logical and it didn't have the boundaries he liked, so he created a few. He had to know there was a way out.

When it came to sex with a woman, simplicity kept him from getting tangled in any morass of emotion. Not one time had he ever told a woman he loved her, and not one time had he ever asked for more than she wanted to give. A discipline of sorts that he'd honed from the day his father slammed the door in his face and he learned firsthand about what happens when you seek and find nothing. Now he sought little, expected nothing and was rarely disappointed. He simply didn't allow any desire he had for a woman to so overwhelm him that he couldn't focus enough to walk away afterward.

And he was determined Elizabeth Healy would be no different, despite his uncharacteristic move the night before of not giving her what she wanted. The truth behind that particular decision didn't bear too close a scrutiny.

One thing he hadn't done when he paid the motel bill was to assume. He'd taken adjoining rooms, wanting to make sure she had every opportunity to back out.

He watched her walk out of the gift shop with a bag in one hand and Julianne propped on her hip. The heavy coat hid her well, but it didn't matter, just as the flannel nightie hadn't mattered. He remembered the pucker of her nipple and the way her breast had blossomed in his hand. The way his palm had pressed the warm dampness that shielded all her potential for pleasure. And her mouth, pulling him into all those deep, deep kisses. Zach felt the rush climb up his spine with all the power of an erupting volcano.

"Zach, I found a china cat that looks exactly like Foggy." She wrestled with the bag, trying to balance the baby, her handbag and the package. "It's got this huge tail and—" She blinked up at him, her smile shrinking. "What's wrong?"

He felt as if every nerve-ending in his body was wired. Now that he'd settled the question of should he, his mind raced with how soon and, of course, the all-elusive if.

"You're scaring me. Is something wrong? Oh, God, it isn't Gordon, is it?"

"Gordon and Naomi are fine."

"Then why do you look so intense?"

There was no way to ease gradually into this, and he wanted to be very sure he caught every nuance of reaction when he told her. In his world, initial reaction was everything. Wanting to sleep with her, to make love to her, to consume her, had so lodged in his mind it scared him. Or was he scared she'd say no? After last night she had sufficient and valid reasons.

He made sure she was looking at him directly. "I took motel rooms."

She almost lost her grip on the tissue-wrapped china cat she'd pulled out to show him. Her eyes widened as she stared up at him while people rushed around them. He took the small object, put it back into the bag and took her arm. "This isn't a big deal. I got two rooms. They're going to bring a crib in for Julianne."

He guided her out the door and along a snowy walk to where he'd parked the car in front of the rooms. She didn't argue, and in fact she hadn't protested, but then she hadn't agreed, either. He slipped the key into the first door and ushered her inside.

The room was modern, clean and ordinary with a standard set of double beds, flowered drapes and a carpet in an undistinguished gray.

She lowered Julianne onto the floor where she sat looking up owlishly from one to the other. Zach started to turn away.

She reached out and gripped his arm to stop him. "You can't just walk away without explaining all this."

He studied her a moment. "No pressure. That's why I got two rooms."

"I sleep here and you sleep over there?" She pointed to the door that connected the two rooms.

"If that's what you want."

"What about what you want?"

"Your decision. Let me get the stuff out of the car."

She was still standing in the same place when he returned with not just the luggage they'd used at the inn, but everything they'd brought from Liberty, including his garment bag. He put it all down and propped his hands low on his hips. "What's wrong?"

She looked at the array, especially the garment bag, frowned and then raised her eyes to him. "I don't know what to say or what to do."

"You don't have to do anything, Lizzie. We can have dinner, come back here, go to our own rooms and go to sleep."

"But if that's what we're going to do, then why not go on to New Hampshire?"

"The other option isn't possible at Gordon's."

"The other option being that we make love."

"Many times."

She sat down on the bed as though glad it was there to support her. Her eyes never left him. He saw her swallow before she spoke. "You're incredible, do you know that? It's as if you're deliberately setting out with a plan to have sex, and then creating reasons to refuse."

"I don't like wanting you."

"I know. Is this another one of your endurance tests?"

"Perhaps something more ordinary, like survival."

"My God."

"I won't push you, Lizzie. And I won't seduce you."

She licked her lips. "I think it's too late."

The motel manager arrived and supervised the moving in of the crib. Elizabeth's comment lay between them as if some invisible gauntlet had been thrown down. The crib was set up and the men left.

Elizabeth put Julianne into the crib, and Zach started for the adjoining room. He then gestured to the suitcase that had never left the car while they were at the inn. It was the one he'd packed with her extra clothes.

"The black dress with all the buttons is on the top."

She frowned for a moment, and he knew she was recalling the conversation they'd had in her bedroom about the dress she'd impulsively bought. "You packed that dress? I told you I wouldn't need anything like that in—" She reached for his garment bag and opened the zipper. His gray cashmere suit and a shirt and tie were inside. She stared for a moment and then at her own suitcase. "My God, did you plan all this while we were still in Liberty?"

"Only that I wanted to see you in the dress." He propped his shoulder against the doorjamb that separated the two rooms. She moved closer to him, and as she did he wrestled with telling her the other reason. Keeping the focus on his own desire was probably more convincing.

"And when was I supposed to wear it?" she asked, coming to a stop inches from him.

He raised an eyebrow at the confrontational tone in her voice. No doubt her independence hadn't suffered any serious dents in the past few days. Even to him his reason for bringing the dress sounded weak and questionable. But then sometimes the truth simply had to stand on its own.

"There's a nice restaurant near Gordon's, and I planned to take you out to dinner before I went back to Liberty."

She narrowed her eyes. "Why does that sound far too innocent for you?"

"Because in this I am innocent. God knows there've been damn few moments with women when I have been, but this was one of them. Seducing you wasn't my intent. The issue was you feeling sexy and sensual and not feeling guilty about others knowing it. Wearing the dress is for you."

She stepped closer to him, and he didn't step away. She laid her hand low on his stomach. Despite his sweater he could feel the light stroke of her fingers.

"I've never known anyone like you," she whispered.

"I'm not sure that's good." He lifted her hand and moved it higher so as to avoid his inclination, which was to press it against the front of his jeans.

"If I wear the dress, are you going to take it off me?"

He skimmed his hand from her hip to her waist and to the swell of her breast. Bringing his fingers forward he traced the path the buttons would take from her throat, down between her breasts to her stomach and coming to a stop at the zipper placket on her slacks. At her gasp, he answered her question. ''There probably won't be time.''

She shuddered, and when he met her eyes he saw his own desire reflected there. The thought of kissing her obsessed him, but he knew that once he did, it would be all over. He felt as though he were caught in a maze he couldn't escape, but beyond that were two more questions. How had it happened? And what if he didn't want to leave her?

Chapter 10

It wasn't until the waiter brought the check that Zach told Elizabeth that she, and not the dress, was stunning.

The black watered silk made her skin seem whiter, the iridescent buttons down the front catching his attention every time she took a deep breath, which she'd done a lot since he told her he'd taken motel rooms.

From the moment they sat down at the table for two, she had barely taken her eyes off him except to feed Julianne. Her own dinner of braised scallops had hardly been touched. Zach had steak, but she had no idea how much of it he ate.

"You never say what most men say," she whispered, her heart skipping a delighted beat at his compliment.

Amused he asked, "What do most men say?"

"They might say a woman is beautiful or sexy or..."

He waited as though giving her time to decide how explicit she wanted to be. He grinned suddenly. "Careful, Lizzie, we have a rule about language in front of the baby."

She smiled a little, not at all sure what he was thinking but not about to appear to be naive. "I wasn't going to say anything like that."

"Good. You might shock me." He took a sip of brandy, watching her over the rim of the glass.

She doubted anything she could say would shock him. Zach was probably shockproof.

He grinned at her. "Men might tell women they're beautiful, sexy or—?" The smile came again and she knew that when he kissed her she wouldn't want him to stop. "Or what, Lizzie?"

She raised her wineglass, wondering if it was the drink or the man who got her into these verbal seductions. "That she turns them on."

"Ahh," he said thoughtfully as though the comment were more profound than it was. "But then you're all three of those all the time."

She put down her glass before she spilled her wine. The persistent ache along her thighs rose and fell with a heavy throb. Her breathing hadn't been even for hours, as though air were an intrusion rather than a necessity.

Zach set aside his own glass and turned his attention to Julianne. Elizabeth had outfitted her in a red ruffled dress, white tights and a red bow in her hair. A bib imprinted with a Christmas elf, compliments of the restaurant, caught the food drips. Zach dipped a spoon into the peppermint ice cream he'd ordered for Julianne and tucked it into her open mouth. Elizabeth pressed her legs together, thankful that the arousal she felt wasn't physically evident.

She glanced at the check, which he had made no move to take, and then realized he might be waiting to see what she would do. He had been upset at the Wisteria when she'd insisted on paying for her own room. Actually he had been determined she would not, and they'd gotten into that whole issue of men and women's roles. Here, hours ago, he'd paid for both motel rooms, and she suddenly realized she'd never questioned it, never even given it a thought. No, her thoughts and her questions had been on Zach, not on trying to prove she could take care of herself.

Julianne had her hand around Zach's wrist as he guided the spoon to her mouth. Elizabeth vaguely recalled mentioning to Zach that night in the car when they'd been eating his candies that Julianne liked peppermint ice cream. Amazingly, he'd remembered. Here at the table he'd carried on an elaborate conversation with the baby about what flavor she liked, as though her choice were of infinite importance.

Elizabeth continued to watch them. Her thoughts, and yes, her desire, were so focused on him and the coming night that she'd completely tuned out what would happen afterward.

Although her sexual experience was limited to Craig at college and her husband, she didn't feel as though she had lived in a sexual vacuum. But with Zach she knew there would be more, for already she'd caught only a fragment of the dark caverns of sensuality. During those moments at her house he'd tapped into something that had since blossomed into a compelling and driving need.

Again she glanced at the check and considered. . . .

Stop it, she told herself. You don't care if he pays it. You don't care about anything except getting back to the room so that you can settle Julianne for the night, so that you can kiss him and let him kiss you and touch you and make love.

At intervals during their dinner, he'd seemed amused, or he'd shown an occasional opposite extreme of stark impatience. At other times, he'd displayed obvious hesitation that she was sure was reluctance or at best wariness. She treasured that reluctance, for it showed her another side of him. He'd always previously seemed so sure of himself, so above every situation, as if he'd figured out the ending before he stepped in.

Julianne concentrated on pieces of a cookie that Zach had broken for her and put on her tray. He settled back in his chair and once again lifted the glass of brandy. Elizabeth thought he, too, looked stunning in his charcoal-gray cashmere suit, which certainly proved to her his earlier words. He had indeed packed her dress with every intention of taking her to dinner.

There was no question they were more formally attired than the restaurant required, and for no reason she could think of, their coming here made the whole evening more special. The restaurant was next door to the motel and catered mostly to travelers. It wasn't fancy, but it had a nice holiday atmosphere, with its festive red tablecloths and arrangements of holly in glass vases.

She couldn't help but wonder if he'd deliberately chosen the restaurant because it wasn't particularly romantic. That was one of the paradoxes of Zach Stone. He almost went out of his way to create romantic barriers, and yet his very presence made her realize that they'd already stepped beyond anything as shallow as romance.

His eyes seem fixated on the top button of her dress as he swirled his brandy glass. As though drawn to touch what he closely watched, she rested her fingers on the button.

His gaze met hers. "Don't. Not here."

Somewhere she had lost all control, and the worst part of it was that she didn't care. Her body felt as though every look, every casual touch, every thought revolved around the man who sat across the table from her. She had a sense of having stepped out of herself to hover a few feet away and observe. She didn't move her fingers from the button.

His mouth showed a touch of amusement. "Ah, your independence is showing."

"You said you weren't going to seduce me."

"And you think that's what I'm doing because we're still sitting here instead of making love."

She opened the button, and she saw him barely catch his breath. "I think your determination not to seduce is seduction in itself."

Seconds crept by before he said, "Perhaps you're right." Then he leaned forward and pushed the check in her direction.

The open button temporarily forgotten, she glanced at him. "You want me to pick up the check?"

"Of course not. I'm simply offering you the chance to refuse."

"And what if I insist on paying it?"

He shrugged. "That's fine. I won't argue."

Elizabeth wasn't quite ready to believe it was that simple. "What's the catch?"

He reached across the table and she felt a sudden pounding in her chest that told her quite definitely that nothing about him was simple, nor ever would be. His fingers toyed with the button she had opened. With the deftness of a man very much in command of every situation, he slowly slipped the button into its closure.

Then in a low voice, he said, "I want you under me the first time."

She closed her eyes at about the same time her breathing came to a halt. Her mind swirled as though she'd tumbled into some exquisite garden. She had no words for him, no thoughts except those she couldn't express in anything but the most private of moments.

Elizabeth paid for dinner and, true to his word, he didn't argue or insist. In fact, he busied himself with getting Julianne out of the high chair so that the waiter would know Elizabeth was paying the bill.

She saw him glance curiously at Zach while she added in the tip, but he and Julianne were busy deciding whether she was going to get another cookie.

As they left the restaurant with Zach carrying Julianne, Elizabeth said, "I expected you to make some remark to that poor, befuddled waiter."

"I considered saying you'd kidnapped me and I was your sex slave, but I didn't want him to fall into the middle of the table."

She laughed, tossing her head back and taking deep breaths of the cold wind. The night felt wonderful, and she felt her own dizzy kind of freedom and joy that she wanted to memorize.

He shifted Julianne to the other arm. "Princess, I think you ate too much peppermint ice cream. You're heavy."

The baby yawned and snuggled deeper against him, and Elizabeth realized the significance of the long dinner. Julianne would go to sleep promptly and they would have the hours they needed uninterrupted.

In her room, she quickly changed the baby into a clean diaper and a heavy sleeper. Zach bent down, kissed Julianne and, without touching Elizabeth in any way, walked into his own room.

He really didn't intend to push her, she thought, trying to ignore the sudden tingles of nervousness. She recalled those moments in her bedroom in Liberty when she'd walked in and found him holding the dress. Then she'd felt an unexplainable quickening as though somehow the sensation had been mere preparation for tonight.

Talking softly to Julianne, she cuddled her for a few moments before laying her down in the crib. She tucked the teddy bear in beside her, covered her with the down quilt and then lingered a few more moments.

Moments of indecision, she wondered, or moments of revelation about herself? Despite their disagreements, and his tendency to set the rules and boundaries—such as he'd done quite masterfully tonight—he made no promises or even held out a thread of hope for later. And there would be a later. After the ransacker was caught, after she and Julianne returned to Liberty, after her life was again normal.

She sighed. Maybe bleak was a better description. Or perhaps lonely. Strange that she'd never considered her life to be bleak or lonely. But then again, her life had been devoid of Zach Stone.

But he had given her choices. Not about later but about tonight. She could cross the room and close the adjoining door and simply go to bed alone. As much as she wanted to believe that he might come in and seduce her into changing her mind, she knew he wouldn't.

Or she could face him and say she thought it would be better if they didn't get physically involved. Because it would be—infinitely better given the circumstances. He was doing a job, and hadn't she reminded herself numerous times she never wanted to get involved with another cop? Neither of those seemed relevant given what she wanted to do with him, but in reality they would be important tomorrow and therefore were valid reasons to sleep alone tonight.

She glanced toward the slightly open door just as he turned out the light. Damn you, Zach Stone. You didn't give me a choice about leaving Liberty and going to New Hampshire. You didn't give me any choice about sharing a bedroom at the Wisteria, and you didn't give me a choice when you decided to take motel rooms for the night. Why are you giving me one about making love when you know I want you?

And she knew he wanted her. She'd seen his eyes, the gray-blue deeper, more intense, and she'd heard the depth of urgency beneath his words when he said, ''I want you under me the first time.''

She shivered suddenly with what she knew was more than eagerness and sexual anticipation; it was a giving of something within herself to him. Perhaps that was her choice. Not the sexual union as much as the giving of herself.

After rechecking the sound-asleep Julianne for the third time, she took a few steps toward the door and stopped to fill her lungs with air. Her body felt hot and tense, her breasts heavy, and the feminine dampness between her legs brought a rush of color to her cheeks. Not embarrassment as much as a realization of what thinking about him, touching him, kissing him ...

He'd barely touched her, and yet she knew he had. Sensually, yes, but deeper. Down in those places that were fragile and vulnerable and not as easily defined as desire and sexual fulfillment.

She slipped off her shoes and reached beneath the dress to peel off her panty hose. Those disposed of, she took only a few seconds to decide also to skim her panties down and off. She wasn't sure what that said about her daringness, but she knew that once she entered his bedroom, she didn't intend to stop anything he wanted to do. Panty hose and panties seemed more a hindrance than sexy.

The dress, of course, was another issue. That definitely had something to do with what they would do. Never had she felt quite so sexy as she moved to the adjoining door. Slowly she pushed it open and walked into his room. The moonlight, a blinking neon sign and the occasional sweep of car headlights from the nearby highway would have given her enough light to see him, but he wasn't in bed or sprawled in a chair waiting for her or standing by the window reflecting as she'd often seen in old movies.

"Zach?" She barely whispered his name, sure that her pulse was louder than her voice.

"Right here, Lizzie." But before she had a chance to jump or be startled his hands slipped around her waist and

pulled her back against him. She knew instantly that he was
naked, just as she realized he made no effort to hide his
arousal. His body felt hot and hard and tense, and for a
fragment of a second she wondered if he felt as unsure about
their joining as she did.

He aligned them, her back to his chest, spreading his legs
apart to brace and balance them and without asking settled
her bottom exquisitely against him. From low in her womb,
she felt a sense of rightness, of this being how it should always be. His mouth moved across her neck in concentrated
kisses, not the scattered touches of impatience, but wet and
hot and deep. He would mark her and she didn't care. She
let her head fall forward.

"God, I'm glad you came," he said with a raspy relief, his
mouth at her shoulder.

"You knew I would." She lifted her hands to reach behind her and tunneled her fingers into his hair. His mouth
moved, nipping and sucking at her shoulder, which in turn
made her arch her back.

Zach groaned as he cupped her breasts. She felt one
thumb skim the dress buttons open. The layers of material
suddenly annoyed her; the watered silk, which could have
been erotic, was simply a barrier. He arrowed one hand
downward gathering handfuls of fabric as he went.

She was shamelessly wet.

Before he touched her his discovery that she wore no
panties almost undid him. "Ahh, baby, you are pleasure itself," he murmured when his fingers skimmed the damp
curls.

His touch brushed as softly as a sweep of feathers, and
she gasped at the instant rush of sensation that skittered up
her spine.

He slipped his other hand beneath the buttons he'd
opened to explore her breast with the same rhythm with
which his fingers strummed the curls. "I don't want to hear

that you weren't wearing panties in the restaurant," he growled in a way that made her wonder if in that case they would have left the dining room much sooner.

She turned enough to see him. "What if I said yes?"

"Please don't." His fingers sank deeper, his eyes dark and heavy.

She felt his pounding heart against her back, wishing now that she had worn no panties then, if only to have caught him in a moment of total surprise. "My bra..."

"Nowhere near as soft as your breasts," he whispered, dipping his fingers into her cleavage.

She swallowed. "No... it matches... the panties...."

"And they aren't as soft..." With erotic eloquence his fingers demonstrated his pleasure at touching her. "Ahh, Lizzie, not as soft as you..."

He dragged the dress off her shoulder, slipped his finger beneath the blue bra strap and then worked his hand down to the cup, to the middle clip and unhooked it. Her nipple was hard before he palmed it. In a husky and raw voice, he muttered, "Why do I have the feeling I lost control of this somewhere."

"You didn't." She skimmed her fingers up the sides of his thighs, taking great pleasure in his indrawn breath. "I just want you to want me as much as I want you."

He hesitated, then slowly turned her around to face him. Her dress was rumpled, the top open to her waist, the bra unhooked to expose breasts that weren't perfectly firm, and yet reminded him of one of his first thoughts about her. Milk and whiskey. Nurture and intoxication that made him want to touch and taste. Her tangled hair and swollen mouth made her seem very young, too vulnerable and more sexually exciting than any woman he'd ever known.

But part of him still wrestled with not wanting to want her. He knew she'd already sent him past ordinary sexual excitement. Somehow she'd slipped beyond his self-imposed barrier. He wanted to say no, that wasn't allowed, no woman could get where he didn't want her to go. It's the tension, he assured himself. Once they made love, once this ache he'd been carrying for days was gone, then he could put her in perspective. He could distance himself from the dazzling, sensual feast she offered. He could forget that she was a woman with an uncanny ability to make him hard by walking into a room. Yeah, he assured himself, it's just tension and sex and mutual greed. Afterward, he would force the barriers back in place.

She drew in a breath and raised her head, her hand brushing his stomach, moving lower, skimming across him.

Slightly hesitant, she whispered, "I want to be bold with you."

He turned her a little and lowered his head. Before he kissed her, he pressed his fingers against the damp curls. "Let's begin here." His tongue swept into her mouth and she tightened her arms around his neck.

She wanted to say no, she wanted to deny she wanted this shimmering release. But as though her body knew her better than her mind, as though he knew her better, too, when his fingers feathered beneath the delicate folds, she tried to bring her legs together to hold him there.

She twisted in disappointment when his fingers stilled.

"Easy, baby. I'm not going to stop," he murmured, his mouth moving to kiss each corner of her lips. "Let me make it deep and strong for you. Trust me."

She shook her head, the throb in her womb tightening as his fingers did indeed make her trust him. The distant pound felt like the approach of a wild storm. Her mouth tasted dry and hot. Again his hand moved away, and she heard herself pleading, "Oh please . . . I can't stop. . . ." And then in some fragmented part of her mind she rejoiced that she was here with him, wanting him and letting him know.

When his hands cupped her face, his thumbs rubbing at the mouth he'd so thoroughly kissed, she knew her eyes glistened with a combination of arousal and impatience.

Kissing her ear, while his fingers played and teased, he whispered, "Do you know how incredible you're going to be?"

She tried to shake her head, but it felt heavy and disconnected, as though his hands and his fingers were all that were holding her in place. She tried to concentrate on framing an answer, but she didn't have one.

Zach brushed his mouth across her closed eyes. "I have a lifetime of sensations to give you."

His hand moved once again to the dampness between her legs, his fingers stroking in an unabashed caress that sensitized her from her womb to her breasts to her mouth, where once again his mouth hovered a kiss away.

She couldn't talk. She could barely think. She felt it begin, and wrapping her arms around his neck she sank down, then raised herself back up.

Zach held her, taking her to an exquisite numbing and bursting level of pleasure that broke through her as though drawn from a reservoir of sensuality.

His sex pounded for release, and he knew in a few moments he would find it, but what she was feeling was a different satisfaction. One he wanted for her, yet one he needed for himself.

At first she tried to slow it down, to savor and capture the denseness. The rush of fire spread and fanned from deep inside her, stripping and scorching her as though no release could ever again be so powerful. From somewhere she heard Zach swear, encouraging her with dark, raw words that heightened the pleasure. She hung suspended and peaked and mindless, then tumbled over with a shuddering gasp.

As though boneless, she sagged against him. Her breaths came in ragged gulps.

Zach held her, his hands on her bottom as though he knew she was too sensitive to touch. He gently kissed her temple.

"Come lie with me," he murmured, sliding his hand down to lift her into his arms.

"I want you to..." She couldn't finish.

"I know. I want to fill you." His mouth settled on hers, while his hands brought her up so that her legs clutched his hips. Her dress flowed around them and he quickly crossed to the bed.

He felt himself teetering at the edge of his own explosion. Days of denial and mental foreplay and two nights of frustration had all culminated here at the juncture of their thighs. And yet for him this time was like no other. She was like no other woman. It wasn't simply the beat and pound of coming satisfaction. Nor was it even her impatience, which he'd been aware of all through dinner. He'd seen it in her eyes, memorized it in her restlessness, felt it in her determination to be cool and controlled. Admittedly, her powerful response—or perhaps her very wet readiness—had thrown him. If he'd indulged in generous foreplay, but he'd done nothing really except open up the possibilities and the potential.

"Zach, please..."

She lay on the bed, her dress not quite to her waist. The open buttons and unhooked bra showcased her breasts and the dying flush of her climax. He stood above her, thinking he'd never seen a woman quite as dazzling. That very reaction proved to him that if there were such a thing as a point of no return, he faced it right now. Once he entered her, once he filled her, once he felt her come around him, then nothing would ever be the same.

He reached for one of the foil packets he'd bought when he made the decision to get the rooms. The head games he'd played were already bad news, for he feared that with this woman he had made a calculated error in logic.

Then, as though she could read his mind, she said, "I scare you, don't I?" In a move as natural as breathing she touched him, her fingers not gripping but feathering over him as though unsure how much he could take.

"I want to walk away in one piece."

She lifted herself up onto her elbows, her eyes shimmering, her mouth wet. "This isn't about walking away. This is about coming together."

"About these moments of coming together."

Had he seen a second of pain, of disappointment in her eyes?

He leaned down, and pressed his palm low on her stomach. "There are no words for what I want us to reach together," he murmured before dipping his head and brushing his mouth across the still-damp curls.

She gasped, and when he kissed her mouth, she could taste herself. The kiss made no apology for its roughness or its intensity. He pulled her up enough to strip off her dress and bra, then flung both aside. Her hand found him, guiding him almost immediately into her. She steamed with heat and he slipped through the delicate folds as though she'd been ready for him forever.

Her mouth opened wider and Zach made no attempt to hold back. Taking her breasts into his hands, he memorized their shape and their softness and knew he'd never forget the sweet sustenance he drew to himself when his mouth closed over one nipple and then the other.

Her hands tangled in his hair, not allowing him to leave her. She murmured, "How can you make me feel so much?"

"Tell me what you feel, Lizzie."

"Like I'll never be able to get enough of you."

God..." Her words hurled him to the crest, too fast, too wildly, and when he knew he couldn't stop, he groaned out a frustrated "Damn." His release roared through him, pouring from him into her with a richness and demand that transcended every other experience, every other woman.

In some distant part of his mind he heard her gasp, felt her lift herself high into him, but then it all shattered as he savored the last, sweet moments of pleasure. Breathing in tandem with her, he buried his mouth in her neck.

Elizabeth stroked his head, keeping her legs clasped tightly around him. They lay a few minutes, neither speaking, both stunned by the swirl of powerful heights they had reached.

Elizabeth felt drowsy. Perhaps it was the sweet, dewy aftermath, but she treasured the hope of having endless days and nights with him. Yes, with him forever. And yet with Zach, even the word sounded complicated. If she expected anything from him, she would have to begin here with the physical.

Her hands swept down his back as he lay heavily on top of her. When he tried to move, she gripped her legs tighter around him.

He brushed his mouth across hers. "I'm too heavy for you."

"No, you're not. I like being under you."

He lifted his head and stared down at her. Her mouth was swollen, her hair swept across the pillow in snarled disarray, her body warm and flushed and replete with just-experienced passion. Her dress hung precariously from the chair where he'd flung it.

"I seem to have done about all I said I was going to do," he said, the remnants of passion still in his voice. "The dress, you beneath me."

"You forgot one," she said, her fingers lightly touching his back, his hips.

"What?"

"You said we'd make love many times."

He shook his head. Rolling off her, he drew her into his arms. "After what you just did to me, I'll need a week to recover."

Delighted with his answer, she laughed and bent her head to kiss him. "Hmm, I'll have to work on you, then, won't I?" Then she tipped her head to the side. "I almost wish…"

He was carefully drawing smaller and smaller circles on one of her breasts as he closed in on the nipple. "What do you wish?" He wished he didn't feel as though making love to her twenty times wouldn't be enough."

"That we had some time together. Just the two of us."

"We do." He lowered his head to her breast. He could feel the slow stirring deep in his sex, and with a smile drew her nipple into his mouth. To his delight she gasped. "We have right now."

She pulled away from him and scooted down so she could kiss his chest. "I mean days and nights, not a few hours."

His fingers in her hair went still. "Days and nights? Alone?"

"You have a very sexy chest," she murmured, kissing the exact center. "Well, certainly alone. I don't want to be with anyone but you."

If she hadn't had her hand there, she would have missed the accelerated heartbeat. "What about Julianne?" His voice held a definite edge of disturbing uncertainty.

She raised her head, and to her surprise his eyes no longer showed any sign of satisfaction or even pleasure. "Julianne? Well, if we took a few days in New Hampshire, I could leave her with Naomi. Or if we were in Liberty, Betsy would keep her."

"Abandon her?"

The word sounded foreign to her, especially in reference to Julianne, but the set line of his jaw told her she hadn't heard wrong. "Leaving her with people I trust is hardly abandoning her. I just meant that we wouldn't—"

"Wouldn't have to be bothered with her?"

"I meant we wouldn't have to worry about her! What is wrong with you? One minute we're making love and the next we're arguing."

But he didn't stop it, and in fact for a brief moment, she wondered if he was deliberately baiting her. Yet, that wasn't like him. She might not know everything about him, but she knew he wasn't devious.

He cupped her chin, his hand firm enough to let her know he wanted all her attention. "We could be sexual and selfish and hedonistic, is that it?"

She'd had enough. She wasn't going to be defensive because there was nothing to be defensive about. The idea of her doing anything as ridiculous as abandoning Julianne was absurd.

She glared at him, forcing herself not to flinch. "Is that so terrible? Isn't that what we just did? What we are going to do more of before the night is over? Is it wrong to want to be together, to be alone, to have time to know each other? It has nothing to do with Julianne and you damn well know it."

"We had sex, Lizzie. We didn't make some eternal commitment about nights and days and God knows how long. You knew when I told you I took the motel room that I wasn't even going to push you to sleep with me."

She sat up, dragging her hands through her hair and sweeping it back from her face. "I can't believe we just made love and you're acting as if I threatened to tie you to me for the next fifty years."

"I don't like being boxed in. I don't like you making plans about days and nights and time together. Tonight was for tonight. It wasn't an introduction into some relationship."

"Dammit, don't put your own narrow interpretation on what I said. I didn't say a relationship, I said a few days and nights."

"Why?"

She took a deep breath and softened her voice. "Because I enjoyed this. Because I liked the way you made me feel. Because I'm glad you brought the dress, and yes, I did feel sexy in it and I'm glad I was able to feel that way with you." She turned her head and took long deep breaths. "And because being open and sexual with a man wasn't always easy for me, and after Jim died I didn't think it would ever happen again. And sometimes, like when I bought that dress, I knew that I hadn't changed, but..." She rolled back and tried to scramble off the bed.

"Ahh, Lizzie, my sweet... Oh, hell," he muttered, hauling her into his arms. She stiffened and pushed him away, but he dragged her back, settling her against him. His voice husky, his eyes as dark as she'd ever seen them, he said, "I want you on top this time."

"I can't. I can't make love after what you said...I...no!" But he silenced her with a deep kiss. "Damn you," she said when his hands lifted her astride him.

"No, damn what you do to me." He steadied her, working his hands along her thighs to position her. Then he slid deep into her.

She caught her breath at the wholeness of his arousal, and at her own unquestioning need to have him inside her.

"Look at me," he whispered, and when she tried to focus eyes already feeling the glaze of desire, he said, "I didn't want to hurt you, but this...this is all I have to give, Lizzie."

He held her hips, raising her and bringing her down. She gripped his wrists. She wanted to cry, It's not enough. But she didn't.

She bit her lip as the sensation began once again to build. She closed her eyes so he couldn't see her tears. She knew and she didn't want to know. He'd told her once that he taught himself not to hate and not to love.

He'd given her passion and taught her deep pleasure, but he hadn't taught her how to not love him.

He would never return love, or accept it.

Her tears were for what would never be.

Chapter 11

"It's about time you three got here. I was about to call out the National Guard." Gordon Healy shook Zach's hand and gave Elizabeth a gruff hug. Past sixty-five, Gordon was tall with sharply defined angles in his face that as he'd gotten older had softened into distinguished character lines. Not as hard-edged as Zach, the retired chief had been equally compulsive when it came to thorough police work. Gordon had set a high standard for honesty and integrity that still was adhered to by the Liberty Police Department.

Naomi, his wife of forty-two years, still had the classic Bostonian-bred beauty that had won Gordon's love. Taking Julianne from Elizabeth, she hugged her granddaughter to her for a few minutes. Her eyes were slightly damp when she kissed the baby's forehead. "I can't believe how she's grown," she said with a catch to her voice. "And she's so beautiful."

"Like her grandmother and her mother," Gordon added fondly, his eyes resting for a moment on his wife. It was a look that said the love and passion they had shared through the years hadn't diminished. Gordon brushed a kiss first on Julianne's cheek, then on Elizabeth's.

Zach stepped out of the reunion scene. He glanced at his watch, calculating what time he'd arrive in Liberty if he left within the next few hours. While he was here, he needed to find out what progress, if any, Buzz had made on the ransacking, spend a little time with Gordon and Naomi and begin to think Lizzie out of his life. She and Julianne were no longer his responsibility. Just as his night with her had ended, he decided firmly, so would all his obsessive thoughts.

"Let me look at you." Gordon took Elizabeth by the shoulders and turned her toward the late-morning light coming in the double-hung windows. With a fatherly frown, he said seriously, "I know you're annoyed and a little resentful of me for insisting you come up here. We fathers tend to be protective, honey, and I know you modern women like to take care of yourselves."

Naomi said to Elizabeth, "I told him he was overreacting, but I'm glad you're here. It seems like ages since I've held Julianne."

Elizabeth gave Gordon an affectionate hug. "It's all right. Sometimes we modern women don't always take care of ourselves in the best of ways."

Gordon studied her a moment, then glanced at Naomi. Zach didn't miss the silent exchange, and for a brooding moment he wondered how much they had guessed.

Then with a quick smile, Gordon said, "Come into the living room and get warm. We're all standing around here like we hardly know one another." He ushered the three of them through the rustic farmhouse, which was decorated for the holidays. There was a sharp scent of pine, and bowls of holly and mistletoe complemented a miniature Christmas tree that sat on a red cloth-covered table in front of one of the windows.

The house was arranged for livability. Naomi's hobby of knitting and crafts as well as Gordon's collection of antique guns were evident in the large living room. A wood stove threw out heat from a wide pipe blower. Stacks of seasoned wood stood nearby.

Elizabeth helped Naomi get Julianne out of her snow-suit. Gordon placed a friendly hand on Zach's shoulder. "You can get the suitcases later. How about a drink?"

"Yeah, I could use one." In truth he would have liked a bottle along with a dark desolate place where he could wallow in a good soul-clearing drunk. Then after a few days to sober up, he'd get in the black sports car and drive at lethal mind-numbing speeds for about a hundred miles.

Gordon walked over to a well-stocked bar. He poured a generous amount of straight Scotch over ice, fixed a soda-weakened drink for himself and gestured to two chairs near the wood stove.

Zach, despite the fact that he was wearing only jeans and a dark blue shirt, chose the chair farthest from the heat. He sank into the soft leather, wishing his weariness could be solved by relaxing with a drink and good company. He stretched out his legs, crossed his ankles and raised the glass to his mouth.

About six feet separated him from Lizzie, but it might as well have been six miles. He watched her get out of her coat, struck suddenly by a sense that he'd been in this scene before. He scowled for a moment and then remembered. It was at her house in the den the day of the ransacking. He'd been fighting exhaustion. Like now, he decided ruefully. He'd conjured up a snowy day and a glass of Scotch while he was stretched out in a leather chair watching a woman come toward him. That day he'd been thinking of mindless sex with no particular thought to who the woman might be. Now he knew.

Her snug jeans were topped by a white cowl-neck sweater with a ribbed waist. It was the first time he'd seen her without her coat since early morning.

Their night together hadn't spilled into the daylight, nor had there been any lingering traces of soft looks or whispered words. He'd gone out to the coffee shop and returned to find her dressed and getting Julianne ready to leave. He'd expected anger, but there had been none. Instead she'd been quiet, distant and, for lack of a better term, coolly independent. She'd spoken in polite monosyllables, carried her own suitcase and refused to drink the coffee he'd brought for her. When he made a last trip through both rooms to make sure nothing had been forgotten, he had found the black dress in the wastebasket.

At first he stared in disbelief, then he got angry and swore with a savageness that in retrospect was probably overblown. It was her dress, and if she wanted to toss it in the trash that was her business. Perhaps she interpreted the act as a roundabout way of dumping him or what they shared, or maybe she believed that what had happened between them ought to be left behind in a motel room. Whatever the hell her reason, it had ticked him off. He'd stalked out, slamming the door hard enough to loosen the screws, and made up his mind he wouldn't ask any questions.

If she'd seen his fury, she'd shown no evidence of it. In fact, she'd acted as though he were what he should have remained from the moment Gordon had called him—just an escort to New Hampshire.

Exactly what he wanted, he'd reminded himself as the car ate up the miles to Gordon's. Incredibly, this time with this woman, he hadn't been faced with trying to untangle himself from some ongoing relationship. She had done it as cleanly and as thoroughly as if the only thing that had passed between them was a friendly handshake.

That annoyed him, and he wasn't sure if it was a blow to his ego or something else. He wasn't about to allow himself to explore what that something else might be, but admittedly, in the same way as the dumped dress, it annoyed the hell out of him.

He took a swallow of Scotch, drowning a vivid string of obscenities at the same time. Hadn't he taken what he wanted? Given her what she, too, had desired from him? Hadn't they exhaustively lavished on themselves and on each other the kind of sex that was as hot and passionate the fifth time as it had been the first?

Leave it there, Stone, before you do something incredibly stupid. In a few hours you'll be on your way back to Liberty, and that will be that.

He hoped.

And even while trying to disconnect from her, he knew if she gave him even the slightest hint of willingness, he'd make love to her again. She'd been too sensational. That was why the taste of her lingered in his mouth despite the bite of alcohol. That was why he couldn't look at her without remembering the way her body opened and flowered beneath him, and that was why he could recall so vividly the way her legs gripped his hips, pulling him into her deep welcoming sweetness....

Welcoming sweetness. Unwillingly, he allowed his eyes to linger far too long on first the snap of her jeans, then the placket that hid the zipper. If they were alone, if she looked at him with the need he'd seen and felt hours ago, he might not only kiss her, but slide the zipper down. Against his palm she'd be all warm and wet and wanting....

He sucked in a long funnel of air, and with more effort than he wanted to admit to, he raised his eyes. She glanced up at that moment and their gazes met. He didn't look away.

Possibly he could stare his way out of this. If he looked at her long enough, made himself recall with infinite detail every warm place, every wet kiss, every wild, sweet sound she had made. Maybe, as had happened in the past with other women, she would fade and merge into nothing more substantial than a good memory.

Gordon cleared his throat. "Pretty deep in thought there, Zachariah."

Zach brought his eyes back from Lizzie to Gordon. "Yeah, I guess I was."

"So, apart from the storm, how was the trip?"

"Too long."

"You look beat. I guess it was a good thing you called and said you were stopping for the night."

"Yeah, terrific." Of all the great, vast decisions he'd made in his lifetime, somehow sex with Lizzie had managed to be both the worst decision and the best one.

"Zachariah..."

Zach sighed wearily. After the silent glance that had passed between Naomi and Gordon, Zach knew exactly where the conversation was going. Hoping to change the subject, he said, "You must have talked to Buzz. Any news?"

Gordon took a sip of his drink, and Zach saw his concerned attention fall on Lizzie as she and Naomi watched Julianne explore a box of toys her grandmother had given her. Finally Gordon sat back in his chair, and put his feet on a needlepoint-covered stool.

Zach wasn't fooled by the seemingly relaxed posture. He knew this was Gordon's way of getting to the real question he wanted to ask.

Gordon peered at him speculatively. "How about if I skip the preliminaries and come right out and ask?"

It was the kind of question that if Gordon had asked it of a junior officer, the cop would have been searching for an answer that would spare him the discipline that would surely follow. But Zach knew discipline was not at the heart of Gordon's probing.

He took another long swallow of his own drink, allowing the Scotch to slide slowly down his throat. In a mild voice, he said, "And then I'd have to call you a nosy son of a bitch."

Gordon chuckled. "That's what I like about you, Zachariah. Honest to a fault. You and Elizabeth are both responsible adults, and you know I wasn't going to criticize."

"I wish you would. I wish you'd tell me to get the hell out of your sight."

"That would be too easy for you." Bringing his brows together in a scowl, Gordon added, "There isn't a doubt in my mind you'd do it and say thank you very much."

Despite his weariness and lousy disposition, Zach managed a grin. "You're right."

"It would please us, you know that. Since losing Jim…" He paused for a moment, lowering his head. With just the slightest raspiness, he murmured softly as though to himself, "It doesn't get easier with time. It should, but it doesn't." Using his thumb and forefinger, he pressed them around the bridge of his nose.

With a barely audible shudder he continued, "Both Naomi and I have been concerned about Elizabeth. She's young, beautiful, and certainly shouldn't stay a widow the rest of her life. Lord knows we want her to be happy, but it's difficult for us to accept the idea of her marrying some stranger that Julianne would call Daddy."

Zach recalled her concern at her house about the Healys' reaction if she got involved in a new relationship. There had to be some kind of weird irony in this, he thought grimly.

He worked one hand around the cramp in his neck and sank lower in the chair. He knew the direction Gordon's conversation was going to take. Zach had always routinely—and deftly—diverted any ideas anybody might have about his settling down into some family-type arrangement, and when Gordon had previously brought up the subject of Elizabeth, he had dismissed it without a second thought.

In fact, he'd regarded the entire concept as about the most preposterous idea Gordon had ever come up with. The retired police chief thought of him as a son, especially since Jim's death. It was clear that Gordon had seen his notion as a simple way to end what he termed Zach's stubborn insistence on living an isolated existence, and at the same time pass approval on a husband for Elizabeth and a father for Julianne.

"Elizabeth is a lovely woman and Julianne is a terrific baby, but I'm me and I can't give them what they should have," Zach said brusquely.

Gordon took his feet from the stool and leaned forward. Bracing his arms on his legs, he studied the liquid in his glass as he slowly turned it around and around between his hands. "You're implying that they are the ones who need something. Perhaps they do, but I think you do, also. Oh, I know you don't discuss the past, and that's fine. I respect that. Hell, all of us have things we'd like to forget or change or undo. The point is—"

"That there is no point," Zach finished for him. He felt uncomfortable. He *had* discussed his past with Lizzie. And not just a few details, but all of it, right down to admitting he'd considered killing his own father. He'd never told anyone that. God, he had a hard enough time facing it himself. Why? Why had he told her? Why had it been so easy, so right? Somehow and in some way she'd not only stepped through the barrier, but she'd unobtrusively destroyed it. When and how? He couldn't answer either question, but he knew that she had.

The way out of this was supposed to be leaving her here with Gordon and Naomi, not getting jammed up in some emotional mess that felt too much like love. He didn't love her. He didn't love, period. Dammit, no.

To Gordon he said, "My past isn't forgettable, changeable or undoable. I know the things I'm capable of, and what you're talking about isn't one of them."

"In other words, she deserves better."

"Exactly."

"So did Naomi when I married her. I told her that about fifty times, but I couldn't stay away from her."

A sense of being closed in without any avenue of escape swept over Zach. He hated conversations where no matter what he said it was countered as if he could be worn down by the disposal of all his reasons. Finally, in a low even voice, he said, "I'm not you, Gordon."

"I know. You're building walls as we talk. I saw her eyes when the three of you came in. Her obvious effort to not touch you or even stand near you wouldn't have been missed by a rookie cop looking for clues. Whatever happened between you two, she's hurt and unhappy."

"She'll get over it," he said, raising his eyes and not even trying to disguise the biting chill of finality in his words.

Gordon, as usual, ignored him. "I don't think so."

"Dammit, she has to!"

Zach glanced up to see both Naomi and Elizabeth staring at him. Julianne's lower lip began to tremble. He closed his eyes. From far away he heard Gordon get up from his chair. Whispers drifted across the room and Zach slowly opened his eyes. Gordon was speaking to Naomi, and Zach saw her nod. A moment later the two women and Julianne left the room.

Zach drew in his legs and prepared to get up. Gordon crossed to the bar and lifted the bottle of Scotch, gesturing to Zach.

He shook his head, and the older man walked to the desk where he picked up a pad of paper. Coming back to his chair he sat down. "I talked to Buzz about an hour before you got here. There's a problem."

The problem was that the Liberty Police Department had put the ransacking of Lizzie's house on low-priority status, which meant that if Buzz stayed there it would be on his own time. The informant had disappeared, and while Buzz continued to track down leads, nothing new had turned up. The neighbors had volunteered to keep an eye on the house, but Zach wanted to get back. He wanted to search the rooms again, and even more wanted time alone to shake this insane notion of being in love.

He assured and reassured himself he was not using the fact that Elizabeth's house had been ransacked a second time as an excuse to talk to her before he had to leave.

After a hearty lunch of homemade beef stew and freshly baked pumpernickel bread, Naomi tried unsuccessfully to persuade him to at least stay for the night.

Zach hadn't been as successful in trying to dismiss Julianne's obvious affection for him. Both Gordon and Naomi had marveled at the way the baby had cried for him to hold her, and then refused to settle down for her nap without him tucking her in.

Now with Julianne asleep, Zach pulled the nursery door almost shut and caught up with Elizabeth in the upstairs hall.

The floor was carpeted in a swirled gold filigree pattern. Light came from hurricane lamps on either side of a drop-leaf table on which Naomi had laid pine branches. The scented greenery was decorated with red ribbons and silver balls.

Gordon had gone to the drugstore for a newspaper. Naomi was downstairs watching an afternoon television program and finishing some crafts for a Christmas bazaar.

Zach stood between Elizabeth and the stairs, thereby giving her no choice but to speak to him.

"I hope you have a safe trip back," she said, not looking at him.

"Before I leave, I need a few minutes to talk to you."

"I don't think so." She met his eyes, her mouth unsmiling. When he took a step toward her, she backed away.

"This has nothing to with us."

"There is no us," she said with a coldness that reminded him of his own words that night at the inn when he told her that nothing had happened between them. "Let me by, Zach."

Perhaps he needed to clear the air by getting her boiling mad, or maybe he needed to voice his frustration. One fact he was sure of: he was damn tired of the silence. "For God's sake, will you drop the scorned-woman facade."

She swung on him, her cheeks slashed with red, the pulse in her throat jumping. "Is that what you think this is? Some facade? And don't flatter yourself that I feel scorned because I . . ." She took a desperate breath as if she'd almost said too much. "Never mind. I don't want to talk about it."

He started to say he didn't, either, but then she glared at him, her words tumbling out as though her desire not to talk about it had been expressed by someone else. "Do you know what 'scorned' is? It means rejected with contempt."

He tried to say something, but she narrowed her eyes, daring him to try to defend himself. "But the only way it works is if the woman clings and pleads and refuses to believe what has happened. Well, I have absolutely no intention of doing that. I believe it, Zach. I don't doubt for an instant you meant exactly what you said."

He hated the fact that in the entire melee of words that they'd exchanged, he didn't know what in hell he *had* said. The only thing he could remember was telling her he didn't like being boxed in, but she must have known that. Hadn't he told her he didn't want to want her? Hadn't he left them both options by renting two separate rooms? Or was she referring to his accusation about abandoning Julianne so they could make love?

But he had had to make it. Her invitation of days and nights would have been a disaster for him. It was tough enough letting go after one night. Immersing himself with her and loving her would make the leaving...

He ignored the direction his thoughts were going in. To Elizabeth, he snapped, "Exactly what I said about what?"

"You don't remember?"

He could try to bluff through this, or allow himself to get angry enough that they'd get into a roaring battle right here in the hall. Then again, did he want to know what had hurt her? And if he did, would it change anything?

"No, frankly, I don't remember."

She looked as devastated as though he'd said he didn't remember making love to her, that she was just a face and a body for the night. She tried to get by him, but he blocked her path.

"Listen, if I don't know anything else, I know I've hurt you—" He cocked his head, then scowled when he heard that the volume on the television had been lowered. Wanting to apologize, or at the very least admit he never should have gotten the motel rooms, he took her arm, intending to lead her into one of the guest rooms so they wouldn't be overheard.

"Let go of me. The last room I want to be in with you is a bedroom."

Zach felt the rope of polite restraint snap. He hauled her against him, sliding his hands into her hair and forcing her to look at him. His voice was low and very controlled. "If I wanted to get it on with you, baby, I could do it right here in the hall up against the wall. Quick, silent and hot."

"You're crude." She tried to twist away from him, but he held her fast.

His mouth a kiss away, he murmured, "That was clean and sweet. You want crude? I'll give you crude."

"Zach, stop it."

"Julianne won't hear this. Just you." He pulled her forward, ignoring his need to kiss her thoroughly. Bending his head to her ear, he caught the elusive scent that on the previous night had enveloped him. He then spoke the words in a raw whisper, words that were short, explicit and, because he wanted to shock her, undeniably crude.

For an instant she simply stood rigid, the red anger that had tinged her cheeks earlier fading to a pasty white.

The pain in her eyes tore through him, and he pulled her into his arms. "Sweet God, what am I doing to you . . . ?" he murmured, knowing it wasn't a question, since he clearly had no answers.

She stood stiff and tense in his arms. "I could hate you so easily," she said with a ragged softness.

"Maybe that's the best way."

She seemed to lose her will to stand and sagged against him. Zach cradled her body with a sudden gentleness as the built-up tension diffused and slid away. Her arms stole around his waist, and she held him, her head tucked beneath his chin, much as they had stood the day he'd come and told her Jim was dead. Perhaps in a bizarre way, their relationship—for want of a better word—now had also died.

She tried to pull away finally, but he tightened his grip. When she once again relaxed, he worked his fingers across her back in a soothing motion.

"This isn't how I wanted us to end, Lizzie," he murmured, rocking her against him.

"It doesn't matter," she said dully.

He tipped her head up, and almost without volition brushed his mouth across hers. There was no passion, no hope of deepening and drawing more from the light touch.

Somewhere inside him a door slammed shut, and he felt as emotionally drained as the day his father slammed the door in his face. He'd considered murder then before he chickened out. Maybe this time he'd killed the love *before* he chickened out and let it live.

Elizabeth, too, seemed almost numb. There were no tears, no clinging fingers gripping his shirt as if he were a lifeline to her future, only a kind of awful, draining sadness.

Days and nights after Zach left to return to Liberty, Elizabeth was still thinking about their final conversation in the upstairs hall.

The kiss had been poignant and gripping in a way that no deep prelude to making love could ever have been. They had simply been two people who had taken too much from each other and were forced to face nothing but the ashes of memories.

She glanced at the sculpture that was taking shape beneath her hands. It wasn't large, only about ten inches, but that was deliberate. She preferred small pieces that didn't overwhelm, and she also believed that emotion could be more powerfully portrayed when the eye didn't have to wander so far.

She'd gone out the morning after Zach had driven off and bought the materials. For something to do, she told Naomi and Gordon when she returned and set to work. Julianne had plenty of attention with no lack of laps and willing arms to hold her. Naomi and Gordon had shown her off to a steady trail of friends and neighbors who dropped in to wish the Healys happy holidays.

The only different period was at night, when the baby cried for Zach, but the tears and fussing were less frequent now.

Elizabeth, too, had cried. Once in the shower where no one could hear her, and again here in the studio she'd fashioned from a small downstairs room that absorbed the northern light. A week had passed since he drove away, and while she had resigned herself to that departure being a symbol of their lives separating, she found herself marking time.

And she was doing something else. Relating time to him. It seemed that all her conversations with the Healys began with some point related to Zach, so that she was beginning to think she had had no life before she walked into her den that day and faced him.

She knew now that her awareness of him then had been a preparation of sorts, just as every step from Liberty to the bed in his motel room had not only added layers of sexual attraction but also fostered a slowly forming friendship. And yet now there was neither sex *nor* friendship.

Now there was nothing, and even when she was feeling most sorry for herself she blamed herself. How could she have expected him to accept what she herself had always hated?

She smoothed her hand down the back of the statue's head, pressing her fingers to make the swirls of mussed hair in the clay. She added some more along the nape of his neck. He wore his hair long, she told herself, just as he wore his jeans tight. She stepped back and studied the form, and had just decided the line of his thigh needed work when there came a knock on the door.

"Come on in," she called distractedly. Perhaps it wasn't his leg, but that the baby needed more defining.

Naomi opened the door, and then lifted a tray with cups of tea and freshly baked Christmas cookies. "I thought you could use a break."

"You're going to spoil me," Elizabeth said, taking a cloth and working the worst of the clay off her hands. Naomi set down the tray and walked over to the clay piece.

"Do you have a name for it?"

"Not yet."

Naomi studied it for a long time, tipping her head to one side and then the other. "It is quite exceptional, Elizabeth."

"They were quite an exceptional pair. At first Zach was so leery of Julianne, but after a shaky start they seemed to respond to each other almost on an instinctive level. I sketched this at the inn one evening when he was holding her."

"You've captured an essence of bonding between the two of them, a closeness not unlike that of a father and child." Naomi glanced up at Elizabeth, and for a moment their eyes met and held in a mutual truth. Naomi brushed a piece of clay off Elizabeth's cheek. "You're in love with him, aren't you?"

Elizabeth walked over and helped herself to a cup of tea. "Is it that obvious?"

"Not all the time, but it shows here in your work. The shape and the detail. There's a quality of life you've infused in the clay that I doubt would be there if he were merely a friend who was fond of Julianne."

Elizabeth sipped her tea and crossed to the window where she'd stood numerous times since Zach's departure. "It was foolish of me to let it happen."

"Love isn't always sensible and predictable."

"With Jim it was mutual and..." Her voice trailed off. Uncomplicated and sweetly predictable, she thought to herself. He'd always wanted to please, to be more than what was expected of him. She'd always had a sense that much of that had been directed toward making his father proud of him, but Gordon *was* proud of his son. Jim had been a good police officer as he had been a good husband, and he would have made a fine father.

Elizabeth said, "I don't know, Naomi, but loving Jim was easy. He made it easy."

"And Zach makes it difficult."

Elizabeth shook her head. "Try impossible."

"As long as I've known him—and I don't know a lot about him—I've found that the concept of family is foreign to him. Gordon has always been fond of Zach, as I have, but since Jim died—and admittedly for our own selfish reasons—we've wanted to treat him as a son. He's fought that almost as if he's afraid that if he allows himself to love us as we love him, something will come in and destroy it."

"He told me once that he had taught himself neither to hate nor love."

"I don't think he's succeeded." Again, Naomi looked at the clay sculpture. "If ever a man loved a child, it is here in your work."

"But it's only clay, Naomi. Powerful and moving, perhaps, but only clay."

Another week passed before Elizabeth finished the sculpture. She examined it, walked away from it for hours and then came back. She went shopping with Naomi, hardly able to believe Christmas was only a little more than a week away. Gordon had already pronounced that she and Julianne were spending the holidays with them, and perhaps by the time New Year's came and went, the ransacker would have been captured.

"And what if he isn't?" Elizabeth asked Gordon one morning at breakfast. "I can't stay here forever."

"Zach called and said that the investigation is moving along. He talked to your manager at The Easel, and she said to tell you the Christmas trade is brisk and not to worry about anything."

"I'm sure Yvette is handling things just fine, but that's not the point. I feel as though I'm suspended in some kind of time warp."

Naomi poured her husband another mug of coffee and rested her hand on his shoulder. "Gordon..."

"Now, Naomi, we've discussed this. I won't have them in danger."

Elizabeth knew the greater danger for her lay in staying. The longer she put off returning to Liberty, the more difficult it was going to be to get her life started again. Facing Zach was crucial, if only to seal permanently that there wouldn't and never could be anything between them. As long as she stayed in New Hampshire, she would feel caught in the time between facing him in her den and watching him drive out of the Healys drive.

She'd settled it all in her head, simply because that was the safest place to deal with it. Her heart, she knew, would never accept it, but she had to test her ability to see him and begin the process of forgetting.

She had to go home.

She pushed back her chair and carried her dishes to the sink. Gordon had lifted Julianne out of the high chair and was feeding her tiny pieces of scrambled egg. Elizabeth thought of Zach and their numerous conversations about baby food and real food.

"What if I compromised, Gordon? I'll leave Julianne here with you and go back by myself."

She knew she couldn't argue her way out with him, and she doubted she could convince him with logic. So she did what she had done so many times with her own parents when they insisted on being too parental: she kissed his cheek and said, "I love you for caring and for wanting to protect me, but I have to do this. I have to go home."

Chapter 12

His black sports car sat in her driveway, as proud and deadly as a crouched panther. Seeing Zach Stone leaning against it as though he were waiting for her didn't dilute the danger.

Elizabeth parked Naomi's car behind his and busied herself unbuckling her seat belt. She gathered up the map she'd used after she took the wrong exit coming through Boston and ended up driving in circles for an hour.

Taking a deep breath, she cautioned herself that the reason her heart was pounding had nothing to do with Zach's being there, but only with seeing him without any warning. During the trip down from New Hampshire, she had contemplated exactly how she would react when she faced him. Her first choice was to keep her distance, but that probably wasn't too practical considering that the ransacker had yet to be caught and that it wasn't yet known what he was hunting for.

However, she had made one decision. Under no circumstances would she make a mistake such as she had at the motel and suggest any kind of relationship. Zach had been very clear about that, and she had no intention of giving him even a hint that she'd been so stupid as to fall in love with him.

All those distracting thoughts had so dominated her concentration that they probably accounted for her taking the wrong exit in Boston. She'd finally concluded, after getting onto the interstate again, that she wouldn't take any chances of being caught off guard by him. Instead, she would take the initiative and make a casual visit to him at the police station.

Well, so much for plans and preparation, she thought grimly. Glancing at him as he walked toward her, she noted that as usual he wore no coat. And since being critical kept her emotions in better balance, she studied him with a scowl.

His hair still needed to be cut, and she told herself she didn't care that she'd liked the way its coarseness had felt around her fingers, across her breasts and against her thighs. She wondered if he had pushed up the sleeves of his gray fatigue shirt because warmer temperatures had come, melting much of the snow, but decided the weather probably had little to do with it. He spent more time without a coat than wearing one. Strange that he never got cold outdoors, but at the inn she had been overly concerned about him being warm at night. Or was it as simple as making him warm against her?

And his jeans. Indecently tight, she mused, allowing her gaze to linger no more than a second where the tightness had the most effect on her. This pair had a slash in one leg above his knee that gave her a too-memorable peek at his thigh.

Briefly she closed her eyes and reminded herself that he looked absolutely no different than he normally did, that there was nothing between them and that any moment...

"You're late," he said in a voice that sounded disgustingly official when she opened the car door.

She managed a bored smile. "Oh? I didn't realize we had an appointment." She couldn't help an inward swell of pride at her aplomb.

"Gordon called me and said you'd insisted on coming home."

With a wide-eyed glance she said, "And you're here to welcome me. How nice." She glanced around curiously. "Is there a band? Balloons? Perhaps a party later?" She paid no attention to his chuckle at her sarcasm.

Why hadn't it occurred to her that Gordon would call Zach? In fact, she should have been suspicious that he hadn't put up more of a fuss about her returning to Liberty than he had. Making up her mind to do something—in this case to try to get her life back to normal—wasn't sufficient reason to assume Gordon or Zach would simply agree. She mentally thanked her good sense at leaving Julianne with the Healys. If she'd insisted on bringing the baby with her, Gordon, no doubt, would have had the entire Liberty police force here to greet her.

Zach commented, "Since the band was booked and I'm fresh out of balloons, I'll compromise and spring for the beer and pizza."

She gave him a withering look as she took the keys from the ignition and got out of the car.

"Give me the keys. I'll get your stuff from the trunk."

She closed her hand around the keys before he could take them from her. "I seem to recall we had a discussion about keys once before."

"Then this one isn't necessary."

"I can manage just fine, thank you." He didn't move out of the way, so she walked around him. She could handle this, she told herself. Be brisk, calm and aloof.

She lifted her suitcases out and glanced at the bundle in the corner. She'd wrapped the clay sculpture in a canvas wrapper so there was no way he could guess what it was. Not that it mattered, but she didn't want to explain, or worse, have him accuse her of trying to box him in by using his feelings for Julianne.

She'd just about decided to leave the bundle until after he left, when he asked, "What's in the canvas?"

Elizabeth jumped at the sudden closeness of his voice. Without asking he had gathered both her suitcases, and was reaching for her makeup case.

She reached it first. "I said I can manage, Zach."

He ignored that and said, "You want that canvas thing or does it stay?"

"The canvas thing stays," she snapped, losing the edge of calmness she desperately needed. "Now, will you please give me my things and go away." It was a statement, not a question or even a plea, but his expression was exasperatingly bland.

He gestured toward the house. "Let's go."

"Dammit, Zach. I don't need your help. I don't want you around and I don't appreciate you waiting for me as if I were a recalcitrant child."

He turned then, an undercurrent of fury in his gray-blue eyes. "Then you're going to have one hell of a time with the fact that you and I are going to be living together."

The ramifications of that comment hit her in less than a second. The two-word expletive she uttered shocked her when it slipped out with all its coarseness, succinctness and, unfortunately, its raw, intimate meaning.

He only raised an eyebrow. "It's a good thing Julianne isn't here. Your language would be a lousy influence."

She should have been relieved he hadn't come back with some comment such as the one in the upstairs hall at the

Healys when she said she wouldn't go into a bedroom with him. But she didn't feel relieved, just madder.

"Damn you, Zach."

"Much better."

"Shut up."

"Even better. Now, if you're finished, I'd like to go into the house—"

"You can go to hell and—"

He touched his thumb to her mouth as though he were giving her absolution. In a low voice he murmured, "I've been there, baby, more times than I can count. Now, I'd like to go into the house because I'm expecting a call from Buzz."

With that he hoisted all her luggage and left her standing in the middle of her driveway as if she were a salesperson he'd told to get lost. He walked across the yard and through her front door as if he did indeed live there.

She slammed the trunk lid, scowled and wondered what he would do if she simply got in the car and drove away. Probably get in that sports car of his and chase her, she decided grimly as she flung her purse strap onto her shoulder.

Finding Zach waiting for her wasn't the only surprise, although the next one was much easier on her nerves and her heart. When she walked into her house she was stunned. She'd thought the mess the ransacker had left would still be there, but every room had been cleaned and straightened. The slashed upholstery in the living room was the only reminder.

Zach carried her things up to her bedroom, deposited them on the floor and said nothing to her as he passed her on the stairs. When the telephone rang, he went into the den and closed the door.

She kicked her bedroom door closed, taking little consolation in the noise. Then suddenly feeling exhausted, she sank down on the bed, reminding herself that she must keep her emotions in check. No more outbursts of expletives like the one outside. She shuddered at the memory. Never in her entire life had she said such a thing to a man, but then no man had ever made her quite so angry, annoyed, unhappy, frustrated, sexually satisfied and, oh God... She wrapped her arms around herself to stop the sudden chill.

Staying unaffected by his presence, and definitely avoiding any verbal sparrings, would be her only chance to get through this in one piece.

And get through it she would. Blinking, she realized she hadn't even asked if there was anything new on the ransacker. The sooner he was caught the sooner Zach would leave.

And the sooner he left the better—

Cutting off her thoughts, she made herself face reality. If there was anything about Zach Stone she was quite sure of, it was a clear understanding of his intentions. From the beginning she had been a job to him. Obviously she still was or he wouldn't be here. If he felt any kind of personal involvement, any kind of nonobjective feelings toward her, he would have sent Buzz to stay here.

Sighing, she got to her feet and began to unpack. Obviously, she couldn't avoid him if he was staying here, but there was no reason she couldn't simply ignore him. If she pretended he was just hired security, she could be polite and distant.

And with any kind of luck, the police would soon find the ransacker and Zach would be gone and out of her life for good.

"Good morning."

He was seated at the desk in the den, reading through a stack of manila folders that she didn't recognize. His hair was mussed as if he'd tunneled his fingers through it in exasperation. His light blue polo shirt displayed a logo for a popular Providence café. On the desk was an array of take-out coffee cartons that looked as though he'd been collecting them for days and some crumpled wrappers from a fast-food breakfast. The phone sat near his elbow and beside that lay his gun and shoulder holster.

"Good morning," he said, glancing up and then going back to his reading. Opening the next folder, but not looking at her, he asked, "Did you sleep okay?"

"Yes. And you?"

"Lousy."

"Oh?" She stopped a few feet from the desk.

"The couch is too short and the lumps are uneven."

"There is a guest room," she said, feeling once again the beginnings of a disagreement. How did he manage to turn the simplest conversation into a confrontation? Or had he so affected her that she'd become one of those women who wanted attention and would take it any way she could get it? No, she didn't believe that. He just seemed to set her on edge.

"I'm not a guest." He lifted one of the coffee cartons, drank and then grimaced.

She folded her arms. "Ah, yes, the cop doing his job."

He closed the folder he'd been reading with enough of a slap to let her know he didn't care for her comment. "Look, I don't like this arrangement any better than you do."

She considered her mind's warning to let the comment stand. She didn't disagree with it, and it required no explanation. And yet . . . "Then why don't you leave?"

"I intend to. And with some cooperation from you, we might be able to wind things up quickly."

"Then you have my complete cooperation."

"Good. There are some things you need to know and some things I want to ask you. Now, before we exhaust ourselves with all this polite conversation, why don't you get yourself some coffee and come back and join me?"

She was about to ask what things when she remembered why she had stopped in the den. "I came in here to call Naomi and see how Julianne is."

He slid back the chair and propped one booted foot on an open desk drawer. Tapping a ballpoint pen on the edge of the telephone, he said, "Don't bother. I already called. She's fine. I said that you were still asleep and that you'd probably call later."

"How considerate of you," she said with a dry sarcasm he gave no indication of catching. She probably should go and get her coffee, but his take-over attitude annoyed her. As he had reminded her earlier, he was doing a job, but that didn't include making her personal phone calls. "I hope you emphasized that I was sleeping alone."

He watched her and continued to tap the phone, then finally, in about the most disinterested voice she'd ever heard, he said, "No one asked."

She clenched her hands into fists. "Well, of course they wouldn't. You are the very trustworthy Zachariah Stone. Being alone all night with a woman when you're doing your job isn't a problem. Not even when you and the woman have already slept together."

He did stop tapping, and tossed the pen onto the folders. "Lizzie, don't make this any more difficult than it is."

"Is it difficult?"

His glance didn't waver, and in fact penetrated so deeply she had to make herself not turn and run out of the den.

Finally he said, "Do you want me to take you to bed? Is that it?" He rose to his feet and moved around the desk toward her.

She didn't move. "No!"

He stopped close enough for her to know that if she'd answered "yes," he would already have had her in his arms. He lowered his voice, but he didn't touch her. "Then stop acting like you do."

This time she did take a few steps back. She didn't like being accused of something she hadn't done, but if he kissed her he'd know.

"Am I down here in my robe? Am I flirting with you? And now that I think about it, have I ever used any feminine ploys to come on to you? Not one time, Zach Stone, and don't you dare say I have."

"God." He sighed heavily and added in a weary voice, "Enough, Lizzie. I'll concede that you won this one. Now, if you're going to make some coffee, I'd love a cup. Then we need to talk about the ransacking."

But she didn't move, her eyes suddenly feeling hot and stinging. She bit her lip, deciding she was acting like a bitch goading him on. It wasn't his fault that he was here or that he made her pulse race or that she certainly did want to go to bed with him.

He studied her for a moment. "Please?"

Finally she nodded, turned and left the room, barely aware of his sigh of relief.

By the time she returned to the den with their coffee, Zach had sat back behind the desk, with both feet propped on the edge, ankles crossed and a folder open in his lap. He glanced up, reminding himself that not taking her to bed was both the most rational and the smartest decision. It was also the toughest.

She set down the steaming mug beside him, and he deliberately concentrated on what he was reading so he wouldn't encircle her wrist and say something incredibly inappropriate.

She sat down in the same chair she'd occupied the day of the ransacking when he'd given her brandy in a champagne flute.

After taking a sip of her coffee, she said, "You had some things to ask me? Or tell me?"

"Yeah. The coffee smells great." He took a careful sip. "Tastes even better."

She lowered her eyes, seemingly to concentrate on the steam rising from her cup. "I should have asked you yesterday, but—"

When she paused, he thought, Yeah, yesterday things were pretty tense for questions of any sort. On second thought, this morning wasn't a hell of a lot better. "Ask me what?"

"The house. Did you clean everything up?"

"I hired a housecleaning service to come in after I spent a few days going over everything again. That was one of the things I wanted to tell you. The ransacker was in here again. The neighbors were keeping an eye on the house and one of them called the station. Unfortunately, the neighbor tried to be a hero and the guy got spooked and ran, so we didn't get him. It happened the day I got back. But from one standpoint it was exactly what we wanted. Now we know that you did indeed interrupt him the first time, and whatever he was after is still here."

"But you haven't found anything?"

"We've drawn some fairly substantial conclusions. We've concluded from these reports—" he gestured to the manila folders "—that what he was looking for is connected to Jim's undercover work."

"But the time gap. If Jim had something he wanted, wouldn't this person have tried to find it right after Jim died?"

"You remember Gizzo Gates?"

"The informant."

"Yeah. We learned that he flew to Mexico a few days before Jim was murdered and returned to Liberty just before the ransacking. Apparently Gates was living it up in Mexico on a lot of money that he couldn't account for. He came back to Liberty because he was broke.

"Street talk is that he was looking to sell some information for cash. A whole lot of cash. Tell me, did you notice anything different about Jim in the week or so before his death?"

She tried to think back. "I don't recall anything different. I always had a sense of when some investigation was coming to a head, because he got kind of wired. He'd always worried about his father being proud of him. He never wanted to make a mistake that would embarrass the department or Gordon."

Zach frowned. "Wait a minute. What do you mean, he worried about Gordon being proud of him? Gordon was always proud. My God, he thought the sun rose and set on Jim."

"Jim was in awe of his father. He always talked about wanting to be as honest and incorruptible as Gordon."

"But he was."

"Of course he was."

"Then why would he talk about it as if he wasn't?"

"Perhaps I was just overly conscious of it. One of my brothers was like that. He never felt as if he was good enough. He always tried to outdo the others. Unfortunately, he tended to get involved in things that got him trouble rather than accomplishments."

Zach put his cup down, closed the folder and tossed it on the desk. "Jim was the only kid. There was no one to compete with."

"There was you." She looked at him a long time as if the impact of her words was as startling to her as it was to him.

"Me! Hell, I was hardly competition. I'd only known Jim about two and a half years."

"But Gordon thought you walked on water. He did, Zach, and he still does. Jim told me once that Gordon viewed you as the quintessential cop. Zach Stone, the cop every police chief in the state wanted to work with."

Zach stood and went over to the window that looked across the backyard. "Strange, because I thought Jim was just about the luckiest guy in the world. Parents, a family, a beautiful wife, a house with permanent possessions."

After staring out the window for a few moments, he turned and said, "Come over here. I want to show you something."

When she was next to him, he dropped a casual arm around her neck and drew her close. He brushed his mouth across her temple, feeling in that moment that having her there with him was as necessary as what he was about to tell her.

"When I was about eight I went to a foster home—the fourth one I'd been in—and there was this tree in their yard that was a lot like your maple tree. I watched that tree for weeks trying to screw up my courage to climb it. When I finally did, I straddled a branch that was about fifteen feet off the ground and felt as if I'd conquered the world. For once I was a winner. I was up and looking down. And from way up there, life, from an eight-year-old's perspective, looked pretty cool. And since I was feeling cool and cocky, I decided that I wanted to build a tree house. A place with walls and windows and security, a place I could go where I wouldn't have to listen to a hundred other kids. A place where I could sleep alone instead of in a room that was more of a warehouse than a bedroom. I had it all planned right down to the kind of wood I would use."

She slid her hand around his waist, her fingers pressing into him almost as though she knew.

He pulled her tighter. "You know, don't you?"

"Just a guess. I felt you tense up."

He knew his shudder was palpable. "They said it would ruin the tree, and that since I wasn't going to be there for-ever like I was their son, they didn't want to have to dis-

mantle it after I left." He turned then and faced her.
"You're a real problem for me, you know that?"

"Why is that?"

"I've told you more about myself and how I feel than I've
ever told anyone."

"And you don't ever talk about your past, or your feelings, do you?"

"No."

"Then perhaps our being together for these days has accomplished something for both of us. Maybe we've just become friends."

He stared down at her for a moment, his eyes searching
as though trying to see more.

"You're too suspicious, Zach."

"Yeah. Comes with the territory." He pulled away and
went back to the desk. "Let's get back to Jim. At the inn
you said you packed a lot of Jim's personal things away to
give to Julianne someday. What kind of things?"

She took a deep breath and went back to her coffee. "The
commendations he got from the department. He was especially proud of the one he got for uncovering those two cops
who stole money from the evidence room."

"Yeah, I remember. Jim was assigned to the evidence
room and when those cops were arrested, Gordon personally gave him the commendation," Zach said, recalling both
Jim's pride that his father had given him the coveted assignment and that he in turn had uncovered two dirty cops.
"At the time it seemed pretty routine, but now, thinking
back, Jim did talk about that particular day for a couple of
weeks afterward. One night we stopped for coffee and we
got into the subject of what makes exceptional police work,
and I mentioned his discovery of the evidence-room theft.
He looked at me and said, 'Yeah, I sure did make the old
man proud.'

"At the time I thought it strange that his pride wasn't in his accomplishment, but in what Gordon thought of him. Now, considering what you've just said, it fits. What else of Jim's did you pack away?"

"His notebooks, mostly."

Zach looked up at the ceiling and grimaced in self-disgust. "Damn. Of course. Jim was a methodical note taker. I must be too preoccupied. I forgot all about his notebooks." He rounded the desk and took her arm. "Let's go take a look."

For the next few hours they searched through boxes and cartons that Elizabeth had stored in an upstairs bedroom. One brief moment when Zach turned too quickly, she was thrown off balance and he grabbed her to steady her. For long moments they stared at each other as though caught in a surprise interlude.

He wanted to kiss her. Hell, he wanted her, period.

She, on the other hand, was struck by the fact that given any encouragement, she wouldn't have objected to anything he wanted to do.

They separated and continued to sort through boxes. Zach put the notebooks in order by date. He went through three years' worth before he turned to Lizzie.

"One is missing."

"But it can't be," she replied, staring at the contents of the boxes strewn across the floor. "I put all the ones I found in these boxes. Jim kept them all on a shelf in the den."

"Except the last one."

"Maybe there wasn't a last one."

"Out of character for him. Jim had kept them since he became a cop. Why would he suddenly quit a week before his death?"

"Maybe the ransacker got it."

"No. He wouldn't have come back if he had. Jim put it somewhere, but the question is where. It sure as hell isn't in here."

Frustrated by the futile search, Zach helped her to repack the boxes. When they returned to the den, she started to gather up his coffee cartons at about the same time he reached for the manila folders.

He took a step at the same time she did, and their bodies brushed. In a moment she was in his arms and he was holding her. It wasn't rough nor was it particularly gentle, more of a resigned reaction. They breathed in rhythm with each other until finally he tucked her hair behind her ears and tipped her chin up.

"This neutral relationship isn't working too well, is it?" he asked as his fingers lingered near her ears, toying with the small gold hoops she wore.

She shook her head.

He slipped one hoop out and then the next one. "Nothing has changed, Lizzie."

"I know." She moved her head from side to side, trying to feel more of his hands.

His thumbs brushed her cheeks. "I have work to do, so this isn't days and nights of sexual satiation."

"Of course not."

He bent his head and kissed her, but it wasn't passionate and she wanted passion. Hot and wild and unforgettable. She slipped her hands around his waist and opened her mouth just as he started to lift his head. It was too much and not enough, and when he backed her over to the couch she didn't object.

This time when he ended the kiss, she grinned. "I thought you had work to do."

He worked the buttons loose on her blouse and pulled it open. Beneath she wore an ecru chemise, and he bent to kiss her breasts through the lace. She gasped at the shiver that ran through her. "I don't want to leave the lady unsatisfied," he murmured against her nipple.

She closed her eyes and brushed her hand across the front of his jeans. "And you could just push me away and walk out of the room, couldn't you?"

"You wouldn't let me," he murmured, proving his words when she clasped his head to her breast. "You want me too much."

She tossed her head back as he kissed his way up her throat to her mouth. She licked her lips, her thoughts distracted by the way his hands had deftly opened her slacks and slipped inside. "It's only because you're so good in bed."

He chuckled and said, "Yeah, I know," and then kissed her soundly.

Just when she wanted his mouth again, his tongue deeper, his hands to cup her bottom and pull her closer, he moved back so that he could see her. Then in the softest of whispers, which sounded almost secretive, he said, "What if I tell you something I've never told another woman?"

Elizabeth went very still; her hands, which had been in the process of working on the snap of his jeans, stopped their motion. A whole treasure of possibilities slipped into her mind. She didn't want to guess; she wasn't even sure she wanted to know.

"Not curious?" he asked.

"I don't want you to say you don't want me." It was a silly thing to say. She knew he wanted her. She could read it in his eyes and in the deep full way he kissed her. She could certainly feel it against the most feminine part of her.

"Not a chance of that and you know it." He slipped his hand inside her panties. "I've never wanted another woman as much as I want you."

She blinked and hoped nothing in her expression had changed. Her entire body wanted to cry, No! That's not what I want to hear. I want to hear that you care for me, and maybe if I give you enough time you might even learn how to love me.

They got their clothes off—awkwardly, but she hardly noticed. In truth she wanted to stop. Not that she didn't want him, she did. Desperately. But not this way, not with no hope of more, no possibility that love might have a chance.

She wrapped her arms around him and kissed him, trying to convince herself that good sex was enough. More than enough.

"Easy, baby..."

"No. I don't want to go easy. I want to see you and touch..." Her mouth moved along his shoulder, her hand sliding around his manhood. "I want to kiss you everywhere."

She slipped down with consummate grace, her hands holding him while her mouth moved closer. His hands tangled in her hair, trying to stop her. "Lizzie, Lizzie...wait. Ah, God, don't...."

But she didn't, couldn't, wait, and she kissed him with an exquisite talent. At his groan, she kissed her way up his body, then pulled him down, sliding and stretching out along the length of the couch. "You like me under you, remember?"

His breath rushed from his lungs. "After that, you can go anywhere you want."

She arched her back and he gripped her hips, bringing them together in a long, smooth stroke as though their union were the discovery of what each had been missing in the other.

His climax came first and hers a sweet hot moment later.

They lay replete, their bodies sticky and warm against the leather couch. He raised himself, kissing her lightly.

She lowered her lashes.

"Lizzie?" He tipped up her chin, his eyes serious and concerned. "You did come, didn't you?"

She nodded.

His relief showed in a slow, lingering kiss. "I thought so. You make this funny little sound and I was sure I heard it."

She frowned. "I make a funny sound? What kind of sound?"

"Sort of a breathless catch that has a satisfied purr to it. I can't describe it, but I love hearing it." He rolled off her and began to dress. He had his jeans on and zipped but not snapped when the telephone rang. Holding his shirt in one hand, he crossed to the desk and lifted the receiver.

"Yeah, what have you got?" He searched around the desk for a pencil and a piece of paper. While he was busy, Elizabeth quietly got off the couch, gathered up her clothes and started to leave.

"Lizzie, don't go."

Elizabeth came closer, her eyes wide. She got quickly into her clothes while he talked.

He dragged a hand down his face. "When did it happen? Tell me we got lucky and the bastard spilled his guts." He swore, shaking his head in disgust and then quickly told Buzz about the notebook search. "We could use a break, Buzz, not another complication. Hell, no, I don't like what it could mean, but we don't have any damn choice. She's here with me. Yeah, I'll tell her."

"What is it? What happened?" she asked the moment he hung up.

"Gizzo Gates is dead. He was trying to shake down some money from a contact and got a little rough, so they shot him."

Elizabeth sat down hard.

He walked over to her. "There is something. Not what I hoped and not pleasant."

"What?"

"They found Jim's home phone number among Gizzo's possessions, and on the same piece of paper a date, a time and a figure of twenty thousand. The date was a week before Jim's death. Buzz checked the log for that date, and Jim had signed out that afternoon claiming he had to take you to the doctor. Did he?"

She swallowed, her eyes unblinking, and he knew she realized the import of her answer. "He never went to the doctor with me."

He touched her mouth, his thumb rubbing. "I'm sorry, sweetheart," he murmured, wishing he weren't thinking what he was. But he had no choice but to follow the lead where it went.

The end result could change a lot of memories about Jim Healy. That fact, in turn, made him hope there was some other explanation than the one edging along his mind. "The department has ordered an internal investigation of the evidence-room records. We think that twenty-thousand figure might be cash from there."

"You think Jim stole money? No! He would never do that."

"You think I want to believe he would? Dammit, of course I don't. No one downtown wants to, but cops don't give out their home phone numbers to informants unless they're doing something they don't want the department to know about."

"But Jim is dead. What possible good will it do to destroy his reputation? And Gordon and Naomi. My God, Zach, you can't do that to them."

"You think I like this? You think I like finding out a partner might be dirty, that he didn't care enough about his wife, his coming baby... For God's sake, that he didn't give enough of a damn about himself not to cave in and allow himself to be compromised?"

"No! I knew Jim. I lived with him, and he wouldn't have done that, I know it."

"Your loyalty is commendable, Lizzie, but hardly objective."

"And what about your loyalty? Where is that? Or is that just another job? Find out the answers and the hell with who it hurts and whose reputation is destroyed. What about Julianne? Do you want her to grow up believing her father was a dirty cop? And what if this is all a mistake? Then what? Jim's reputation has been destroyed, and for what? So you can prove that you're the perfect cop? You already have everything he wanted. Gordon and Naomi think of you as their son. Julianne adores you and I—"

"You what?"

"Nothing."

"You're not going to tell me you're in love with me, are you?"

The question washed over her, and she thought how simple it would be to say yes. But there was a warning tone in his voice, a warning that he didn't want to hear her answer, that stopped any such fanciful thoughts. All her energy seemed to drain out of her. She quickly glanced down to the floor.

Finally she said, "No, I'm not going to tell you that."

Chapter 13

Two days after she almost admitted she loved Zach, Elizabeth found the missing notebook in the garage. There was nothing especially different about it in comparison to the ones they'd gone through in the house.

Except that Jim had usually used black books, and this one was a muddy brown and fat with hastily inserted extra pages. She pressed her fingers into the cheap imitation-leather cover as though to keep it closed and secret.

She drew a deep breath, feeling a drag of disappointment that finding it had been so anticlimactic. A ransacker had turned her downstairs upside down, had gotten into the house another time before Zach had returned from New Hampshire, and just the previous evening, her neighbor, Betsy McGann, had called to say she'd seen a strange man crossing between the yards.

Zach had gone out to take a look, but just as on that night before they left Liberty, whoever it had been in the yard had disappeared.

Staring down at the notebook now, she realized that the man who wanted it was nowhere near as important as what the pages might reveal. This wasn't television or the movies or some suspenseful mystery where catching some unknown assailant would automatically bring on the happy ending. This was real life, and the notebook was the unknown assailant.

And therein lay her fear. She knew that whatever was written here would probably provide the answers that hadn't been found in the reports Zach had been through. These pages could very well confirm what the internal investigation of the evidence-room records had found—that the missing money had been traced back to a few days before Jim's death. And they would probably reveal things about Jim.

Revelations that would both bring a solution and create a problem. The solution for all of Zach's and the department's questions, and a problem for Jim's memory.

Whether her husband had been guilty of anything was still a question. Elizabeth wanted to think the suspicious facts were all circumstantial, but Zach was proceeding as though they were not.

They'd said little in the past two days—living together but not sleeping together and talking only when necessary.

The previous day, she'd taken the clay sculpture from Naomi's trunk and set it on the kitchen counter, but left it wrapped in its canvas covering. She couldn't deny that her motives weren't suspect. Secretly, she hoped he would take the covering off, see what Naomi had seen and decide that loving her wouldn't box him in. Fanciful in the extreme, she knew. Zach not only never removed the canvas, but he never even asked what "the canvas thing" was.

Both relieved and disappointed, she finally decided she would simply give it to him, but not while her feelings were so exposed. At a later time, a few months from now when he wouldn't think her gift was an obvious ploy to tie him to her because of Julianne. It was a decision that pleased her, for she had convinced herself that in a few months she wouldn't feel so vulnerable, and perhaps she wouldn't love him so much.

Her decision, earlier this morning, to go down to The Easel had been so she could give her employees their Christmas bonuses and give herself some space from Zach. Since her return to Liberty, she felt as though she were existing in a vacuum. Loving him and knowing she could never tell him had become a swirl of contradictions. He feared she'd box him in. She feared he'd shut her out.

She hadn't resigned herself to the idea of forgetting him—she knew that wouldn't happen, but she wanted him gone, the investigation finished and Julianne home.

For those reasons alone, she should have been pleased that she'd found the notebook. She'd been about to get into her car when she spotted the rows of plastic shoe boxes on one of the garage shelves. Jim had used the boxes to store everything from small tools to papers and instruction books that came with the lawn mower and the snowblower.

She had opened four boxes before she found the notebook. Ironic, she thought, it was here in plain sight all the time. Not hidden as though it contained secrets, and not in the house where the ransacker had assumed it would be.

Well, of course, now that she thought about it, Jim had told her once that the safest place to hide something was in plain sight. Safes and secret drawers and cubbyholes are beacons for a thief. So he'd put the notebook in plain sight, in the garage, and yet managed to hide it from both the police and the ransacker.

Her discovery didn't solve problems; it created new ones. And yet she held on to a hope that perhaps there was nothing damaging to Jim written here as there had been nothing in any of the others. But she knew differently, simply because it wasn't with the others. In his own way he had hidden it, and the very fact that it was in the garage and not in the house indicated that it contained more than just notes made by a methodical cop. Zach would want it, and that possibility set her pulse racing.

She stood rigidly in the chill of the garage and seriously considered destroying the notebook. The idea came easily, coldly and with unflinching realism. How easy it would be to simply put the notebook back in the box and tuck the container into the trash. No one would know. And if she didn't open it, or read the pages, or pay any attention to Zach's growing suspicion that Jim was a cop gone bad, then nothing would change.

Elizabeth pressed the notebook to her, the sudden pain in her chest burning and sharp. Yes, if she threw it away she could preserve his memory for Julianne, for Gordon and Naomi and for herself.

She'd never thought of herself in the role of someone who sheltered, who tried to protect, who would keep away the bad news because it was so painful. In fact, she'd always been the opposite, hating to be smothered and coddled and kept in the dark because life didn't yield all the perfect answers. Yet here with this one small notebook, she was seriously considering and, perhaps worse, justifying to herself, the destruction of evidence to protect Jim.

"Lizzie?"

She swung around, startled, clutching the notebook to her heart.

He stood in the kitchen doorway that led to the garage. Dressed in jeans and a sweatshirt, he gripped a mug of coffee. The steam rose in a curl in the cold air. "I thought you were going to the shop."

"I was…I mean, I am." She wished she'd gotten into the car and left immediately. Then at least she'd have had time to think this through.

He stared at her hands, but he made no move toward her. "I talked to Gordon a few minutes ago. I told him what we had, and the possibility that Jim could have taken money from the evidence room."

She hadn't wanted him to call Gordon, and in deference to her she knew he had waited. But now she wasn't feeling very grateful for his patience. "You told him Jim was a thief, didn't you? How could you when there isn't any proof." Yet, she knew there probably was, that she held it there in her hands.

"The media are sniffing around. I wanted Gordon to be abreast of the developments from me, not from some reporter who decides to call him up and ask questions that won't be kind or subtle."

"Is he all right?"

"He's upset and disappointed, but he wants the truth. Naomi was stunned, and like you she believes there's another explanation. Oh, and by the way, she said to tell you that Julianne was the hit of the Christmas bazaar, and for you not to worry about her."

Distracted by the mention of her daughter, she said what she'd been musing over for the past couple of days. "I think I'll go and get her. I miss her. Also, I need to return Naomi's car."

To her surprise, or perhaps disappointment, he didn't argue with her. "How do you plan to get back?"

"I'll stay over the holidays and come back on the bus." Was she really standing here holding a casual conversation about her holiday plans as if everything was normal? She took a step toward her car, glancing at him to see if he would stop her.

He sipped his coffee, squinting his eyes against the steam. "And when were you planning to tell me you found the notebook?"

For a few moments she simply stared, the notebook suddenly feeling awkward. Although the distance between them was more than eight feet, she didn't need to see the chill in his eyes to know he was angry that she hadn't come in and shown it to him immediately.

"It probably isn't important. Just as the others weren't."

"You know better than that."

"No, I don't know better," she snapped, holding it closer to her. "I haven't even opened it."

He took a step back and set his mug of coffee on the kitchen table. Then he walked down the two steps into the garage toward her. It wasn't the quick, let's-get-this-settled kind of movement, but almost a sad movement, as though he, too, hoped this notebook was no different from the others.

He brushed his fingers down her cheek, but she twisted her head to the side. She didn't want to be comforted or pacified or told that she was doing the right thing.

In the softest of whispers, she said, "I hate you, right now."

"I know," he said in a resigned way, as though acknowledging her words might make them easier to accept.

Then slowly, without using any force, he worked the notebook from her fingers. She felt numb and defeated, and when he took her arm to indicate he wanted her to go inside with him, she almost balked. She wanted no part of whatever he might find, and yet if she really believed Jim was innocent, she couldn't ignore anything that might help to prove that. She couldn't destroy the notebook.

In the kitchen, she stood beside him at the counter with her coat still on. Despite the cozy warmth of the house, she felt chilled and shaky. Zach opened the notebook. There were pages of notes and he read quickly and thoroughly. As he turned the pages, his expression grew more confident. Elizabeth felt as if she were waiting for a guilty verdict.

Then a green spiral-bound notebook that had been tucked into the larger one fell to the counter. Zach laid the larger book aside and opened the green one to the first page. To Elizabeth it looked like a long list of names and numbers.

It was far more significant to Zach. "I'll be damned," he muttered in a voice that sounded relieved as well as amazed.

"What is it?" she asked.

"An account book and a proverbial gold mine. This is the link the department has been trying to find to the drug network that has been flourishing in the state." He read through the pages again, running his finger from the names to the corresponding dollar amounts. "Political names, a couple of judges, cops. Here's the name of an officer we got for selling drugs out of his squad car last summer. A lot of these people have been under ongoing investigations, but we haven't been able to pin anything on them substantial enough to hold up in court. There are a few names here that to my knowledge haven't surfaced."

Elizabeth gripped his arm, a sense of euphoria rushing through her. "See, didn't I tell you Jim wasn't a thief? He'd gotten all these names and probably hadn't had the opportunity to show you or anyone else."

He placed his hand over hers as if to hold her fingers against his arm. "I'm afraid not, sweetheart."

"How can you be sure?"

"For one thing, if the department was in on this, Jim would have turned the names in immediately. For another, the last date listed here corresponds to the date on the paper we found in Gizzo's possessions."

"But maybe that was just the last day he took any notes."

"It was the date he handed over the money and acquired the green notebook. No, this book is the connection to the missing money, and no doubt this is what the ransacker wanted." He continued to read and Elizabeth knew he was mentally filling in the blanks.

When he finished, she thought she felt him sigh. He drew Elizabeth close. "Relax, you're getting yourself all wired."

"How can I relax when you're about to destroy Jim?"

"Because I'm not going to destroy him. He probably was guilty of poor judgment, and was no doubt frustrated and annoyed with the red tape. My guess is he took it upon himself to take the evidence-room money, planning that later, after he got all the details into an airtight case, he'd turn in this green notebook along with his notes. He probably figured no one would be too upset because what he got as a result of breaking that rule was a whole lot more important. The end-justifies-the-means theory."

"Then he wasn't a dirty cop." She whispered it as though saying it too loud might make it untrue.

"Too eager, too determined to win Gordon's approval, but not dirty."

Elizabeth scanned the notes while Zach slipped his arm around her. She'd been aware of how Jim felt about Gordon, but she'd also seen Jim's deep admiration of his partner. References to Zach were all through the notes, giving him credit for the success of a buy-and-bust raid, commenting on Zach's insight when it came to probing the drug dealer's mind, noting questions and theories he'd wanted to toss back and forth with Zach. Yet if she hadn't read the notes herself, she knew Zach would have glossed over any influence he might have had on Jim.

Zach continued, "From what Jim wrote here, it's apparent that Gates offered him these names for a price. Jim had bought information from Gates in the past and with positive results. Since he had charge of the evidence room, and consequently any confiscated drug monies, Jim decided that he would buy this green book from Gates. The problem he ran into was red tape. The department often buys information, but there is paperwork—signatures required, and acquisition procedures that must be followed. Gates was probably itchy to get the cash and get out of town before the missing book of names was discovered. Pressure on Jim by Gates, and his own self-imposed pressure not to let this opportunity get away, spurred him to take the money without permission.''

Eagerly, Elizabeth added, ''Jim probably believed that if he'd had the time his request for the money would have been granted. He simply bypassed the red tape.''

''Yeah. Jim paid Gates, got the book here, and Gates took off for Mexico where he spent it—''

''I always said you were too good a cop, Stone.

Elizabeth jumped. Zach swung toward the back door.

With a deftness that Elizabeth didn't expect, he tucked her behind him so that she was wedged in where the counter squared into an L. An instinctive move, she knew.

In a voice that Elizabeth decided was too calm, Zach said, ''Ah, Mushroom, and here I thought you'd moved on to the big city. Last time we had contact, you were running a major crack house. What happened? Run out of customers or coke?''

The intruder had a flat, square face that looked as if it were molded from a grocery sack. His eyes were long and narrow and very blue. A hunted blue that seemed to hover on the edge of a quick viciousness. His skin—overly smooth and the color of spring mushrooms—confirmed his name.

He held the gun in both hands and had it aimed directly at Elizabeth and Zach, moving it back and forth as if to make sure he didn't miss either target.

In a low snarl, he said, ''Can the wisecracks, Stone. I don't want no hassle from you. Slide the notebook down the counter nice and easy like, then I'll be history.''

''You know I can't do that.''

''You better do it, or I'll do some painful damage to your woman.''

"Then I'll kill you, Mushroom." The dead calm in Zach's voice left absolutely no doubt in Elizabeth's mind that he would indeed do just that. No hesitation. No backward look and not a shred of regret. Coldly, he added, "No gun. Nothing messy. Just my hands . . ." Zach paused, staring at the intruder's throat, then added, "Nice and easy like."

Mushroom swallowed, swore savagely, then moved a step back from Zach, but a step sideways and a little closer to the notebook. Zach moved again, which in effect put more of his body between the pointed gun and Elizabeth.

He folded his arms and turned his head enough so that she could see the throb of the pulse in his jaw. "Mushroom and I go back a long way. We even ended up in a few of the same foster homes, before he got adopted. While I was thinking about finding my old man, Mushroom here was slinking around dark alleys and working on his reputation as a serious drug dealer."

If she hadn't been able to see the gun or the flat-faced intruder, had just been listening to Zach, Elizabeth might have thought he was discussing old times with a suddenly found friend.

Zach asked him, "Been hearing some interesting things about you from upstate. I'm a little surprised you've stooped to ransacking houses."

Mushroom's eyes gleamed with pride, obviously taking Zach's remarks as a compliment. "Gates tried to shake me down for more bucks than his lousy life was worth. He sold the notebook to Healy, and if I'd known that—"

"Known it the night you killed Jim?"

"Hey, he who plays, pays," the gunman said with the disinterest of a man who simply disposed of what got in his way.

Elizabeth was appalled at his indifference to killing. Zach said nothing.

"Whatsa matter, Stone? Ain't that the answer you wanted to hear?" Mushroom laughed, a hollow sound that held no amusement. "You cops are a piece of work, you know that? In case you ain't noticed, I got the gun." He slipped his hand into his jacket pocket and pulled out something that to Elizabeth looked like a short metal cylinder.

She placed her hand on Zach's back and felt the tense muscles.

"You'll never get away with this," Zach warned.

"This little silencer will make the shots sound like a pop-gun." Mushroom took aim once more. "Now move the hell away from the counter, Stone, or I'll spray you over your girlfriend."

"Let her go, Mushroom. Then we'll cut some kind of deal."

There was no question that her presence put Zach at a disadvantage. She guessed that he was trying to stall for time while he tried to figure out a way to get the gun without her getting hurt....

"No way, man," Mushroom snarled. "I'm not Gates. I don't deal with cops."

The gunman slid his finger around the trigger. Zach shoved Elizabeth behind him with one hard, sharp movement. The motion threw her off balance. She flung her hand toward the counter to balance herself and brushed the canvas-covered sculpture.

Her mind raced even as her fingers closed around the clay. Did she dare try it? Was it insane or too risky? Zach would be furious at her later, but she would welcome his anger. The thought that this man who killed Jim could do the same to Zach terrified her far more.

Mushroom closed in and she heard Zach call him a raw, crude name.

Mushroom only laughed, while at the same time he made a reach for the notebook. The gun came closer and closer to Zach. "Say your prayers, Stone, and say them good...."

Her heart pounded, for she knew there would be no spare seconds for error once she had committed herself.

Making sure her grip was solid, she flung the statuette awkwardly so that it sailed off the counter and onto the floor.

Mushroom whirled, firing the gun at the instant the clay sculpture crashed into chunks and slivers.

The bullet nicked Zach's shoulder, and Elizabeth cried out, "No!"

Zach moved. Bringing up his knee, he caught the ransacker in the groin. Mushroom still held the gun, but all Elizabeth saw was a growing bloodstain on Zach's shirt. She flung herself at the ransacker, her terror and her fury exploding with more force than the bullet that had hit Zach's arm.

The ransacker howled, more from the sudden surprise of her landing against him than in pain. Zach knocked the gun away and it fell to the floor with a dull thud. Instantly, Zach had Mushroom turned around, twisting his arm up his back until he yelped.

Elizabeth sagged against the counter, her body drained and numb.

She reached out to touch Zach's arm, but he swung around, glaring at her. She saw the fury in his eyes and she also saw the pasty gray of fear in his face. "What in all that is holy did you think you were doing? Goddammit, Lizzie, you could have been killed!"

She couldn't talk, she could barely swallow as full realization drenched her and pinned her against the counter for support. The clay lay scattered across the floor in broken pieces, but she hardly noticed.

Mushroom tried to move and then winced when Zach tightened his grip. "When I get some answers, I'll ease up."

He turned to Elizabeth. "Call the station." When she simply stared at him, at the broken clay and at the gun, his voice sharpened. "Lizzie!"

She stared back at him, her eyes glazed, the idea of Zach being dead locked in her mind as tightly as a deeply embedded knife.

Zach surveyed her face, the sag of her body and the strewn clay. "Sweetheart," he whispered in a gentle, reassuring voice that was a marked contrast to the scene before her or to his earlier tone. "It's okay to scream. It's okay."

Whether it was his voice, his words or the memory of the other time, the time when Jim was killed, she drew herself up with a kind of invincible courage. She became aware of her surroundings as she raised her eyes and looked at Zach.

No words were needed. None were spoken.

Mushroom tried to move again. Zach snarled, "Talk, you bastard. Now."

"Like hell."

Zach twisted the arm higher. "Trust me, I'll break it without a second thought."

"Hey, that's brutality."

"If you want brutal, just keep stalling," Zach said in a low, clipped voice.

Apparently Mushroom didn't want to test any limits. "All right. Hey, let up a little."

Zach didn't. "You the one who shot Jim?"

"Yeah. Come on, man, you're killin' my arm. It ain't my fault Healy got wasted. We were all nervous about the missing notebook and trying to figure out who had it. I didn't know he was a cop."

"You murdered Gates, too, didn't you," Zach stated without any pretense of a question.

"Hey, why should I pay for what I already know? I knew the notebook was here, it was just a matter of time before I found it."

Elizabeth leaned against the counter, her legs shaky, and picked up the phone. She told the officer who answered what had happened.

"You bastard," Zach muttered. "If that bullet had hit her I'd have killed you and taken great pleasure in it."

Still wearing the blue wool dress that she'd put on earlier to go down to The Easel, Elizabeth watched the last police car pull away along with the emergency medical team that had been sent when she told the police that Zach had been shot. Zach had dismissed the "flesh wound," as one of the EMT's had called it, as no more serious than a minor cut. The medics had cleaned and wrapped it, and Zach had promised to stop at the hospital to get it taken care of.

She hadn't given more than a passing thought to the broken clay sculpture, which gave her a strange feeling. She knew without pride or ego that it had been her best work, and yet even as she threw away the shattered pieces, she had had no regrets. The piece had served a purpose far beyond being presented as a gift. The suspicion around Jim's name would be cleared and Zach was alive.

She took a deep shuddering breath and turned when she heard him come into the living room. He was wearing the familiar jeans and a clean fatigue shirt, but she thought he looked tired and, yes, older. The pasty gray color she had seen after she threw the sculpture had left his face, but was replaced now by a kind of resolve. No doubt he was anxious to leave, to get on with his life now that this assignment that Gordon had given him was finally complete.

Trying to memorize every tiny detail about him for all the lonely days ahead, she thought of his promise to come and hold Julianne. How she wished the promise had included her. With an almost painful longing, she wanted to close the distance between them to curl into his arms and kiss him just once more.

"I guess I'm all set," he said, watching her as though waiting for her to do something, to say something.

"You didn't forget anything, did you?" She could tell by the way he favored it that his arm hurt. On the floor beside him sat his nylon bag of clothes. When he didn't answer, she clasped her hands tightly so he couldn't see them tremble and said, "You won't forget to stop at the hospital, will you?"

"Why did you do it?"

His question immediately put away any thoughts of casual parting conversation. Her impulse was to shed all her hesitations, all her ragged reserve and say that she loved him. "I didn't want him to get the notebook."

"He wouldn't have. You're not answering my question."

She took a deep breath for courage. "Why did I do what? Throw the clay sculpture? Did you want me to just cringe behind you?"

He came toward her while he talked. "Ever the independent woman," he said softly, as though finally resigned to the fact. "You're not the cringing type. I've known that since I walked in here the day of the ransacking. No, I wouldn't have ever expected hysterics from you, but to throw and break your work when there was no need." He came to a halt very close to her, but not close enough to touch her.

"No need! If he'd gotten that notebook and escaped, then there would have been unanswered questions about Jim forever."

"Is that the reason you threw it?"

"Yes!" But it wasn't the only reason, and if she was as fiercely independent as she claimed she was she would tell him that the most important reason had to do with being in love with him and not wanting anything to happen to him.

"Then I can pick up my stuff and leave and you won't try to stop me."

She lowered her lashes and looked down at her hands. They were clenched so tight the knuckles were white. The room seemed eerily alive with powerful sounds: her heart trying to find an even rhythm, her pulse thumping, his erratic breathing, his booted steps on the carpet as he closed the gap between them.

Then, in an almost desperate need, he slid his arms around her, stroking down her back in soothing motions that had more to do with the need to touch than to comfort.

"I saw the sculpture. It was incredible, Lizzie," he whispered against her hair, drawing her in as though she were far more valuable than any object she could create.

She felt her heart swell with his compliment. "Why didn't you tell me you'd seen it?"

"Probably because I didn't know what to say. The first thing I saw when I came in the day of the ransacking was a broken piece of your work. It was of Julianne when she was an infant. When I looked beneath the canvas covering and saw the emotion and the love that you'd captured in the clay, I felt instantly connected to you as well as Julianne. I knew then that there was something very powerful between us. I also knew that Julianne would always be like a daughter to me." Zach set her back enough so that he could see her face. "Why didn't you show it to me?"

She searched his eyes, but saw only softness in the gray-blue color. "I didn't want you to think I was trying to box you in by using your feelings for Julianne. You asked me once about a father for her. I was afraid you might see the sculpture as some sort of emotional bond that included me. That night at the motel when you said..." Her voice trailed off, and she had to swallow down the words that were so linked to that night and to her memories of it.

Zach brushed his mouth across her cheek, lingering to catch her warmth. "One of my finer moments, wasn't it? I not only accused you of trying to box me in, but of abandoning Julianne. It was all one monstrous excuse, Lizzie. Cruel to you, but crueler to myself. I wasn't throwing away what we had because I believed any of those excuses." He paused, and then as though he had mentally stepped through some barrier, he said, "I knew and I didn't want to know. I kept telling myself it was impossible."

She felt his heart pounding against her breasts, and she slipped her arms around him, wanting to tell him she loved him but knowing he needed to explain.

He lifted his eyes and for a moment she saw an almost grateful defeat. "Since I was a kid, I've always planned ahead of time how to get out of situations. That way I always had an escape route. I've used it in police work and with women who wanted more than I could give. But nothing I planned worked with you. The crazy thing was that I kept boxing myself in."

He tucked her head beneath his chin, and murmured, "Even after you threw the clay piece, even while I was stuffing all my clothes in the bag, I kept telling myself I was walking away and it was for the best. Best for you and for me."

"Oh, Zach."

Then in the stillness he whispered, "So many times since you walked into the den that first day..."

When he hesitated, she brushed her finger across his mouth as though to coax out the words. "So many times what?" she urged in a hushed murmur.

He captured her finger and pressed his mouth to her palm, then closed her fingers around the moist kiss. In a raspy voice he said, "I kept sinking deeper and deeper into feelings for you that I didn't want to have, feelings I didn't understand. Ones that scared the hell out of me. I've always left myself options to get out. I never committed myself. I never pretended or told any woman there could be anything more than a transient relationship. Even with you..." Again his words trailed off as though he still couldn't quite grasp what had happened between them.

She felt a sheen of tears glaze her eyes. "You were always honest and straightforward about how you felt."

"Only because that was the only way I knew how to deal with it. To deal with you. I thought that after I came back here and got back to work that you'd fade as every other woman had. But you didn't. And the fact that you were so determined not to trap me began to really bug me."

She blinked, remembering the strain between them from the moment she had returned from New Hampshire. "Is that why you asked me that day in the den if I was in love with you?"

He nodded, but not with any pleasure at the memory. "I wanted you to say yes, while at the same time I was scared you'd say no. Real logical, huh?" He let her go then and crossed the room to glance out the window. His sports car was parked in the driveway, and she wondered fleetingly if he wished he were in it and driving at death-defying speeds.

Slowly he turned back to face her. He glanced at the bag that held his clothes and then at her front door as though considering options.

She wanted to stop him from going. She wanted to say that it was possible to love and not smother. Oh God, she thought with a sudden understanding. She knew exactly how he felt. She should have made the connection sooner. His fear of being boxed in was very much like her own fear of being smothered.

Then with the distance still between them, he dragged his hands through his hair as though whatever battle he was having with himself was finally lost.

"Come here, Lizzie."

She didn't hesitate. In an instant she was once again in his arms.

He sighed, gripping her to him as though he could never let her go. "I don't know how to leave you, Lizzie. I know how to hurt you and I know how to spend long nights without sleep trying to rid myself of the need for you, but I don't know how in hell to walk away."

She knew then without the words, she knew by the way his hands cradled her, by the way he seemed to meld against her as though they were one.

"I love you," she whispered and then, tipping her head back, she said, "I don't know how I could have said goodbye."

"Dear God," he murmured in prayerful relief. He winced some when he tightened his injured arm around her. "I love you, Elizabeth Healy, and if you promise to never say goodbye, I'll promise to never leave you."

She pulled his head down for a long kiss that he deepened while his hands worked beneath the dress to find the edge of her panties.

She felt an exuberant delight not only at his touch, but at the joy she knew was now theirs. No more barriers and restraints. No more fighting a love that was more powerful than their ability to restrain it.

His fingers pressed into her satin-covered bottom. "You feel sensational," he murmured, kissing her throat, her chin and finally her mouth.

"I was planning on taking them off," she said, teasing him, loving him, wanting to absorb him. She nipped at his earlobe.

He groaned and slipped his hands beneath the lace that edged her thighs. "Speaking of panties and other things."

She feathered her fingers through his hair, deciding she could never touch it enough. "What other things?"

"I owe you one black dress."

She stilled her hands, letting them glide down to his shoulders. "You saw it in the trash, didn't you?" At his nod, she continued, "I threw it away because I knew I'd never be able to look at it or wear it again and not think about you." She hugged him tighter. Then with her voice breaking, her eyes glistening with tears, she whispered, "And how much I loved you."

"Ahh, Lizzie..." he murmured against her mouth. He kissed her thoroughly before adding, "I want to buy you another dress that will look even more sensational on you, but..."

She searched his face. "But what?"

"The occasion I had in mind is a little too festive for black. How about white?"

"White? Like in snow."

"Like in a wedding dress."

She could only stare, her mouth dry and her heart threatening to leap from her chest. She realized with a new joy that with his proposal he'd thrust aside all the avenues of escape and stepped into the most permanent situation of his life.

"Yes," she said quietly, because there was no other answer that she wanted to give. She felt his long sigh of release and joy. "When?"

"Impatient?" he asked, his eyes filled with his own eagerness.

"To be with you and live with you and love you? Yes, I'm very impatient."

"Now, how can I argue with that?" With his uninjured arm around her he guided her toward the stairs.

"I don't want you to hurt your arm," she said, but then couldn't stop her giggle.

He growled, "I got something else that hurts a lot worse than my arm." He hesitated just long enough to press her against him. Then he lowered the zipper on her dress. When his hand slid across her back and around to cup her breast, she shivered.

"I love you," they whispered in unison.

As they climbed the stairs to her bedroom their words grew more intimate, their bodies more stirred in anticipation. Both knew that their impatience now would soon be satisfied. But their future together would be built on the slowly deepening power of love.

*   *   *   *   *

Bestselling author NORA ROBERTS captures all the romance, adventure, passion and excitement of Silhouette in a special miniseries.

THE
CALHOUN WOMEN

Four charming, beautiful and fiercely independent sisters set out on a search for a missing family heirloom—an emerald necklace—and each finds something even more precious . . . passionate romance.

Look for THE CALHOUN WOMEN miniseries starting in June.

COURTING CATHERINE
in Silhouette Romance #801 (June/$2.50)

A MAN FOR AMANDA
in Silhouette Desire #649 (July/$2.75)

FOR THE LOVE OF LILAH
in Silhouette Special Edition #685 (August/$3.25)

SUZANNA'S SURRENDER
in Silhouette Intimate Moments #397 (September/$3.29)

SILHOUETTE·INTIMATE·MOMENTS®

IT'S TIME TO MEET
THE MARSHALLS!

In 1986, bestselling author Kristin James wrote A VERY SPECIAL FAVOR for the Silhouette Intimate Moments line. Hero Adam Marshall quickly became a reader favorite, and ever since then, readers have been asking for the stories of his two brothers, Tag and James. At last your prayers have been answered!

In August, look for THE LETTER OF THE LAW (IM #393), James Marshall's story. If you missed youngest brother Tag's story, SALT OF THE EARTH (IM #385), you can order it by following the directions below. And, as our very special favor to you, we'll be reprinting A VERY SPECIAL FAVOR this September. Look for it in special displays wherever you buy books.

Silhouette Books®

Take 4 bestselling love stories FREE

Plus get a FREE surprise gift!

Coming Soon

Fashion A Whole New You.
Win a sensual adventurous
trip for two to Hawaii via
American Airlines®, a
brand-new Ford Explorer
4 × 4 and a $2,000
Fashion Allowance.

Plus, special free gifts* are yours to
Fashion A Whole New You.

From September through November, you can take part in
this exciting opportunity from Silhouette.

Watch for details in September.

* with proofs-of-purchase, plus postage and handling